FOREIGN SOIL

FOREIGN SOIL

FOREIGN SOIL

AND OTHER STORIES

MAXINE BENEBA CLARKE

37INK

—

ATRIA

NEW YORK   LONDON   TORONTO   SYDNEY   NEW DELHI

37INK
ATRIA

An Imprint of Simon & Schuster, Inc.
1230 Avenue of the Americas
New York, NY 10020

First 37 INK/Atria Paperback edition October 2017

37INK /ATRIA PAPERBACK and colophon are trademarks of Simon & Schuster, Inc.

For information about special discounts for bulk purchases, please contact
Simon & Schuster Special Sales at 1-866-506-1949 or business@simonandschuster.com.

The Simon & Schuster Speakers Bureau can bring authors to your live event. For more information or to book an event, contact the Simon & Schuster Speakers Bureau at 1-866-248-3049 or visit our website at www.simonspeakers.com.

Interior design by Kyoko Watanabe

Manufactured in the United States of America

10 9 8 7 6 5 4 3 2 1

Library of Congress Cataloging-in-Publication Data is available.

ISBN 978-1-5011-3636-8
ISBN 978-1-5011-4051-8 (pbk)
ISBN 978-1-5011-3637-5 (ebook)

For Mali Langston and Maya Lou

Let no one be fooled by the fact that we may write in English, for we intend to do unheard-of things with it.

—CHINUA ACHEBE

CONTENTS

FOREIGN SOIL

FOREIGN SOIL

David

SHE HAD a shiny cherry-red frame, scooped alloy Harley handlebars and sleek metal pedals. Her wire basket carrier was fitted with a double-handled cane lift-out. If I'd learned anything from Ahmed before we split (and Lord knew there wasn't much I'd gotten from him over the few years we were together), it was how to spot a good set of wheels. And this push-bike, she was fuck-off beautiful. The jumble of wheels, frames, spokes, and assorted handlebars crowded around her in the window display at Ted's Cycles made me think of the bike dump round back of the Fitzy commission tower.

Before we had Nile, Ahmed and I used to hang at the bike dump with the boys. I'd watch them all piecing together patchwork bikes from throw-outs we'd scabbed off curbs or pulled out of Dumpsters. They were crazy, some of those contraptions Ahmed and them built: tiny little frames attached to oversized backward-mounted handlebars and gigantic heavy-tread wheels. Insanity in motion. Ahmed's mum was always going mental about him getting chain grease on his school clothes.

Hadn't seen Ahmed's mum since forever. Not since I fucked off with Nile and got my own council place. I knew what she would have been saying about me, though. I could hear her voice like she was standing right next to me outside the bike-shop window. *These children, born in this country, they think they can behave like the Australian children. They have no idea about the tradition and respect. In Sudan, a good wife knew how to keep her husband, and a good mother would not leave. My son and my grandson's mother—did you know they did not even get marry? Not even marry!*

I shifted my backpack on my shoulders, leaned in for a closer look. BARKLY STAR, read the shiny bronze sticker across her body. Strapped to the bike's back rack was an orange and blue baby seat: reality, barging right on fucking in.

Black clouds were on the move as I wheeled her out of the shop and onto Barkly Street—the fuck-awful Melbourne rain about to come through. I pulled up the hood of my jumper, the one I lifted from the Footscray Coles after they fired me, the winter before Nile was due. Snot-colored, Ahmed had reckoned when I got back to the flats with it. Jealous shit. I was always better at swiping stuff than him.

I'd had no car ever since Ahmed and me split, and Nile rode too fast on his trike for me to keep up walking beside him. I'd end up running along behind, yelling at him to wait up. Community Services were on my back then too, about weekly check-ins. Those wheels were gonna change my life, I knew it. Sure fucken thing. I spent most of my welfare money buying that beauty, but the rent was already way behind. It was gonna be a fortnight of porridge and potatoes, but half the time I cooked other stuff Nile wouldn't look at it anyway.

These children, born in this country, do you think they feed their babies the aseeda for breakfast? Do they drop it on the little one's tongue to show them where is it they come from? Do you think they have learned to cook shorba soup? I tell you: no! They feeding them all kinds of rubbish. McDonald's, even. They spit on their grandmothers' ways. They spit in our bowls, in our kitchens.

Wheeling the new bike up Barkly Street I noticed a woman, standing on the footpath, gawking. She was the color of roasted coffee beans, a shade darker than me, wearing black from headscarf to shoes, carrying a string grocery bag. She cleared her throat, started on me. "Little Sister, is that your bike?"

———

This young woman, she walking down Barkly Street with that red bike, brand-new and for herself even though she look like she Sudanese and a grown mother too. Straight away, she remind me back of David. She remembering David to me.

Way back when things were better more good, before the trouble in my Sudan, a man in the village, Masud, who used to being mechanical engineer, he make my boys a bike. With own two hands, he builds it. I don't even knowing how he make it from scrap of metal around that place, tin cans even, but he did. And my little David, seven then, he look at that bike like he never saw a more beautiful thing. His brothers were too small to ride without adult helping, but David always on that bike. He riding it from one end of village to other one, poking his little-boy nose in about everything that going on.

Little David riding that bike so much that Masud tell him about country call France, where is very long bike race which will make you famous if you win. Long bike ride is call the Tour of France because it goes all over that country. After the day Masud told David about the famous bike race, every time David passes him on that bike Masud calls out to him. "Here come David, on his Tour of Sudan!" he call.

My David, he would grow the biggest smile ever you saw when Masud say that.

"One day, David," Masud say, carrying on to David to make him all proud and smiling. "One day you will be so famous because of bike riding that they will name after you a beautiful bike."

David so dreamy he believe that might come true.

———

"Little Sister, is that your bike?" the woman said again. She was my mother's age and looked like a Sudanese too, so I knew nothing I said was gonna be the right thing. Anyway, it wasn't really a question, just a kind of judgment, like when Mum found out I was knocked up; she never even looked up from her maize porridge. Mum never liked Ahmed. Liked him less than his mum liked me. Probably that was the reason we were ever together. To piss them the fuck off with all their whinging and nagging.

I ignored the woman, made myself busy fitting my backpack into the bike basket, looked down at the weed-filled cracks in the pavement, at the shiny silver bike stand—anywhere but at her.

These children that born here in this country, they so disrespectful. They not even address us elders properly. Do not look us in the eye. Back in Sudan, you remember, we used to say Auntie and Uncle. We knew how to speak to one another with proper dignity. We would never ignore Auntie on the street.

"It is my bike, Auntie. Yes."

The woman touched the back of the baby seat, looked me up and down. "What will your husband think, when he sees?"

I wanted to laugh and say, "What husband? Who even cares? My boyfriend was no good, so I left him. Now he's off with some slag down the Fitzroy Estate. But seriously, she can have him, bless the desperate thing! I've wanted a bike like this ever since I was six. So please, lady, hands off and back away from my childhood dream."

You children, you have no respect, no manners. When you have lived long as we have, you will realize everything we said, it is for your own good. You should show us respect, like real African children. You may have been born in this country, but do not forget where is it you came from.

I smiled sweetly. "Oh, my husband won't mind, Auntie. After all, for better or worse, he has vowed to love me."

The woman sucked her yellowing teeth, adjusted her headscarf, did that one-eyebrow-raised thing at me. "You don't *have* husband. Do you?"

———

We had been thinking about how the army would come and destroy the village, since they took my husband, Daud, and his friend Samuel two year ago. But somehow, they leave us alone. Before, when we thought the Janjaweed must be about to come and burn our houses like they did to many others, we were always ready with bundles of food and clothes, but after years pass, we were thinking they don't care about us anymore—maybe they busy in Khartoum or near the border where there are more things to steal.

One day Amina, my friend and the daughter of Masud who build David his bike, she come running, tripping through the village screaming, "Army! The army coming near! They just now burn the whole of Haskanita to the ground. It is the Janjaweed! We got to run!"

Everybody around us terrified, packing all what they can.

"Quickly, Asha, where your little ones?" Amina say to me. "Where your boys are? No time to gather, you just bringing water and the boys!"

I am standing very still because is like when they come for my husband and Amina's husband and put them in the jail in Khartoum, like when last I saw my Daud.

Amina grab hold of me and put her hands on my face and hold my face to look at her face. "Asha, already we lost Daud and Samuel—already we lose our husbands, but that is past now. Where the boys, Asha? Where your children? Or are you also wanting to losing the not-yet-men you give birth to, as well as the man you make them with?"

———

"Yes, I do have a husband." Fuck her, for making a judgment on me.

These children, born in this country, they doing the sex and having babies and then not even wanting get marry. Oooh, if we did that back in Sudan, we would be cast out. The government would not give us money to raise our babies. Can you imagine us asking?

Rain was starting to fall now, and the rush-hour traffic along Barkly Street was bumper to bumper. I wheeled my bike quicker along the pavement, but Auntie kept in step with me.

"What does your mother think about the cutting of your hair off like that? Is not like a woman. So short Afro. Is she all right about you wearing the jeans and riding around on the street? And where is your baby, Little Sister? The baby who going go on that bike seat? Baby will be missing you!"

They put the babies in the childcare and they let them looked after by strangers. Strangers! When the babies are not even yet out of nappies. Did you ever hear of such thing? Why they having the babies if they do not want to look after?

"It's okay, Auntie, I can handle myself. Bikes are awesome, though. If you want to, we could go up a side street where no one will see. I'll hold the back while you have a ride. Then you can have a proper turn." It came out of my mouth before I had time to rethink.

"You are wicked," Auntie choked, like she was trying to stop herself from laughing. "You so funny, Sister. You Muslim girl?"

"No."

She waited for my explanation.

"What religion you are, Little Sister?" she nosed again, scratching the outside elbow of her robe, shifting to one side of the footpath so an old Chinese man with a cart could pass by us.

"None." I shrugged, kept wheeling.

The woman's eyes opened wide. The whole of Barkly Street seemed to go quiet.

———

Everything around me silent. I suck the air into my mouth but I cannot talk. Amina, she push into the house and I turn around, following her. Clement and Djoni playing in the house with David.

"Boys, like I tell you would happen, the time is here, we must leave quietly, quietly," I say. I get the water container and quickly roll up some bread and put some blanket in the bag. When we get out of the house, Masud and Amina are waiting, but David, he say he going get his bike, he not leaving without it. Before we can catch him, he run. David run so fast toward the middle of the village where all the children play in the big fiori tree. That is where he left his bike. So fast he run away, his little legs kicking up the dirt.

"Get Asha and the boys to the edge of village. I will go back to get David," Masud tell Amina, and he walk quickly after my boy. Masud was not young man anymore, and he did not run, but fast, fast he walk.

Amina pulling my arm. "Don't be stupid, Asha, you got two boys with you and David safe with my father."

The others in the village are running past quickly, quickly. Amina is pulling me to come away. Clement and Djoni, they crying. Masud disappear into the village and it swallow him up the way two minute ago it swallow little David.

One of the boys is on my back, the other on Amina's. Nothing else about that walk I am remembering, even now. When we get to edge of the village, we hide in the spot where we can see back a little bit. In the bushes. Some other people from the village there already, quiet, quiet. When we look back, the soldiers are not coming after us. The village is smoking and the soldiers busy smashing, burning. We hear a woman voice then, and she is screaming, screaming. Amina and me put our hands over Djoni and Clement ears.

After some hours, the boys fall asleep in the bushes. Amina hold her hand over my mouth while I crying.

"Don't worry. My father keeping your David safe."

She crying too, and we both know she is not talking about safe in our village, safe in Sudan, safe from militia, safe alive. The village is burning, and David and Masud are gone. I am praying then. Amina praying also because her husband and now her father she has lost. Because of his love for my boy, her father is also gone.

———

Auntie walked along next to me, talking to herself. "This girl! She has baby but no husband. *Tsssk.* She ride bike and she doesn't care even who see. She even going take the baby on it. *Tsssk.* No religion. No God. She cut her hair short and wear the jeans. *Tsssssssk.*"

The rain was getting heavier. I wanted to cut across the rail line and head up Geelong Road to Nile's kindergarten, test out if this Barkly Star really did know how to shoot and shine.

"Auntie, nice meeting you," I lied, flicking the halfway-down bike stand right up.

Auntie turned the corner beside me, grabbed my wrist tightly and whispered loudly in my ear, "I have second husband. I very lucky. My first husband, he die back in my country. I have five children now. My husband, he is good man, but he would not like me riding. Here, nobody is watching. Quick. I can try and have a turn just this one time. You hold the bag."

———

Hours, hours must be passing. We waiting for dawn light so can creep away from the bushes to another place without walking into dangerous thing. Sudden in the darkness, we hear a rattling. It is coming out of the smoke, louder, louder. Rattling, rattling. The boys still asleep but Amina and me, we are looking, looking through tree to see.

———

I laughed, sure that she was joking, but Auntie handed me her string grocery bag. She pulled her skirts tight around her legs to stop them getting caught in the chain, eased herself onto the bike and held on to the handlebars.

"Um . . . Auntie, have you ever ridden a bike before?"

Auntie shook her head no. The man who'd just passed us with his shopping turned curiously, stopped to watch.

"I'll hold the back for you. Are you sure you want to have a go?"

"Yes. I want to ride it, Little Sister. Thank you. I will have a try."

———

It is David. Somebody hear my prayer because that noise, that rattling, rattling, it is David. He riding that bike to me fast, fast. He is pedaling, pedaling. Three men chasing a little bit after him, but he is soon leaving them in the distance. Some small piece of metal fall down off the pedal but that bike with my David on it is going faster, faster. David is almost to where we are hiding, and he is laughing. My David is riding to me, smiling. The metal on that bike, it glinting, glinting in the darkness, like star or something.

———

Auntie was heavy—not overweight, but it was hard for me to hold her steady on the seat.

"Hold the handlebars straight," I said. "Move the front wheel where you want to go, and push the pedals."

Auntie was zigzagging all over the place, as if she'd never steered anything in her life. It was a struggle to keep her on the bike.

"Steer it like a shopping cart," I suggested.

The bike straightened up then, and Auntie started pushing the pedals. I ran along behind, her grocery bag heavy over my shoulder.

"Slow down. Hey. *Shit*. Slow down!"

My foot caught on a crack in the pavement, and my fingers lost their grip on the bike seat. Auntie kept riding, pedaling faster, more furiously, until she was a few hundred meters away from me.

———

Then out David's laughing mouth come roar like a lion. Bright red roar like fire, like sunset, tomato-red roaring. David, he stop pedaling but the bike still rolling, rolling straight toward us. The roar spilling out behind the bike now, the red roar spraying from David's mouth out onto the bike, splashing onto the dirt and leaving dark patches where the dry ground drinking it in. David, he falling. The bike is falling. The men in the distance have stopped chasing, stopped coming toward us. The men in the distance look now very small. They are not men. Like David, they are boys. Two of the soldier boys are cheering and another one he is smiling and holding over his head a gun. Up and down, the boy with the gun jumping. I understand then, the Janjaweed soldier boys were racing my David, for the fun.

———

The bike swerved suddenly, skidded sideways. Auntie's skirt became caught up in the pedals. The bike toppled, and Auntie with it. Fuck. *Fuck.* When I reached her, she was untangling herself, shaking, crying, the scarf beneath her chin wet with tears. But the oddest thing was, with those big tears running down her face, Auntie was laughing.

"My David. He used to have the bike, back in Sudan. One day I saw him ride, ride that bike, so fast like he was flying."

"Oh."

"Thank you, Little Sister. Thanking you. When I ride that bike I remembering my boy, riding toward me, laughing, how he laughing . . ."

I felt awkward, had no idea what she was talking about, but felt like I was somehow supposed to. Auntie took up her grocery bag from the ground, smoothed some dirt from her skirt, walked away slowly, down toward West Footscray Station.

I stood there for a minute, staring after her. The rain had stopped. A small puddle of water had settled in the baby seat. Nile would be getting testy. It was half an hour past when I usually collected him. I threw my leg over the bike, started pedaling down the street. The Barkly Star was a dream to maneuver—smooth gliding, killer suspension, sharp brakes. Felt like I was hovering above the wet tar, flying. Like there was nothing else in the world except me and my wheels. David. I slowly rolled her brand-new name around in my mouth.

Harlem Jones

HARLEM LEGS it from the job shop soon as the sour bitch pushes the button for security. Shoots like the fuckin' wind. She won't call the coppers, he's sure of it. Old cow's just trying to give him a scare. As if he'd been serious anyway, about that shit.

Harlem rockets out onto Tucker Street and takes the back laneway through the park, long legs striding out on the cracked concrete path. His still-new black work shoes strain at the seams, creaking at each push off the pavement. Usually Harlem's mind goes blank when he runs. Only thing he can hear is his own even breathing, wind rushing past his ears. This afternoon is different. As he sprints away from the place, all he can think about is that fuckin' Mark Duggan. It's the mug shot from the paper that rises up in front of him—not a real mug shot, but practically. The hard eyes, angry frown;

the papers always drag out photos like that when London Met bullets get themselves lodged in some poor black bastard.

Harlem pushes the man's face from his mind. He's not Duggan; the pigs won't catch him. He's more fuckin' Linford Christie. Harlem reaches the Finsbury Park flats in less than five minutes, four even, not the slightest bit out of breath. Only reason they'd kept him on so long at school was because he ran cross-country like Wile E. Coyote on crack. Even his running hadn't been enough for them to keep him on in the end.

Harlem opens the door to the flat and dumps his rucksack in the hallway. He showers and dresses again, leaving his sweaty Tesco's uniform in a heap on the bathroom floor. The kitchen still smells like that disgusting yellow porridge his ma cooks in the mornings. Harlem opens the fridge, starts digging into the jerk chicken and sweet potato left over from last night's dinner. Devours it cold, he's that fuckin' starving, the whole container of it gone. When his ma comes back from her shift down at the youth center, she'll make some more.

Harlem raises his right arm and aims the empty plastic container across at the sink. "And the crowd goes wild. Harlem Jones! Harlem Jones has the ball! And he shoots. The ball is going in! I don't believe it, it's going in! And it's a score! It's a basket! Harlem Jones has won the game for them!" Head thrown back, arms over head, he runs mad circles on the small square of scuffed linoleum.

After filling his rucksack with the spray paint cans hidden on top of the fridge, Harlem shrugs on his new hoodie and opens the front door.

"Harlem Jones," the tall copper says, knuckle poised to knock.

Ain't a fricken question, they know damn well who he is. Harlem curses. Course they have his fuckin' address. For all he knows they might be the same filth that sent his brother down. Not that Lloyd hadn't deserved it. Janelle was real pretty before Lloyd lost it with her that night. When Harlem saw his brother's ex a few weeks after, everything on her face looked swollen and crooked.

"Been making death threats against ladies down the job office, Harlem?" the ginger copper says.

Death threats his skinny black arse. Even the crazy job-shop broad ain't dim enough to really believe that. Harlem went to see about quitting the Tesco's job. Got his first pay yesterday and the whole lousy shelf-stacking month gave him just twenty quid more than being on subsidies. Fricken slavery's what it is. Time he pays his Oyster card fare he's actually behind.

"Sorry. Don't know what you're talkin' bout. You got the right person?" His word against fuckin' hers. Stupid cow told him if he ditches the Tesco's job he won't get benefits for three months. Casual, like she was used to dumping no-hopers like him in the shit. Fuckin' stuck-up bitch.

Harlem locks the front door behind him and steps out onto the steps, forcing the coppers back toward the footpath.

He'd lost it at the job-shop broad, with her fancy clothes, the posh way she talked. Fuckin' raged out on her, and once he got started, he couldn't do nothin' to stop himself. Not that he would have fuckin' wanted to in any case.

"What's dis goin' on?"

Jesus, his mother has bad timing. She's looking from the coppers to him like she's gonna have a heart attack or something. Seeing her so worried makes Harlem feel like shit. He doesn't mean to rub up against the law so much. He's just so fuckin' angry, all the time.

"You this lad's mother?"

"Don't be foolin' wid mi, ye know mi damn am."

He bets the pigs never counted on goin' up against his ma. She can be a drag sometimes, but she always fronts up swinging when they come for her own. Harlem drops his rucksack off his shoulder, fishes out his ciggies and sits down on the step to watch the spat.

Three minutes with her, and the coppers turn back down the path. She's getting smarter at this shit, his ma. Harlem makes to leave as well, but she's not finished with him. She blocks his way out of the front garden, right aggravated. Sweat's pouring off her forehead like it's her own chubby self that done that run.

"Ye need te pull yeself together, Harlem." Them veins in her neck are popping like the American weightlifters' on the Nike ads. "Ye father an I never come te dis country te raise delinquent children. No chile-a mine gwan threaten a woman! Ye nat readin' de news? Ye wan end up like dat udda black boy dem kill?"

"He was a grown man, Ma, not a boy." It's on the tip of Harlem's tongue to remind her about Lloyd, but he doesn't want to risk a slap across the face with the workbag the woman's wielding. Besides, his ma's still in denial about Lloyd being inside. Won't talk about it, even to Harlem. Tells all them mates down the West Indian club that his brother's in Trinidad for a while, doing some work for her builder cousin.

"Harlem, mi don't wan ye turnin' out like ye good-fe-nothin' dadda is all. Ye raise bettah dan dis, ye know it. Look at mi, bwoy!"

Harlem can't look at her. She makes him too fuckin' irate. She always dumps on his dad whenever Harlem does anything wrong. Ten years since the man pissed off, and she still can't stop slagging on him. Harlem flexes his trembling fingers. He wants to fuckin' strangle her, his own mother, who gave birth to him. *Really* strangle the woman. He wants to wrap his fingers firmly around that fat neck and squeeze until her face goes purple.

———

Toby's late. Even after the holdup with the cops, Harlem reaches Seven Sisters before him. Dragging smoke deep into his lungs, Harlem sinks down onto the station steps and squeezes his eyes shut.

Fuck.

He exhales slowly. He can't get Duggan out of his mind— the cocked head, the scowl on the bugger's face. Harlem takes one last puff of his rollie and crushes the glowing stub into the step below him with the heel of his right sneaker. Gazing down at the running shoe, he spits on his right index finger and carefully wipes specks of London grime from the light gray Adidas stripes.

He and Toby were both shit-faced yesterday when they

agreed to meet up, but he's sure they said five thirty on the steps at Seven Sisters Station. Toby's a lost cause when he's on the piss, though. Could be the dumb fuck's forgotten all about it.

Harlem runs an anxious hand over his buzz cut, pulls his iPhone from his hoodie pocket and scrolls down to find his friend's number. Absentminded as his mate is, Toby can pack a nasty fuckin' punch, and tonight isn't something Harlem wants to be walking into on his own. He presses Send on the text message, then stops to examine his reflection in the mobile screen. Funny, he didn't realize before how much he looks like that poor dead geezer.

Running late. Got caught up @ home. Soz. Harlem reads Toby's reply, annoyed. What the fuck was Toby doing up in Brixton to keep him late? *Caught up.* Messing around with one of those Walker sisters, Harlem guesses. One of these days they'll find out he's horizontal with both of them. Watch the shit fly then. Harlem can't never figure out what the girls see in his mate. Tobes is all pale English skin, sticking out ears, lanky arms and legs.

Harlem stands, strides two at a time up the station steps, draws a gob of phlegm to the back of his throat and spits thickly on the curb.

Fuck the stupid git.

He swapped his Tesco's shift with Ayana to make it tonight. The only shift she'd swap for his four-hour evening at the supermarket was an eight-hour Saturday. Done him right over she had, even though she'd figured out what he wanted the night off for.

"You goin' down Tottenham way, innit?" she'd whispered triumphantly from the other side of the wire shelving where she was restacking cartons of pomegranate juice. "Better be careful. Cording to Facebook it's gonna be fricken war."

Harlem hadn't bothered responding, just continued turning the Yorkshire pudding packet mixes around so they all faced the same way.

He reaches into his trackie pocket and pulls out his gray beanie, jams it down over his head. It's summer, but the clear evening has a chilly edge.

Tardy shithead.

If he waits for Tobes he's gonna miss the action. Harlem crosses the road, turns the corner and heads down Woodgreen. It's been a few months since he came right into Tottenham. Several more Caribbean grocery shops have sprung up. Through the grimy windows Harlem glimpses shelves lined with jerk seasoning, tinned ackee, smoked saltfish and bruised plantain: all the shit his ma cooks from back home in Trinidad that Harlem mostly can't stand.

On the corner of Woodgreen and Martin a new bookstore's opened: kids' books in the window showing bright, happy-to-look-at pictures. *Jalawah and the Beanstalk, Jet Black and the Seven Pygmies.* Harlem stops to read a few of the titles, smiling to himself. Black hair salons spill onto the footpath with baskets of hairpieces, dreadlock wax and netted sleeping caps—all that rubbish them girls back at school spent hours messing up their heads with. The barbershops are filled with brothers. They man-clamp, bump fists and chat, as barbers carefully pattern-shave the sides of their heads.

"Harlem! Thought you were gonna fricken wait for me!" Toby jogs into step beside him.

"You're late, you shit." Harlem stops to touch knuckles with his friend.

"Yeah. Sorry bout that. It was Camille. I kept tellin' her I had to go, but she wanted me to, y'know, finish what I, uh, started." Toby grins, gold-capped front tooth glinting from his pale face.

Harlem grimaces. "Too much fuckin' information. You know where this place is, then?"

"You're joshing me, right?" Toby stops to stare at him. "You ain't never spent a night in the Tottenham pigpen?"

Harlem ignores Toby, flicking through Google maps on his phone.

"Fastest way is up High Street." Toby flicks a thumb over his shoulder.

"Nah, we should go Beaconsfield, then Philip Street. Back way."

"True. Don't wanna get searched by filth." Toby pats his bulging blue backpack.

"Fuck you got in there?"

"Something I will not mention in questioning, and may later disown when evidence is given against me." Toby grins like a madman.

Harlem undoes the zip a few centimeters, peers in. Molotovs. Bloody hell.

They step up their pace as they turn the corner past Marcus Garvey Library. A bunch of elderly African men on the steps of the library building stop their chatting to watch the two of them pass by.

"Careful, sons," a man in a brown plaid bowling hat calls over the fence. "Lord watch over you all tonight."

"Fuck was that bout?" Toby asks Harlem, as they pass the bus garage.

"You know what?" Harlem smiles and squares his shoulders. "I think that's ole grandpa's way of sayin', 'Go on, boys, you have our full permission to burn London to the fricken ground.' "

Toby throws back his head and wolf howls as they skirt round a trio of parked cop cars.

"Holy fuckin' shit." Harlem stops to stare at the rippling crowd.

JUSTICE FOR MARK. STOP POLICE BRUTALITY. MET MURDER. DUGGAN IS ALL OF OUR SONS. They pause a moment to survey the signs: professionally sign-written, home-printed, handmade, scrawled in large childlike handwriting, dripped on with red paint to look like blood. Most of the placard-waving lot look Harlem's ma's age or older. Harlem's well surprised about that, though he guesses he shouldn't be. After all, it's all of them povo lot that are being royally fucked over—anyone down here, where him and Toby are.

Toby pushes through the closely packed crowd, elbowing his way closer to the cop station. Harlem sticks on his mate's tail, eyes glued to the blue backpack. Swallowed up by the throng, Harlem feels at home. Angry chatter hums over them, rising, collecting, pulsing like the gathering of a bee swarm.

The evening sunlight hits Harlem's face. They've reached the front of the crowd. The coppers are out in force, ringing the whole police station four or five deep. They're strapped into bulletproof vests, wearing clear riot masks and carrying shields.

"We are *all* Mark Duggan, we are *all* Mark Duggan, we are *all* Mark Duggan . . ." A woman somewhere in the crowd starts the refrain on a megaphone, static electrifying her words. Within a minute, her voice has been joined by several hundred. The bloke standing next to Harlem, a burly middle-aged man still wearing his fluoro council-worker's jacket, raises his right fist and repeatedly punches the air to the staccato mantra echoing around them.

"We are *all* Mark Duggan, we are *all* Mark Duggan, we are *all* Mark . . ."

Harlem wishes they'd fuckin' stop. He—*they*—are not Mark. Duggan is dead. Shot by the cops, at almost point-blank. Mark's mother has lost her child. Mark's children have lost their father. They are not Mark Duggan. *He* is not Mark Duggan. He is Harlem fuckin' Jones.

The cops shift in their positions, ears trained on their radios. Something's going on. Harlem looks over at Toby. His friend is several meters away, has stopped mid-chant. Their eyes meet. Toby whisks his bag from his back and disappears beneath the crowd. Harlem watches the spot where his friend was standing, holding his breath.

A smashing sound comes sudden, shotgun-like, scattering the crowd. A Molotov. Harlem breathes out. He and Toby cocktailed a car once—that dickhead principal's back at the Comprehensive. It was fuckin' magic; crystal rain glittering everywhere, flame bursting into being from nowhere.

The crowd has thinned. People have been startled in every

24

direction. The pigs step forward, shields raised in a single movement. Harlem steps back, eyes scanning the sixty or so youths left in front of the station. Toby's next to him now, passing him something. Harlem's fingers close on the glass bottle. The rag taped around it reeks of kerosene. His friend fishes in his jeans pocket, quickly tosses him a red plastic lighter. The coppers are moving forward now, pushing them back toward the road.

"Don't be stupid, son." Muffled by the riot mask, one of the coppers tries to raise his voice above the smashing, shouting, running, in the distance, stares Harlem down.

Harlem smiles. The pigs have no fuckin' idea what's coming to them. It's not just him this time—won't be just the few of them left behind to fight after the main crowd has scattered. There's an army of them, all over London, just waiting for the word. They're all angry; they're all armed. They're all Harlem Jones.

Harlem flicks the lighter on with his thumb, holds the flame up in front of his face. "My name," he says, "is not *son*. My name, my fuckin' *name*, is Harlem fuckin' Jones."

Holding the neck of the Molotov, he touches the flame to it and quickly pulls back his arm.

Hope

AT ALMOST fourteen, Mildred Lucas was already a beautiful young woman. Cappuccino-skinned, she had inherited what her mother called "good hair," tightly coiled like telephone cord rather than the dense frizz that crowned her seven younger brothers and sisters.

"Dat dere be Spanish blood dat done come tru de bloodline, chile. It frum ye fadda's grandaddy," Mrs. Lucas would tell her daughter, fondly stroking her curls as Millie worked at the family darning late at night after the younger children had gone to bed. "Folk, dem seh im was a pirate, ye know. Sail de seas an all. Ye tink im would leave nough treasure te keep im family outta want, but all im did leave was dis yere ringlet curl on top ye head."

Millie was born, and grew up, in Cidar Valley, Saint Thomas. Her home was nestled in an emerald dip at the foot of the Blue Mountains, some ten miles east of Kingston. The place was a small town, run on coffee and community. Most Cidar Valley residents worked with the coffee bean, in the local fields, factories, and processing plants still owned by British expatriates.

The Lucas family steered clear of coffee, except for utilizing discarded grounds in the tending of their livelihood—a small block of land on which they grew bananas and yams and kept a large coop of chickens, producing both eggs and meat. A small community of black growers and farmers surrounded the family.

Millie loved her childhood home. The way the mountains glistened shiny shades of jade at the height of wet season. The way the warm summer winds whispered softly through the cracks in the door of the Lucases' small cabin. There was little privacy at home, but there was always a fat-nappied, pumpkin-faced baby to be squeezed, and Millie loved the per-cussion of myriad hopscotch stones simultaneously scraping across the dirt driveway, the rhythmic slosh of her mother's spicy flying-fish stew being dished into ten wooden bowls at dinnertime.

But Millie knew her father wanted more for his children than this place, beloved to him as it was. In the dark of night, spooned up against the warm body of her twelve-year-old sis-ter, in the bed they'd shared since Millie was two, she pondered what life might have in store for her.

The neighborhood school in Cidar Valley was a one-room building run by the Pentecostal church. Though adequate, by island standards, in syllabus and staffing, it did not offer classes beyond those mandatory for a basic primary education. In a rural village, where jigging school for the day meant an extra pair of hands in the kitchen or garden, the school had ongoing problems with attendance. Learning the King's English played second fiddle to loosening hardened ground soil to dig a yam bed. Eldest daughters grew up rising at five to pummel maize meal for the family's porridge, and fell asleep at night sitting on wooden washing stools, chins slumped to chests.

Mr. Lucas had greater aspirations for his daughter. He knew for sure that something extraordinary rested in the fingertips of this child. Millie was no genius, but he'd watched her at her sums and spelling of an afternoon: the way her long tapered fingers pressed the pencil firmly down on the paper of her exercise book. He watched her at the kitchen sink on Sunday afternoons, plucking feathers from the still-warm bodies of fat garden chickens, yanking the strands from the flesh with a sharp flick of her wrist.

Millie's mother was a strong woman, stockily built with broad shoulders, coarse practical hands and earthy fingers not given to the delicate duck and weave of a sewing needle. At the age of eight, Millie had become responsible for the household darning, and within a year this had been extended to the fashioning of basic clothing items for the younger children, and mending for several other families in the village.

What to do with beautiful Millie had kept her father tossing and turning in his bed at night for almost twelve months. One evening he resigned himself to the logical conclusion. He turned to his wife, their old wooden bed creaking as he moved. "Ye know we gotta send dat girl te Kingston?" he asked, gently shaking her shoulder. "Edna, ye damn know it gotta be done." His wife played asleep, refusing to roll over or reply. She would protest his decision, the man knew it, but eventually she would come to see the light.

Mr. Lucas had no inkling of where in Kingston he was going to send his daughter or how he was going to get her there, but he had faith that the Lord would offer up a way. He knew that scraping that little something out of nothing was the legacy of the city, sordid as its beginnings were. Centuries back, the harbor of Port Royal had been multiculturalism at its fighting best. Swarthy Spanish pirates ate in dark taverns next to Roman Catholic priests before returning outside to deliver leftover scraps to the African slaves who'd been minding their horses. Located on the shipping route between Spain and Panama, Port Royal was the Sodom of the New World, a place a woman could do well, given the right body and inclination.

The Baptists of Jamaica believed the earthquake of 1692 was comeuppance for the depraved trading hub. The earth beneath the port opened just as the city was retiring for lunch, swallowing brothels, gambling dens, and trading shops filled with spices, silk, and doubloons. Quaker meeting houses caved in, churches crumbled and local synagogues sank: the wrath of a furious God against the golden gleam of sin.

The earth cracked in so many places that there was nowhere left to run, the ground parting wet and panting like a thousand lusting mouths, suctioning lives and livelihoods into fierce vacuums of quicksand. In truth, the quake was the result of an ever-adjusting Earth and shortsighted planning. The city was built flat against the sprawling palisades, founded on long sandy beaches prone to shifting with the tide.

Refugees moved inland, away from the death rubble and decay, and the smaller village of Kingston swelled to the occasion, gathering up those who had lost everything. Weeks turned into months, months turned into years, and years turned into decades. One day people looked up and a city had been built around them, bustling between the mountains and the sea. Old people were buried, new life birthed, and eventually all talk of leaving ceased. Somehow, Mr. Lucas knew that things would come right for his daughter in this place, that the girl was full of a kind of promise that would surely shrivel and wilt in that valley of theirs.

To this end, he planted an extra plot of sugar bananas in the back garden. He tended them especially carefully, circling them with coffee grounds to keep pests away, gently prodding curled baby leaves to unfurl under the yellow heat of the tropical sun. "Come, banana, come. Nothin' te be scared ov. Ye gwan be teyk care ov, jus ye concentrate on de growin', Mr. Lucas yere worry bout de rest. Ye gwan be mi daughter dere passage fe a new life, so grow, fruit, go on an grow. Curl out dem leaves an jus grow . . ." And slowly but surely, over the course of ten months, the stalks thickened. Large red-purple buds emerged, strong, fat, and blooming clusters of white flowers.

Millie watched her father from the kitchen window of their cabin, peered eagerly at the way he patted down the rich black grounds around her banana future with the toe of his weathered brown work boot. The plants were a testament there had to be something more out there for her than Cidar Valley, and that *something more* was drawing toward her, she could feel it.

Millie's younger brothers and sisters, knowing the fruit crop was intended to fund a better life for their elder sister, nicknamed her Banana Girl. The name soon caught on with the other Cidar Valley children. As Millie passed by, ferrying an apronful of yam to the kitchen to prepare for dinner, they'd jokingly hum strains of the "Banana Boat Song" under their breath. "*Six foot, seven foot, eight foot bunch, daylight come an we wan' go home* . . . Dere go Banana Girl again."

The other young men and women in the village tittered among themselves. "Wat greatness her daddy tink dat yellow flesh inside peel gwan bring?"

"Ye nyah haffi tell mi bout dat one. Her daddy, im tink her de brightest star in blackest sky. But twelve month come, de girl be still yere darnin fe whole village, or in de factory, sortin de bean."

"Hear, hear. First ting dem Pentecostal teach us up de school be dat pride a sin. An yere she is, swannin aroun tinkin she bettah dan all ov us."

Millie was a dreamer, with the city in her sights and a dream in her heart, and she wanted to do her family proud. The odd time she turned her mind over to it, the thought of staying in that there valley made her tired right down to her bones.

In the black of night, after the rest of the family had retired to bed, she padded barefoot across the garden, past the tomato, spinach, and yam plots, and stared at the banana plants. Seemed to her like they were speaking to her, all that bending, winking, and rustling in the wind. *Shee cah heeee tsssssss. Teeeeka sssssss heeeeeee.* Millie stood there listening, desperately trying to determine her destiny.

From the age of nine Millie had accompanied her father on rare journeys into Kingston to replenish hardware and sewing supplies. Regular black folk in the village wishing to fetch provisions were obliged to wait until a lorry in the area was going. The driver would make a tidy profit charging for a space in the tray of the truck, often so crowded the vehicle sat low to the ground, tires groaning all the way to town. Once arriving in the city, passengers were given a time and a place for the return pickup. Many a village man, having indulged in city overproof, was left stranded in the capital for several days, until the next lorry visited.

On their arrival in Kingston, Millie's father would walk her to Willemina's sewing shop on Port Royal Street, then cross town to seek out the hardware, cooking, and gardening supplies the family needed, before returning to pick up his daughter. Willemina was a striking woman of sixty-five with perfectly roller-curled silver-white hair framing her dark face. Wary of nimble-fingered children, the shopkeeper had trained her sharp gaze on Millie's every move as she worked her way around the shop with her basket on her first visit.

After several shopping trips and a few polite conversations, Willemina realized that in spite of her youth, the courteous girl knew exactly what she was looking for. Millie knew how to clothe a large family with the cheapest of material. Hessian bags from the hardware store were bleached then softened in boiling, soapy coconut oil and water. This material formed the tough outer layer of much of the family's clothing. From Willemina's store she bought cotton lining, thread, buttons, thimbles, and other sewing accessories, always quizzing the shopkeeper about the products prior to making a purchase.

The midyear visit of Millie's fourteenth year was different. As Millie browsed the cotton thread selection, she could feel the older woman's eyes following her. Willemina, for her part, couldn't believe what she saw. The child who had provided her store with custom since she was no more than knee high had almost grown into adulthood. The woman thought about what might be in store for the girl back home, helping care for her army of sibling pickneys. She thought about the shake in her own fingers when she threaded a needle these days, the ache in her back when she bent to stock the lower shelves.

"Dat chile go te school?" she asked Mr. Lucas curtly, when he arrived to pick Millie up.

"Course she go te school! Wat, ye think both she an mi dat foolish?" Mr. Lucas scolded Willemina.

"De girl sew?" Willemina kept her eyes on the length of cotton she was measuring out with a meter stick.

"Ye know she can, woman. Half de village run aroun naked iv nat fe she!" He placed a proud arm round his daughter, who in all her growing had now stretched up almost to his shoulder.

"She sew wid machine?" The aging woman tried not to sound too eager, could hardly believe her luck. "Mi can teach her dat, iv she so inclined. Long time now mi run likkle sewing school out back de shop on weeknights. In mi old age, mi lookin' fe help in de shop. Board, meal, an sewin' tuition fe right-minded girl."

Millie stood stock-still at the sewing shop counter. Her head felt giddy, and when her vision started blurring, she realized she was holding her breath. The woman was looking at her now, with those knowing eyes, as if between the two of them was a delicious secret.

"Mi tank ye kindly fe offer, but de girl only fourteen, an still gat half an one year in de village school te finish up. Mi put de proposal before de girl mudda an return fe give decision." Millie's father screwed up his face as if in thought, but in truth the man liked the idea and his mind was made up before the old woman had even finished her sentence.

The bananas Mr. Lucas had planted to fund his daughter's future grew like the young girl's fate was meant to be: almost spherically fat, full with white flesh, in such thick heavy bunches that the man had to prop them up with stakes lest the trunks break or bend to the ground.

That October, the wet season was unforgiving. The rains fell like the ocean would, if the entire seabed were yanked from underneath. For three whole weeks the wet did not let up, and with the steam of the following heat rush came Panama disease. The fungus first attacked the feeder roots of the banana plants, freckling them lightly with tiny brown spots. Mr. Lucas, crooning to his daughter's future-crop with a deep, velvety calypso as he tended the plot after the rains, noticed the disease when, starting at the outer edges, the jade-green leaves started to yellow. Within two weeks the tiny Panama freckles expanded to dark pockmarks, and the man knew his daughter's dreams were in trouble.

Millie's mother and father were away collecting coffee discards down at the processing plant when the area's agricultural inspector arrived. Millie watched from the kitchen window, fat tears welling in her eyes, as the large man let himself into the garden, almost wrenching the gate from its hinges.

"Jesus, iv ye listenin up dere, ye gatta help us now," the desperate girl appealed as her hands busied themselves with the washing-up. The man's heavy boots clumped around the banana plot, and after several minutes, he raised his head toward the house and stared at her through the cracked windowpane.

That night Millie watched her parents through the door slit of the room she shared with her four sisters. Her mother and father sat with their heads bowed, but she could see the tears, fat and wet, splash down their cheeks and into their laps. Snuggled back in bed, Millie thought about the woman in the sewing shop, the future that had somehow passed between them. Something would come, Millie knew it. Something would come.

Mr. Lucas was nothing if not resourceful. Hailing the next lorry into Kingston, he purchased as much marshmallow and spiced pig meat as he could carry. The Lucases' bonfire could be seen for miles around, raging flames dancing a glowing tangerine across the charcoal sky. As with all Cidar Valley gatherings, the whole community flocked around. Millie's father stood at the front gate, collecting ha'pennies for entry, laughing off the tut-tuts and annoyed teeth sucking of neighborhood scrooges. Millie and her mother manned a small stall near the burning banana brush, selling marshmallow and sausages by the stick while the younger kids stoked the glowing bonfire.

———

"Ye call Miss Willemina *Auntie*, ye hear, an ye gatta respeck her like she one an all."

Millie smiled, and watched her father try to blink away his pride-tears with scolding before he turned on his heel without a backward glance and headed for the return lorry to the valley. The girl was more than happy to bestow the honorary title on her guardian, a kindly woman, though stern in a well-meaning, grandmotherly sort of way.

Millie was a hard worker and the old woman congratulated herself often on her good fortune, rarely voicing a criticism about her apprentice's work. Around six every morning, Millie rolled out dough for bammy cake, which she fried up with banana chips and fresh fish for her and Aunt Willemina's breakfast. Once her tiny room was tidied and the breakfast dishes washed, Millie was free to amuse herself until the shop opened at nine.

The only sewing and haberdashery store in central Kingston, Willemina's was as busy as a market, but Millie managed to keep proceedings under control with her quick thinking and able fingers. Under her guardian's watchful eye, she embarked on a series of practical measures to streamline operations in the shop: dividing the large open room into clearly labeled sections, and precounting and bagging buttons so that the old woman's creaking knuckles did not have to do the job with every purchase. The girl firmly cut off credit when accounts reached a certain limit, where Willemina previously hadn't had the heart to do so. When customers commented on the old woman's good luck in finding her protégée, Aunt Willemina frowned at the girl's puffed-up chest. "Cha, chile, it be de death-a ye fe gwan get silly-proud an a big fat head, ah?"

On Tuesday, Wednesday, and Thursday nights, Millie attended the sewing school Willemina ran in a small shed out back of the shop. The room contained a blackboard and six sewing stations, and the walls were lined with shelves holding all manner of patterns and sewing implements. Aunt Willemina's sewing course ran over a twelve-month calendar year and, other than Millie, the class included five local girls of varying ages: the youngest about ten, the eldest close to eighteen. All materials for the classes were provided, but there were no set fees, the demand for dressmakers being so high in Kingston that acceptance into the unregistered and informal course was by highest bidder. Apparently unaware of their good fortune, many of the girls complained about the long hours and repetitive training.

"Mi nyah wan come te dis stupid sewin school, fe cryin out loud. But mi dadda seh if mi nat gwan finish secretary school, mi gatta haff a trade."

"'S if we nyah haff bettah tings te do wid our time, eh?"

While the other girls moseyed about before each evening's class groaning over their lot, Millie felt fortunate to be in attendance. But at night, snuggled down lonely in her big bed, shifting to find the warm spot her sister's body once afforded her, Millie dreamed of the banana plot, swaying and whispering in the wind.

Millie liked to walk along Kingston Beach during her recreation time, curls a-fly on the wind. It was a new and foreign sensation for a girl from the mountains to feel sand squishing in the spaces between her toes. The majestic sight and sound of the flat ocean filled the young woman with wonder. Millie rose way before dawn some mornings, creeping out to catch the bronze-flecked sun easing up over the shimmering water before breakfast preparation time. It was during one of these morning walks that she met Winston Gray.

Winston cut cane for a living, the only work available to an uneducated seventeen-year-old in his home region of Montego Bay, now that the war was over. The war had taken Winston's elder, and only, brother nearly four years back, fool that the young man had been to volunteer. Even though the fighting was now finished, Winston had decided to steer well clear of the armed forces.

Cane cutting was backbreaking work: bent down double under the scorching sun, Winston swept his sharpened machete a hair's width from the ground to harvest the plant. Once severed from the root, the cane stalk was shaved of leaf, sliced into even pieces, and the roughage discarded for later incineration. Then the whole process started again. In an irony the young man never came to appreciate, the cane forming the finest, sweetest sugar grew from a swamp of cow dung, mud and the burned ash of previously processed crops. Winston started work before five in the morning and cut until sundown. By midday, horseflies would be arriving to drink at his salty brow. All day, cow-itch nettles bothered and bruised the young man and his colleagues' shins.

But the day he met Millie, in the second-to-last week of his 1949 off-season, Winston wasn't thinking about work. He had money in his pocket, sand beneath his feet, and forty-eight hours left to kill in the capital. Walking toward Millie on the beach, he fell for the gentle young thing at first sight; after he'd passed her he turned on his heel and dropped into step next to her. The two remained silent for a kilometer, trotting side by side, before he took her hand. "Ye nyah mind if mi teyk liberty like dis, young lady?"

"Ye nat gwan get lovin', if dat de ting ye after. Mi nat girl like dat, fe sure."

He laughed at this, flashing his straight white teeth and shaking his head as if the very idea of it was ludicrous. Millie could have fit her whole world onto that smooth tongue of his. The girl's heart flipped and thumped like a flying fish thrown up on the beach, and she promptly fell in what she assumed must be that thing called love.

Some nights in the small cabin in Cidar Valley, Millie and the others would hear their parents together—the heavy breath of them, the creaky rusting springs of that saggy old bed. To Millie, that thing between her parents was all routine: warm, rhythmic comfort, just one of the many noises of their weathered wooden house. She was sure the sound of their loving must have thudded her to sleep as a baby—and probably it had, because look how many more babies her mother and dad had made since then.

But this was different: Winston's hands were so alive she could feel the pulse in them as they slid over her smooth body. His breath was hot and salty down her throat, stubbing out her own. She could have stopped him, she knew that, but she wanted the full of it. Millie knew what was coming and she settled into it. Winston's broad chest crushed down against her and she could feel every blade of beach grass digging into the soft skin of her behind as he expertly eased her knickers down below her knees.

"Dis a dream?" he queried in her ear as he pushed down into her. Millie closed her eyes, smiled at the bittersweet pain of it, and asked herself the same question.

It was after their glistening, sweaty bodies had clutched at each other in the sand dunes, when they were walking hand in hand in the cool morning air, that the young man told her he was leaving for Montego Bay in two days' time. Millie was heartbroken, but could not countenance her foolishness. Instead, she chose to believe Winston when he assured her he'd come to see her at his first opportunity. In her lover's eyes, she was certain she saw truth.

"Mi nat gwan forget bout ye, girl. Sometin' deep tellin' mi we gat future. Wide-stretchin' future. Mi write ye at de shop. An iv mi privileged, den de young lady will respond." He held her to him, gently wiping away her tears. Millie, a simple mountain girl who had never known such feelings, felt so full with happiness she thought she might die with the lightness of it all.

———

Willemina was not surprised to learn from a neighboring shopkeeper that her young charge had been seen being courted by a visitor to Kingston. Whereas women used to come to the store alone, these days their husbands often came with them, and the girl's gentle curves and budding breasts had also begun to turn the heads of young men on the street. Fear in her heart, Willemina had already sat the girl down and warned her to concentrate on her schoolwork and the shop. "Big up dat belly-a yours, ye ain't gwan do nuttin' but be stuck in dat dere valley ye grow up in, chile."

"Yes, Auntie." Millie had tried not to show her amusement.

"An don't roll ye eyes at mi, chile—ye tink mi crazy even mention it but, girl, mi know wat is a-comin'. Happen te many a young woman come te de city frum mountain or de plantations, chasin' big dreams."

"Aunt Willie, ye nyah haffi worry bout mi. Though mi tank ye greatly fe concern. Mi only come te Kingston te sew up an find mi way in dis yere big, big world. Only ting gwan big up dis belly-a mine is ten ton-a bammy cake an lots ov ackee fry-up."

Willemina watched the girl walk away, remembering her own young self and that handsome man who had promised her the world to entice her to stay on the island and make mischief outside his marriage. And by God, that mischief was sweet and worth making. But now here she was, alone and taking care of someone else's child in that godforsaken shop he'd bought to keep her there.

HOPE

When Millie returned from the beach that first day, Willemina quizzed her about where she'd been all morning. The doe-eyed girl told the old woman she'd been "wandering." Willemina was no fool. The girl had *wandered*, true enough. She'd been seen by gossip's eyes, holding hands and giggling with that Montego Bay boy. Willemina had had enough young girls through her classes over the years to recognize the dreamy step of a child who felt she had just become a woman.

"Ye fool, hear mi? Fool. Dat farm boy nat gwan return fe girl like yeself. In any case, ye far bettah dan dat kind ov youth." She cupped her hand tight beneath Millie's chin, spoke firmly, though she understood the heartbreak of it all.

Millie had heard stories about the root of Aunt Willemina's wealth. About the wealthy Haitian man with a wife and children who had set her up on the strip with her own sewing shop in her own name when she had been feisty and beautiful. She took the older woman's speech for half a lifetime of regret.

———

Millie had seen enough of her own mother's pregnancies to know what was happening when her breasts began to swell and she couldn't keep her morning bammy cake down, but she wasn't afraid. Winston would come back calling for her. So she waited. For five months, she waited.

For her part, Willemina pretended not to notice the gradual swelling of the fifteen-year-old's figure. During quiet spells in the shop, Millie examined dress and sweater designs to find those which would best conceal her indiscretion; her frowning guardian watching discreetly from behind the counter.

43

Millie had no confidantes in Kingston to speak of. The other girls in her sewing class shunned her—a hick from the hills who wore quaint, homemade clothes and spoke with a heavy patois that was hard work to decipher. Millie wrote regularly to her family in Cidar Valley, but knowing what great things they expected of her, she had no heart to tell them of her situation. Circumstances being what they were, they could ill afford to visit now that her sewing income had disappeared.

The first letter arrived some five weeks after Winston left Kingston, the postwoman winking and raising an eyebrow at Willemina as she slid the scented envelope across the sewing shop counter. The delicate cream rectangle screamed out against the olive green of the countertop. The boy's loopy cursive handwriting surprised the woman, given the cane-field loafer he was.

"Dat chile don need no more trouble," Willemina whispered to herself as she carefully tucked the small, thick package into her apron pocket.

When Millie reached the six-and-a-half-month mark, Willemina still hadn't mentioned the change in her figure. One day, though, after overhearing customers gossiping about Millie's predicament, she approached her charge with a proposal.

"Maybe bettah iv ye work out back de shop, mi bin tinkin'," she gently suggested after closing. "Ye demonstrate capability in de classroom enough te start customer alteration instead-a counter an shop tings. Wat seh ye work out de back nex few mont?"

The girl nodded gratefully as she sorted through the bucket of orange buttons, bagging them into groups of ten. "Mi sorry, Auntie. Mi nevah mean te get meself in dis yere trouble. Mi nat know iv ye can manage on ye own." Head bowed to the button sorting, she was afraid her eyes would well up with tears.

"Course mi can, chile, wat ye talkin' bout? Tough ole woman like meself can handle few mont tendin' te civility. Mi nat grave bound yet, God bless." Willemina had been awful lonely before the girl came along, and most of the time she was even secretly glad for the expectance of a newborn in the house.

Millie barely left the house during the last three months of her pregnancy, being by then unable to conceal her shape. On the one occasion her father made a shopping trip to town, she pretended to be bedridden with a cold: pulled the sheets up to her chin and peered at him over them, curled on her side. Mr. Lucas had sat gloomily next to her, thinking the sweat on his daughter's brow was the feverish kind.

Millie had no idea what the future held for her, and with an extraordinary mix of optimism and denial, she never allowed herself to think beyond the next day of living.

———

Willemina watched as the customer slowly made his way around the shop, running his fingers over button boxes, ribbons, and meter rolls, occasionally glancing up at her. She eased herself off the service stool behind the counter and made her way toward him, under the guise of tidying shelves.

"Where's the young helper?" the white man asked casually.

Willemina suddenly recognized him as the goods driver who hauled her sewing stock from the port every other month. "She nat in today," she replied, busying herself with a feather duster.

The man wasn't happy about that. He frowned, tapped two fingers impatiently on the elastic rack, as if he wanted to pursue the matter.

"Scuse me, ma'am?" Another voice came from behind Willemina. She turned to see a thin, nervous-looking woman. A shy girl of around thirteen stood anxiously next to her.

"It bout de school?" Willemina didn't mean to snap, but she was tired of the inquiries and anxious to get rid of that man. "Mi nat takin' application fe twelve mont now, mi sorry. Dere a list on de counter if ye wan put down ye detail an how much ye wan pay." The woman looked bitterly disappointed, but her daughter appeared relieved.

Turning back to scan the shop floor, Willemina realized the man had vanished. Was she ever glad for it. She couldn't recall the fellow's name but she'd heard talk about that one around town. Word was he had a habit of wandering those dirty-nailed fingers of his just where they were most unwanted.

Out in the back shed, Millie couldn't get the backstitching right. It was hopeless. The shed was like a steam room, and she could barely breathe. But then, maybe it wasn't that hot: sometimes the heat just got at her like that these days. Her stomach moved to and fro as if the baby were boiling up in the heat of her like a dumpling in oxtail soup. Millie stopped fiddling with the needle for a moment, wiped the sweat from her brow with the bottom of her white cotton blouse, then froze. A shadow had fallen across the sewing machine. And there was a hand. Thick white fingers resting on her shoulders.

"What's yer name?"

That voice was familiar somehow, but the hands were so firm on her shoulders she didn't dare look up to see who it was. The right hand was moving now. It was sliding down into her blouse, squeezing the top of her breast, which was already swollen from the baby and the heat. He either didn't care about the baby or couldn't see it there against the sewing table. Her lower back ached. The first cramp hit her hard and fast so she couldn't breathe.

"No need to be scared, miss," he assured her. "You and I are going to get along just fine. I've missed seeing you in the shop, you know."

Millie was confused. He was leaning into her now. Glancing up, she could see dirty yellow stubble on his chin. His voice was thin and rusty. She still couldn't place it.

Another cramp hit her, like a blow to the lower back. The baby was coming. "Uuughm." Millie slumped forward over the sewing machine, braced herself against the sewing bench.

"Best ye step away frum de young lady, ye hear mi!" From the door of the shed Willemina could see the man's back, as he bent down over the seated child. His right hand was out of sight and the woman didn't like to think about what he was busying it with. Willemina had known something was wrong, felt it in her bones. Lord, she should have checked on the girl earlier.

"No need for that, Miss W, the girl and I are getting along

just fine, aren't we, sweetheart?" His hand was still there, down her blouse, sliding down toward her nipple, the jagged nails grazing her skin.

"Mister, mi seh step away frum de girl. Mi nyah gwan ask again." Willemina took a step into the shed, edged sideways toward the meter stick leaning against the wall. Both his hands were at it now, and she could tell by Millie's breathing that the baby felt her fear.

"Get on away and leave us be, woman! The wrong trouble round here could bring strife for your license."

Bastard. Willemina knew he drank with the police up the boulevard; some Sunday mornings on her way to church she had seen him there, still swaying from the night before.

"Wille . . ." The girl was panting now, slouching lower over the sewing machine. The man's hands stayed where they were.

Willemina swooped up the meter stick, took four quick steps forward and brought it down hard on his head. The stick connected with his skull, holding there for a moment with static, then splintered suddenly in two. In the silence that followed, the man half turned toward the shopkeeper, stunned. Eyes glazing over, he dropped on top of the girl, his body looped over her shoulder, his face falling slack on the sewing desk. Millie screamed under the dead weight of him, her entire body convulsing as she pushed the unconscious man off her.

Before Millie could stop it, a terrified scream escaped from her throat. "Lawd, de baby. De baby, Auntie! De baby gwan come!" She immediately clamped her mouth shut, looking toward the open door of the shed. Willemina rushed toward

Millie, stooped down, grabbed the man by his boots and wedged his limp ankles under her arms. Drawing strength from God knew where, she leaned back and dragged the body out of the hot shed.

Returning, she told Millie, "Mi sarry, mi dear, but dere nat time fe move ye now. Dis baby on it way, though why it gatta choose such time fe come gwan baffle mi till end-a mi days." She gently closed the door of the sewing shed.

Millie could feel her insides pulsing. It was as if the baby had suddenly decided it wanted no more of her. She bit down hard on her trembling lips and tasted blood.

The birth was quick, but ripping. Just fifteen minutes of pushing. Puddled in blood on the unpolished concrete floor, Millie looked down at the tiny wriggling thing lying faceup between her legs. The three-weeks-early baby stared around him, squinty-eyed and suspicious as if scanning the place for something untoward, then opened his tiny throat with a piercing squeal.

"Wha ye lookin' so surprise fe?" Millie addressed the newborn. "Look like ye nyah know wat world ye comin' in te. Mi nat gwan bite, ye know." She loved the thing. How strangely and immediately she loved the little thing.

Willemina tied the umbilical cord close to the baby's stomach with thread from the wall rack and let the exhausted girl be, disappearing to close up shop and fetch a tub of warm water and some towels. The no-good driver was nowhere to be seen, the outline of his body-drag just a swirl in the dirt outside the shed door.

On her return, the shopkeeper tended to Millie so casually

it seemed she'd carried out the ritual countless times before. "Wait till it all come out an den go an clean yeself, girl, in de shower." She bustled about mopping the red from the floor.

Millie barely heard her. She was dumbstruck. This warm, scared little thing had been spun out of her, growing all that time while she tried to ignore it. Well, she couldn't now. Here it was, mouth open and searching for her. What should she care about that no-good Winston? What should she care if he never showed his face again? This here was a beautiful thing, this baby. A miracle.

"Eddison. Eddison William." Millie repeated the name, then pushed her rough, black nipple into the baby's open, waiting mouth.

———

Things soon returned so much to normal that, but for the baby, Millie sometimes thought Winston and the nine months following their encounter had been a dream. Mr. Lucas, shocked by his daughter's waywardness, nonetheless offered to take in the baby, have his wife raise it in Cidar Valley as their own. Willemina would have none of it. "De girl ole nough fe mek baby, den she ole nough fe look affer it fe nex fifteen year as well," she insisted. Millie thought herself immeasurably lucky to be kept on under the circumstances.

As Willemina's health deteriorated, it became clear that the young girl was being groomed to take over the sewing shop. Staffing the shop by day and working on alterations in the early evenings, baby Eddison slung tightly around her chest, Millie never had time to stop and think about whether the shop was the good fortune she had wanted for herself. At least, not until the day Winston turned up again.

One evening after closing time Millie was upstairs in the house looking over the accounts when she heard the raised voice of Aunt Willemina down in the shop. The girl hurried down in her white nightgown, the baby tied across her front, and found the old woman bashing a young man over the head with a stiff cardboard meter roll. Recognizing him immediately, Millie darted between them, confiscated the weapon from the old woman and began beating him with it herself.

"Ye lyin' field bwoy! Tink ye gwan waltz inte mi life jus like dat wen mi nat heard frum ye almost one year now. Mi nyah wan none of ye. Be off, ye hear mi, before mi do some real damage te dat handsome face-a yours so ye cyant go usin' it fe trickin' udda unsuspectin' girls! Go on, be off!"

Eventually Winston retreated out through the shop's front door and down the steps. "Send a young woman lettah, money, don hear frum er even affer she lead mi on an mi believe wi life together an she mi sweetheart!" he screamed. "An mi wonder why ye don write back. Mi don listen te udda worker on plantation. Dem seh mi crazy but mi seh nah, mi see it in er eye, dis woman gwan be mine if mi haffi kill fe getta. But de udda worker right, ye crazy woman. Crazy!"

Millie stared at him from the doorway. "Lettah? Ye nyah send no lettah, ye lyin' Montego Bay bush pig!"

Winston noticed Willemina retreating into the shop, pointed a forefinger at her. "Ask de ole woman. Mi send lettah without fail. Each mont. An money too."

Caught out, Willemina moved slowly to the cash register

and removed a stack of unopened envelopes from the locked cupboard underneath the till. "Sweet lawd, whatevah will be now will be," the old woman said, shuffling away in resignation.

Millie snatched them from her angrily, sat down on the front step of the shop and ripped open the letter postmarked earliest. The young man sat down next to her, silent as she opened and read through each of the letters, removing the pound notes one by one until a pile of five or so were stacked under the heel of her right foot.

"It gwan be our passage." Winston smiled shyly at her. "Te bettah life fe woman like yeself. Fe Inglan. Mi send more. Every mont till wi depart. What ye seh, miss? Ye gwan come make a life fe yeself wid a young man dat love ye wild? Marry mi! Even though some will seh it is madness an ye don know mi well enough te be mi wife."

"Winston, mi gotta tell ye sometin' true . . ." Fat tears streamed down Millie's cheeks.

Suddenly, he noticed the baby. How he'd not seen it till now he didn't know. It was a tiny thing, couldn't have been more than two months old, tied across the front of her white nightgown with a train of peach-colored linen. Winston's heart stopped. He stared at it. Was it? Couldn't be.

"Who dat?" Winston's eyes were wide. He sat rigid on the step, transfixed.

"It Eddison," Millie offered, tentatively. "Eddison William. But mi call im Sonny. Sonny fe short."

Foreign Soil

THE DRIVER Mukasa had booked had gone to look for a luggage cart and Mukasa was busy speaking in Luganda to the woman behind the customs desk, so Ange decided to go and look for a toilet. As soon as she walked away from her boyfriend, a man dressed in the Entebbe International Airport uniform sidled up to her.

"Gim sum din."

Ange stared at the man, petrified. This was it. She was being arrested. Somebody had somehow planted drugs on her, in her luggage. Images of a stricken Schapelle Corby being carted away by the Bali police flashed across her mind. She would be all over *A Current Affair*. There would be *Woman's Day* covers. The man was speaking to her in Luganda, gesturing to her handbag and pockets.

"I don't speak . . . Let me go and get my . . ."

Frustrated, the man rubbed his thumb and forefinger together. "Money. Gim sum money. Or sum din else. You pay."

"Oh. Okay . . ." Ange wasn't sure what the money was supposed to be for—maybe he was offering to carry their bags to the car. She and Mukasa already had the driver, but she didn't think an extra pair of hands would do any harm. She only had Australian dollars on her but she opened her purse and gave him a five-dollar note. Glancing behind him to check whether anyone had seen the exchange, he quickly pocketed the note and vanished into the crowd.

As Ange left the women's toilet and started making her way back toward the customs area, a second uniformed man accosted her. He was short and dumpy, with what she thought might have been tribal scarring on his cheeks. His English was better than the first man's.

"My friend said you gave him something," he said without blinking. "Now give me something too."

Ange stared at him, asked him to repeat himself.

"Give me something, miss. Now, please. Right now."

Shit. Mukasa had warned her about beggars, but these men *worked* here, for Christ's sake.

"Miss. Miss! Your husband is wanting you." The driver arrived then, shooing the man away.

"He's not my husband." She wasn't sure why she'd bothered to correct him.

"Well," the driver looked at her disapprovingly, "that *man* you came here with. The doctor. He is asking where you are. He is waiting on you." He gestured back toward the customs area. "Miss, if anybody here see you handing out money for free, your purse is going to be very empty."

Ange felt the heat rising in her cheeks, knew she must be flushing red. "Please. Don't tell my boyfriend."

————

Mukasa Kiteki had walked into the George Street salon one morning, asking for a haircut. The senior stylist, Penelope, had agreed to the cut then left him standing at the front counter while she hurried out back.

"There's a guy out there," she said, reaching for a cigarette, ignoring the no-smoking signs Dean had pointedly placed in the staff area. "He wants a haircut. I can't do it."

"Why not? He an ex-boyfriend of yours or something?" Dean had quipped. "God knows, we must have styled hundreds of them."

"No more than yours," Penelope replied matter-of-factly. "He's a black guy. I've never cut an Afro before. We never did that at college either."

"Don't look at me!" said Dean, looking over at Ange. "Go on, Angie. It's just hair, right? How hard can it be?"

The man was around six foot, with chocolate-brown skin and a wide white smile. Ange ushered him to a seat and he lowered himself into it slowly, watching her in the mirror as she nervously set out an array of hairdressing tools. He seemed quietly amused. "Don't worry. I'm not going to eat you. Just use the clippers. All over on a three blade, then tidy up the edges with the scissors or that razor thing."

His English was perfect. Ange felt silly for being surprised about this. There was a gentle accent wound around his soft, rumbling vowels. The way he spoke took Ange back to year nine choir practice at Mount Druitt High School. It was as if each word had a pitch, was notated somewhere in his brain for length, feel, tone. Ordinarily, Ange hated the obligatory chitchat that accompanied her job. She didn't give a fuck who thought their husband was having an affair, or whether red or burgundy was going to be this winter's must-have coat color. But she wanted to hear Mukasa speak again, so she racked her brain for suitable questions.

"So, where are you from?" Fucking stupid. She might as well have just pointed out that he was black. It had just kind of slipped out.

Mukasa had rolled his eyes slightly, looked down at the salon floor. Not in a mean way, but in a way that told her that question was probably the standard opening to most of his conversations.

"You know what?" she said quickly. "Seriously, I have no idea why I even said that. You must get so many dopes asking you where you're from. As if you want to be recounting your life story every five fucking minutes."

Mukasa looked up at her in the mirror. His mouth hung open for a while. "No, umm . . . it's okay. I'm actually from . . . You know what?" He laughed, his cheeks swelling against the pull of his smile. "You're absolutely right. Ask me something else. Let's start properly."

Ange liked the way he said that, *start properly.* As if it wasn't just a haircut. As if this were the beginning of the rest of their lives.

"Well. I don't know. The pressure's on now!" She slotted the blade-three attachment into the clippers and plugged them into the outlet. She could see Penelope in the background, raising an eyebrow at her flirting. "I guess . . . why *this* hair salon?"

He laughed again, and she was surprised at how giggly it was—shoulders trembling into his chin. "Oh, so profound." He nodded his head in mock seriousness.

"Okay. You're taking the piss out of me now." She smacked at his shoulder.

"If you really want to know, I tried every salon between here and Chinatown. You are the only person who agreed to tame this mane."

"Oh." Ange looked over at Penelope, but her manager had suddenly become intensely interested in sterilizing a set of combs.

By the end of the buzz cut, each of them had come away with the skeleton of the other's story. He'd said to her that she didn't seem to belong in a place like this. Quietly, as if the fancy salon was some kind of low-class brothel.

"Yet here I am, belonging," she'd laughed.

Mukasa's hair hadn't felt at all like Ange thought it would. It was cotton-wool soft, with a lot of give: an easy trim that had taken only fifteen minutes.

"Any chance you're free for dinner this evening?" he'd asked, after settling the bill.

Ange wasn't free. She was supposed to be meeting some of the girls at Bondi Icebergs for Penelope's birthday drinks, but Penelope was out of earshot, and something in Mukasa's face had made her say she was. All her life, Ange had felt she didn't belong to the drudgery around her, to her ordinary world. But here, right in front of her, was a chance at something remarkable.

———

It was stifling in the airport. The air-conditioning was apparently on the blink. The carefully sculpted haircut the Toni & Guy's staff had given Ange as a farewell present had flopped. The feathered chestnut ends stuck limp and sweaty to her neck as the driver walked with her back to the customs desk. She'd have been better off leaving her hair long—at least then she could have tied it back. The line behind Mukasa had grown to wind right round the back of the large room in a mazelike coil. He looked up, annoyed, as Ange joined him.

"I'd hate to be working in there right now." Ange gestured toward where the customs staff were busily opening cases and handing out forms.

"Oh, they do all right. Don't they, my friend?" Mukasa looked pointedly into the face of the man behind the desk in front of them. Her boyfriend had that impatient look on his face, the one he got at the grocery checkout, or in theater queues way back in the beginning when he used to take her out on dates at every opportunity. He jiggled his right leg, flexed his fingers. He didn't like it when things took too long. Mukasa never liked waiting, for anything.

———

The evening they left Australia, Mukasa and Ange had stopped off in Mount Druitt, to say one last good-bye to Ange's dad and mum. Mukasa had insisted on staying in the car with the engine running. There had been more tears, of course. Ange's mother was distraught, shaking as she held on to her daughter.

"Come on, Mum. I'll be back to visit by the end of the year. Kasa will look after me."

"Yes." Her mother had taken a deep breath, stepped back and wiped her eyes with her sleeves. "I guess he will."

As they pulled out of the driveway, thunder had rolled across Mukasa's face. "Thirty-five minutes," he'd said. "Thirty-five minutes I've been waiting out here by myself, Angela."

"I was saying good-bye. You could have come in." Ange sniffed, wiping at her eyes with a tissue. The drive would take fifty minutes at most, and there were still two hours till check-in.

Mukasa's hands were gripped tight around the steering wheel, his thin brown fingers turning almost tan as the blood drained out of them. "What for? So I could listen to your parents weep about me abducting you to the end of civilization?"

Ange had stared at him, shocked. This person wasn't Mukasa. He was always so gentle, respectful even. He was stressed out, that was the problem. He hadn't been back home for almost four years and had been busy frantically organizing things so the new hospital could open on time. Besides, she could hardly blame him for not wanting to witness her parents' grief at her leaving the country for a year. His own parents had died in a car crash in Kampala when he was just fifteen.

———

The customs officer stared back at Mukasa, unblinkingly.

"Can you check your suitcase, Angela?" Mukasa snapped, turning the open bag around to face her.

Ange lifted up a few T-shirts. The suitcase was less full than she remembered. Her jewelry box and the souvenirs she'd brought for his family were missing. After conferring with her, Mukasa listed the items. The man looked blankly at them and shook his head.

Mukasa cleared his throat angrily and pulled out his wallet. After counting through with his fingers, he slapped a wad of money down on the desk.

"How much is there?" the man asked quietly without looking up from his paperwork.

"One hundred thousand shilling," Mukasa said through clenched teeth.

Forty dollars. Ange guessed it was probably worth it.

In one quick movement, the man slid the money over the desk and into his pocket. He rose, taking the suitcase with him into the back room.

"This fucking piece-of-shit country," Mukasa raged under his breath. "No wonder it's going to the dogs. No wonder no one can get anything decent happening here!"

Guilty as it made her feel, hope turned over in Ange's stomach. In the three years she'd known him, Mukasa had never criticized his own country before. Much as she loved him and wanted to be part of his world, at the back of her mind she had worried that once they arrived he'd never want to leave this place. She feared that to be with him, she'd have to forgo everything that was hers. Ange felt ridiculous whenever these fears niggled at her. Mukasa had hardly given her any reason to believe he'd ever do anything other than try to please her.

After a few minutes, the customs officer returned with the case.

"Can you check the suitcase, please, Angela?" Mukasa undid the zip.

The case was fully packed again, including the missing items. Mukasa looked at her, one eyebrow raised. "Welcome to Uganda," he said.

———

For the first two years that Ange was dating Mukasa, it had all been a bit too *Guess Who's Coming to Dinner* for Ange's liking. Not that she blamed her parents; they weren't racist by any stretch, but Mukasa certainly wasn't what they would have expected for their only daughter—their only *child*. From the moment they realized he was African, her mum and dad hadn't wanted to know anything about him. For almost two years, they'd closed their ears to their daughter's happiness. Ange had learned not to even mention Mukasa when she visited them. Then, out of the blue, her father rang and invited Mukasa and her over for Friday dinner.

Her olds had been courteous, as they were with all their visitors, but every time Mukasa turned his back they'd both sneaked furtive glances at him, as if they couldn't quite believe what they were looking at. Ange couldn't remember any other person with brown skin ever having been in their family home. When Mukasa excused himself to use the bathroom, her mother's shoulders had slumped, deflating with the effort of it all. In the end it was too much for her father. He worked his way through half a case of beer and started banging on about how beautiful Ange was, how she looked just like her mother had when he had first met her.

"I guess that's not strange, is it?" he'd slurred. "I mean, really everybody wants to have children—a family—that look like them. Don't you think, Cash?"

"It's not Cash, it's Kasa." Ange had been mortified.

"I told you it wouldn't go well." Mukasa had shrugged as she walked him out to his car.

"I'm really sorry about that," she said. She wished they hadn't come separately, that she could climb in the passenger side and drive away with him in solidarity.

"Don't be," he said. "It's the first time they've met me. All I am right now is a big black penis that's boning their precious white princess."

He was laughing when he said it, but Ange could hear the bitterness behind his words. She'd kissed him through the driver's-side window. When the car pulled away, she noticed her parents' neighbor staring open-mouthed across the lawn, a look of revulsion distorting her face.

"What does he do, anyway, to be able to afford a car like that?" Her mum was still staring through the lounge-room curtains after Mukasa when Ange came back inside.

"He's a doctor," Ange snapped as she gathered her coat and bag.

Her mother and father had looked at each other in disbelief. She'd promised she would stay the night, spend some quality time with them, but she couldn't. She just couldn't.

———

Kasubi, Mengo, Nsambya, Nakasero . . . No matter how many times Ange repeated their names to herself, she could only ever remember three or four of the Ugandan hills at any one time. The entire first month in Uganda she spent in front of a map book. She had no need to leave the house on Makerere Hill, and didn't really want to. The house was a six-bedroom walled compound that had been in Mukasa's family for generations. He had grown up there, until his parents' accident, when he'd gone to live in Nairobi with his mother's sister and her children.

Though Mukasa scoffed at her fear, Ange felt safe at the compound in comparison to the Kampala streets. On the outskirts of the city, beggars and hawkers confronted her at almost every turn. They leered through the windows of the car, skin thick with the sweat and dust of not having washed for weeks, black dirt visible between their outstretched fingers. Ange knew they couldn't help it, and felt bad that they disgusted her so much. She just wasn't used to seeing people like that.

"That's what *actual* poor people look like, Ange. That is called poverty. Real poverty is not welfare cheats in hundred-dollar jeans and cozy housing-commission flats."

She hated the way Mukasa said it, laughing at her as if she'd been born sucking on a silver spoon. What had happened to his parents was a tragedy, but he was the one who'd been born into wealth.

At the house in Makerere there was a housekeeper, a driver, and a gardener to cater to just the two of them.

"This is ridiculous," Ange guffawed when Mukasa had introduced her to the staff the first morning. "I have two hands of my own, and there's nothing else for me to do here but housework."

"People will talk if we don't have enough help," Mukasa said.

Ange laughed again, thinking he was joking, but Mukasa looked at her with pity, as if she wasn't capable of understanding.

"One day, you will realize what it's like here," he'd said, closing the door softly behind him as he left for work. The staff had just stood there, staring expectantly at her.

Since the second day they'd been in Uganda, Mukasa had left for work at six in the morning, and returned at around eight at night. "Things, they will get easier," he assured her, "when the hospital is up and running."

But three months later he still rose at dawn and headed off to work, leaving her in the house with the help. Ange spent hours on the phone with her mother, and Penelope and Dean back at the salon, lying through her teeth about how well things were working out.

Now that she had the time to think about it, she and Mukasa had never spent great quantities of their time together. Even back home, after they'd moved in together, she was sandwiched between shifts, meetings, sleep, patients, lectures. Not that she'd minded; attending several of Mukasa's stuffy work functions early in their relationship had confirmed that she was more than happy to live on the periphery of his work life.

Now, though, she was starting to wonder how much of a person she could actually know if she only caught him in gaps and glimmers. She began to wonder if the real Mukasa Kiteki was another country entirely, whether what happened between them had always been carried out with the choreographed care and watchfulness brought on by foreign soil.

———

Ange rolled onto her back and ran her eyes across the bold printed headlines of the *Bukedde* newspaper. The letters *looked* the same as in English. It couldn't be *impossible* to learn Luganda.

It wasn't that she needed to speak her boyfriend's language. Just that, for some reason, Mukasa had reverted to it. Unless he was addressing Ange, or a hospital supplier overseas, he had barely spoken English since they arrived in Uganda. As a result, he'd rendered her mute in almost every encounter: with shopkeepers, colleagues, the help. Ange would stand to one side, waiting patiently for the interaction to finish, while Mukasa organized dinner, the landscaping, or a hospital night shift. Sometimes Ange caught Lucinda, the housekeeper, glancing at her apologetically as Mukasa held extended conversations with her in their mother tongue.

Giving up on the newspaper, Ange swung her legs over the side of the bed, slipped her feet into her slippers and padded out to the kitchen. Lucinda was standing at the counter, finely dicing meat on a blue plastic chopping board.

"Need any help, Lucinda?" Ange asked, already anticipating the young woman's well-rehearsed reply.

"No, thank you, miss." Lucinda didn't look up from the knife. "The Doctor would not like it."

Ange picked up a piece of carrot from a wooden chopping board and popped it into her mouth. "Yeah, well, the *Doctor* is a pompous arsehole sometimes."

Lucinda paused, knife poised above the lamb shank, and turned her head to look at Ange. Their eyes met, and after a moment of silence they both collapsed with laughter.

"Have you almost finished up?" Ange asked, wiping the tears from her eyes. "Once the stew is on, come drink some *waragi* with me."

Lucinda looked to the door, as if afraid Mukasa would return any minute.

"He has a late meeting," Ange said.

———

Without her headscarf, sitting comfortably on the leather lounge, and with her somber expression softened by half a cup of *waragi*, Lucinda looked almost as young as Ange.

"Miss, you are not what I expected," she smiled, "when the Doctor said he is bringing home with him a wife."

"I'm not his wife," Ange corrected her.

Lucinda looked genuinely surprised. "You don't seem happy here. And I thought that if you are not married to him and . . . not happy, then a woman like you would not be staying."

A woman like you. Ange set her glass down on the table. She shouldn't worry about it. Lucinda was just a simple housegirl— Mukasa was always reminding Ange of that. Lucinda didn't understand Ange's situation.

"A long time, I have known the Doctor," Lucinda said. "My mother worked for his mother in this house, when I was young. We lived out in the back house until the accident. The Doctor . . . even then he could be . . . very persuasive." Lucinda looked down, into her drink, as if she'd suddenly realized that what she held was a very tongue-loosening liquid.

The front door opened then. Mukasa stared at the two young women as he quietly closed it behind him, standing in the small entrance alcove that led into the lounge room.

"Have you not got dinner to cook or something else to do that I'm actually paying you for?" he boomed, taking off his jacket and holding it out to Lucinda.

The English, Ange realized, was for her benefit.

"Sorry, Doctor Kiteki. I am so very sorry, Doctor Kiteki, forgive me." Lucinda scuttled over to take the coat.

The look on Mukasa's face was one of satisfaction, as if he relished the young woman's fear. When he turned and saw Ange watching him, his face softened. Calmness came to his voice.

"Don't socialize with the servants," he said.

Ange felt sick to her stomach. *Servants.*

"I don't pay her to be friends with you."

She stared at him, lost for words.

———

Mukasa climbed into bed several hours after Ange did. She lay as far from him as possible, pretending to be asleep, the pillow underneath her head wet with tears.

"Where are you, Angie? Come over to me." Mukasa's

drunken fingers fumbled beneath the sheets. She could smell that awful Konyagi rum he'd taken to drinking.

"I'm tired, Kasa. And to be honest, that is the last thing I feel like right now." Ange pushed his hand away but it kept coming at her, insistent, annoyed. She rolled over to face him. He wasn't there, Mukasa. Just a masked man, nothing behind his eyes but urge. He was looking at her face but not really seeing. He climbed on top of her, groaning as he pushed his way into her body. Ange lay there quietly, her trembling body bracing itself against him, searching his eyes for something, *anything*. Him.

———

The first time Ange had seen Mukasa naked was in the studio apartment she was renting. It was about six months after that first date, and Penelope and Dean were really starting to rib her about the sex thing.

Penelope never tired of quizzing Ange about it. "Any action yet? Y'know, I've been thinking, maybe it's a religious thing. Maybe he's a closet Muslim and you're gonna have to marry him to see it. Or maybe it's too big, and he's scared that you'll jump out the window when he whips it out. You know what they say about black men."

"Oh, shut the *fuck* up, Penelope." In the beginning, it had been amusing to Ange as well, but she and Mukasa had been together now for almost half a year. Mukasa was always a gentleman, even asking for her permission the first time they kissed. There was no way he could misinterpret her advances, and yet when things got too heated he slowly backed out of the embrace—went to put the kettle on, or started talking about his day at work. She was sure he was probably just being considerate, careful.

Still, some nights Ange had stood in front of the mirror, staring distastefully at her body. Her legs were thin and lanky. Her slim white thighs were longer than she thought they should be. They'd served her more than amply when she was younger and used to run, but now they were a regular annoyance to her, particularly when she was trying to buy jeans—there was only flatness where the curve of her bottom should be. Her hips were narrow—barely existent, and without the underwired bra she usually wore, she felt practically flat up there. They were almost a B cup, which was something, but she couldn't help thinking her boyfriend's reluctance had something to do with them. She thought about the African women she'd met through Mukasa: friends who'd studied with him, or whose families had known his back home. They were mostly built like *real* women, Ange thought. Their hips curved out from their waists. Their firm thighs shaped upwards into impossibly rounded bottoms. As if the shape thing weren't enough of a turnoff, there was also the translucent whiteness of her naked skin.

Then, one day, Mukasa had come over straight from the hospital. They were due at the Theatre Royal at eight. A patient had given him free tickets. Mukasa was completely uninterested in musicals, but Ange had begged him to take her, and he'd eventually acquiesced.

Full of liquid bravado from the Crown Lager she'd nervously downed while waiting for him to arrive, she opened the door to her tiny bathroom and pushed his discarded work clothes aside with her foot. Through the shower glass she could see water streaming over the shiny mahogany of his smooth, tall body. He turned to look at her, surprised, but she started unbuttoning her blouse with one hand. She raised the other and pressed her index finger to her lips.

Three hours later—the musical well and truly missed— they lay exhausted on her bed, limbs intertwined, skin soaked with sweat. Ange was speechless. It was a word used in novels all the time, but she actually *couldn't talk*.

The minute Ange had walked through the salon door the next day, Penelope had looked her up and down and squealed, "Fucking no fucking way!"

Ange hadn't even said anything; it was there somehow, just in her walk.

———

Mukasa was standing over the bed when Ange woke up the next morning.

"Lucinda's gone. I dismissed her. From now on, you will do the cleaning and cooking." He bent at the waist and kissed her on the cheek, then fastened his tie and left the room.

Ange slowly wiped the sleep from her eyes, sat up in the bed. This couldn't be happening. It was a dream, all of it. If she closed her eyes, the alarm clock in her and Mukasa's sunny Strathfield apartment would start ringing, and she'd have to hurry to get to the station in time to catch the 8:10 train into the city.

She could walk out of the house now, out of the compound, call a taxi to the airport. All she needed was her passport. She didn't need to take her things. There'd be enough money in her account to get on the first plane out, or she could phone her parents to wire some. But Ange didn't want to leave, even now. She loved Mukasa, and she would make it work. She *could* make it work. She was angry about last night. The memory of Kasa's body pushing down on her made her feel sick. But it wasn't his fault. That wasn't him. She just had to somehow find the man who had walked into Toni & Guy that winter, that caring man she'd fallen in love with. Besides, the thought of returning to her old life—to asymmetrical inner-city haircuts and two-tone dye jobs—made her bored beyond desperation.

Ange slowly climbed out of bed and made her way over to the large walk-in wardrobe. She took out her navy-blue sweater dress, some sheer tights and her red ballet flats. Mukasa loved the outfit: he'd told her several times that it was one of his favorites.

After showering, she put on the clothes, dug her curling wand out of the bathroom cupboard and started working on the ends of her hair. Her leaving cut had long grown out. She'd asked Mukasa to let the driver take her to a place in Kampala to get her hair cut.

"Western hairdressers are hard to find," he'd said. "I'll ask around at the hospital and when I hear of a good one I'll get them to drop by the house."

Ange examined herself in the mirror. It was a long time since she'd made this much effort. No wonder Mukasa had started taking her for granted. She didn't have to let herself go to rack and ruin just because she didn't get out of the house all that much.

She smoothed a curl into place, turned on her heel and made her way to the kitchen. The fridge was enormous—a hulking three-door chrome beast of a thing. She'd barely had occasion to look inside it before, because most times she went within a meter of it Lucinda had somehow materialized from nowhere. She opened one of the doors and started pulling out onions.

Ange had always wanted breasts like this—a few sizes bigger, a little more pert, a touch rounder. She turned to one side. Her stomach was starting to swell. She didn't know much about pregnancy, but she guessed from the end of the morning sickness that she must be about four months along now. Lucky she wasn't showing yet. She was going to have to tell Mukasa soon. She was waiting just two more weeks, until the tickets for their first trip back to Australia had been booked. At first, not telling him had been about making sure she still made it home for the holiday. Then it had become a whole other thing. She felt stronger, more powerful, knowing she was concealing someone from him. Mukasa still spent twelve hours each day at work and came home to her and told her nothing. She'd been in Kampala for eight months now and the only people she'd met were his work colleagues and a handful of cousins. When she complained, he'd looked her up and down suspiciously. "Who else is there that you want to meet?"

But now she had this thing he didn't know about, not

only right under his nose but growing and breathing, taking up even more space, drawing ever closer, and he still couldn't see it.

Three weeks back, Ange's passport had disappeared. One day it was in her bedside drawer, the next it was gone. She'd told herself not to panic. Mukasa must have put it in the safe at work in case one of the house staff took off with it, or maybe he'd needed it to get the visa for the trip. She didn't fancy an argument, so she'd decided not to mention it. There was no malice involved, though, Ange was sure of it. It was just the prejudice she'd been brought up with that made her mind fly to the conclusions it did—her mother's hysterical voice ringing in her ears.

Whatever happened, she knew Mukasa loved her. She knew if she waited long enough, showed him that she wasn't planning on going anywhere, things would eventually go back to the way they were before.

———

Mukasa made it home for dinner at seven, an anomaly Ange appreciated. The millet bread had come out perfect, on her third attempt. She'd found an old stash of African cookbooks at the back of a kitchen cupboard, and they'd proved a godsend after Lucinda left. Never much interested in cooking, she now spent most of her day preparing elaborate dinners for when Mukasa came home.

Ange watched Mukasa take his first mouthful of stew, waiting for his nod of approval. He swirled the stew around in his mouth, swallowed it quickly, then broke off a bit of bread. Raising his head to look at her, he put the fork down slowly. "How long," he asked casually, "have you known you are pregnant?"

"Pardon?" She chewed the meat slowly, stalling.

"Well, have you actively been keeping it from me, or are you really so stupid you haven't even realized it? That's what I get for marrying a fucking hairdresser."

"We aren't married." The heat rose in Ange's face before she realized how angry she was. Once she started speaking, though, there was no checking herself. "You hear that? We're not fucking married, Mukasa. And even if we were, that wouldn't give you the right to treat me like shit!"

Rage was written all over Mukasa's face. He picked up the bowl of stew and threw it across the room. She saw his hand coming before she heard the bowl land, but she didn't have time to move. He reached out and wrapped his long fingers around her neck, jumping up from his seat so fast her whole body was lifted from the chair. The other hand came for her, fist crushing into her back.

Ange lay on the ground, gasping for air. Mukasa leaned down and grabbed her by the hair, bringing his face close to hers. She could smell the rich spices of the groundnut stew coming off his hot breath.

"You just remember," he spat, "who the fuck you are talking to here." He let go of her hair. Her head dropped suddenly, thudded against the polished wooden boards of the dining room floor.

Ange curled around her stomach, terrified he'd come at her again. Through the blur of tears she watched Mukasa's polished black shoes walk from the room. The front door slammed, and his car started up in the garage.

Behind her closed eyelids, Ange could see the outline of the African continent. She still looked at the map most mornings, made a game of memorizing the geography. Now, she traced the borders of Uganda in her mind, shutting out the dull ache at the back of her head, the shooting pains in her stomach. This country was crouched deep in the Nile Basin, sloping its way down into the wet marshes of Lake Kyoga. On the other side, it curved back up to the green giant, Mount Rwenzori. Uganda was locked by land. South Sudan, Rwanda, or Tanzania were the farthest she could run. Every escape would be ever more foreign soil.

Shu Yi

KELLYVILLE VILLAGE was made up of a bizarre assortment of dropout hillbillies, market gardeners and young one-income families. The center of village life was a short strip along the main artery of Windsor Road featuring ten or so locally owned businesses and small-goods shops and the public school, the prominent red-and-black emblem—a kookaburra on a shield—fixed to the front gate displaying the motto PLAY THE GAME.

It was typical everyone-knows-everyone-else's-business-and-can-I-borrow-a-cup-of-milk-for-the-kids'-breakfast-please suburban blond-brick Australia. The white-picket-fence dream was alive, kicking its calloused toes determinedly against apathy in rubber Franklin thongs. In summer, sprinklers rotated perpetually on lush front yards. Swimming-costumed children skylarked beneath the cool spray. Doors were left unlocked for neighborhood children to come and go as they pleased, and the dinnertime call from mothers was often boomed in a succession of megaphone-volumed reminders from a front step or porch. Extra table settings were standard in every household. If you played your cards right you could have dinner and dessert three times a night.

Nineteen ninety-two was the hottest summer on record, at least since I'd been born. Salt-N-Pepa were all over the airwaves. In our tiny suburb, between crimping bangs and rearranging fluoro bobby socks, all the other grade-three girls were singing "Let's Talk About Sex," too young to realize the real revolution wasn't bumping and grinding at eight and a half, but two unbroken young brown women giving the finger to the world on *Video Hits*.

Forget talking about it, I didn't even really know what sex *was*. Most of all, though, I didn't want a bar of Salt-N-Pepa, or any of their black-as-me friends. I hated my brother's MC Hammer flattop (lopsided, with a two-blade undercut) and happy pants, and my sister's hyper-color bodysuit and British Knights shoes. Mac Daddy from Kris Kross did not make me want to jump crazy up and down in high top shoes.

The real Aussie girls crimped and permed to get frizzy post-eighties Afros, but I was busy begging my mother for hair extensions, or saving up for Soul Pattinson's straightening goo. My blackness was the hulking beast crouched in the corner of every room, and absolutely nothing was going to make it seem cool.

Salt-N-Pepa. I wanted to be as far away from those two condiment shakers as I could possibly get, and if further change was on offer, then thank you very much, I also wanted to be a little less like me. I wanted less springy black Afro curl, eyes less the color of wet potting mix. I craved skin a little milkier than the specific shade of strong-coffee-with-a-dash-of-milk I was.

I never for one minute wanted to be Madonna or Olivia Newton-John or Kylie Minogue. I was already a realist. Besides which, I thought Melinda Meyer, the most popular girl in grade three (who looked most like I imagined Madonna or Olivia or Kylie would look up close), looked odd. Melinda's yellow curls were two shades lighter than her sun-tanned skin. Her eyes were the exact green of the Friday-night beer bottles my dad drank from, and drained just as empty. Looking like Melinda was the last thing I craved. All I wanted was to be a little less me, but nobody understood this, and I didn't know quite how to articulate it so they could.

Every lunchtime, instead of playing Catch and Kiss, I read in the library. I liked it in the library, though I knew enough to suspect that in real life the mothers of Stoneybrook would never have let Jessi, Claudia, or any other brown-skinned girl anywhere near their immaculately blond-bobbed children, even with the endorsement of the rest of Ann M. Martin's Babysitters Club.

———

The knock at the classroom door rapped out so loudly the whole class knew it was Mr. James, the school principal, and almost all of us froze. The only time Jailhouse James knocked in person was when a child was wanted for detention or there had been a complaint about a teacher. Us kids most feared the former, but in this case, the latter was distinctly possible.

Mr. Wilkinson, my grade-three teacher, was a renegade, by local standards. His thick, dark brown hair was always slicked back into a ponytail that hung down between his shoulder blades. He lived in a caravan out on an acreage property on the edge of the village, and preferred jeans and band T-shirts to the pleat pants and short-sleeved collared shirts the few other male teachers at the school wore. According to Melinda Meyer's mother, who was head of the Parents and Citizens Committee, Mr. Wilkinson was a *layabout hippie*.

"Class, there's somebody new and exciting we're going to meet!" Mr. Wilkinson grinned around the room as we hurried to pack away the brightly colored times-tables cards that had been stacked in the middle of each cluster of desks.

The door opened and Mr. James walked briskly in, scanning the room with his scary fake smile. "Good morning, 3D," he barked.

"Goood moooorning, Miister Jaaames," came the singsong reply.

Local rumor had it that Mr. James had been to Vietnam, in the war. Something evil had happened there, something odd, even for wartime, and the myth was that because of that thing, he had been guaranteed a cushy public-service job on his return. Melinda's mum reckoned the Viet Cong had captured him and done God knew what to make him the way he was. I didn't know who the Viet Cong were, but they sounded fierce and exciting, and if they could take someone like Mr. James hostage, I was in absolutely no doubt as to their power. In summer, Mr. James always turned off the ceiling fans before he entered a classroom. Melinda Meyer said the fans reminded him of the slit-eyed Chinks, up there in choppers, coming for him.

Mr. James surveyed the schoolyard most lunchtimes as if inspecting the ranks: hands clasped behind his back, head raised as he marched the concrete path that wound its way from the main cluster of buildings, down past the basketball court, through the primary play area and then back up through the infant school. During inspection Mr. James never strayed onto the grass but walked the path in short, sharp movements, the soles of his polished black lace-ups falling heavily on the pavement. In the event he spotted unacceptable behavior—a perfectly good sandwich being thrown out, a shoving incident on the basketball court—he'd stop dead. "Oi! You!" he'd shout, extending the index finger of his upturned right hand, beckoning the culprits over to him.

A skinny pair of legs and bright red Cooper Hill Public School backpack poked out from behind where the principal was stiffly standing. Mr. Wilkinson walked over to Mr. James and took the new student by the hand. Her lips trembled as she stepped into view. Mr. Wilkinson pulled his sweaty Eurythmics T-shirt away from his chest, airing himself. He rested his pale hand on the new girl's shiny black hair.

"Kids, this is Shu Yi."

Shu Yi was the most beautiful creature I had ever seen—seemed so otherworldly I was convinced she was from another planet entirely. Her skin was a little lighter than mine, and her eyes a little more almond in shape. She blinked over caramel-colored irises, nervously touched the straight charcoal hair cut close around her high cheekbones. The strands of Shu

Yi's hair were thin and wispy, like the black threads that hung from the Hiawatha skirt my mother had made me for the book week parade earlier in the year.

Shu Yi was exactly what I would have been like, if I were a little less me. Where I was flat white with an extra shot, Shu Yi was colored weak Milo. My soft, thick lips could suck a McThickShake through a yellow-and-red-striped straw no problem, but the new girl's features were delicate, as if crafted from fine porcelain. I stared, mesmerized, as her nervous wafer fingers brushed the hair from her face again.

The new girl was always quiet: head bowed, hair drawn across her face like a heavy black curtain. She sat alone during recess, fingertips disappearing into her round red Tupperware lunchbox and emerging tight around spicy-smelling clumps of rice.

The day after Shu Yi started at our school, we were in the back corner of the library during reading time, and Melinda Meyer said, "My mum said this country is going to the fucken dogs. We're thinking about moving out to Windsor because even Baulkham Hills is starting to look like another fucken country."

She said it in the kind of loud whisper you use when you really want everybody to hear. Melinda's mother's word was gospel on our playground, and her daughter a willing oracle.

"What country is this place starting to look like?" asked Glenn Hopkins.

"I don't know. Maybe Africa or something." Melinda smirked across the reading circle toward me as she turned the page of her Golden Book.

Shu Yi's life became a misery. When she walked out the back gate in the afternoons, misshapen spitball constellations stood out against her satin hair. She returned from snack time missing frilly socks, scrunchies, or sparkly hair clips, her eyes puffy and downcast.

I buried my face in the library's big Hans Christian Andersen, hunkered down in the worn gray bean bag in Fairy-tale Corner. Wondrous as she seemed, Shu Yi wasn't a problem I wanted to take on. Besides, with her arrival my own life had become easier: Melinda and the others hadn't come looking for me in months. At home, my thankful mother had finally taken the plastic undersheet off my bed.

———

My mother always went quiet when she wanted to talk to one of us kids about something serious. If she cleared the plates from the kitchen table after dinner in ponderous silence, you prayed it wasn't you she had to talk to, and tried to make yourself scarce. On this particular evening she cleared away the almost-full plates of apricot chicken without so much as a reprimand.

"Ava? Stay here a minute," she said. My brother and sister crept from the kitchen, relieved.

I sat staring at the woven cane placemat, digging a stray pea from one of the holes with my finger.

"I was just wondering, Ave," she said, sitting down across from me, patting her curly hair in place, "how that new girl's getting on. What's her name again?"

"Shu Yi." I willed the conversation to finish.

"Shu Yi. Well, she doesn't seem very happy," she said softly. "I mean, I never see her walking with anyone on the playground. Do you talk to her?"

"Um. She doesn't really speak much English."

"I see." My mother's eyes were boring into me. "When you start at a new school, it can be really difficult to fit in. Sometimes, if you're different, it can be difficult to fit in even if you've been there since the very beginning."

"Whatever."

She stared at me expectantly.

Our mother had worked tirelessly to fit our brown-skinned family of five into the conservative white suburbia in which we somehow found ourselves. Our entire neighborhood seemed built around the Mecca of Mum: the school cafeteria worker, school fete organizer, and office holder for the Kellyville Reciprocal Babysitting Club. On rare occasions, though, I would see another side of her. We'd be in the Castle Hill shopping mall searching for winter pajamas or piling into the car on Saturday after Little Athletics, and suddenly the woman would freeze, eyes wide and fixed in the other direction staring at something. Then us kids would be unbuckled at the speed of light and bustled across the road, or shoveled into the shopping cart as it screeched over to the other side of the supermarket. We came to recognize the cause of these impromptu dashes: my mother had spied, lurking conspicuously on the periphery of our whitewashed surburban lives, another black woman.

A *visit* would usually follow closely after, and inevitably there'd be other black children present. Directed by the adults to *go play outside*, we'd stand gaping at each other: *them* and

SHU YI

us—total strangers somehow expected to bond as kin. As with any family gatherings of this kind there were sometimes connections, firm friendships leading to reciprocal *visits*. Then there were those other encounters, in which, despite our mirrored scuffed-gray knees, knotty Afros and way-too-smart-for-Aussie-children special-occasion attire, the kids we visited with were as unlike us as the local louts who threw stones at us at the BMX track on Greenwood Road.

Right now, my mother had that *visit* look on her face. "I was thinking maybe we should go and speak to Mr. James about what's going on."

"What are you talking about, Mum? Nothing's *going on*." I felt sick to my stomach. "It's nothing to do with us if Shu Yi can't make her own friends."

"Tomorrow morning," my mother said, in the tone that meant the conversation was closed. She rose slowly from the table, disappointment etched into her face.

———

The school bell rang, and from where I sat in the front office, I could hear several hundred feet thundering across the asphalt. I wanted to join them—to grab my bag from the floor, throw it over my shoulder and stumble down the stairs into morning assembly.

The school creed drifted up through the office windows. "This is our school. Let peace dwell here. Let the rooms be full of happiness."

I had never been so close to the principal's office before. I fidgeted on the scratchy chair, wiping my sweaty palms on the woven seat covers. The school secretary looked over again, in disapproval.

"Let love abide here: love of God, love of one another, and love of life itself," came the chorus from the playground below.

My mother's raised voice drifted out of the principal's partly open door. "No, Ian, I'm not saying she should be treated any differently from any other new student. It's just pretty obvious to all and sundry that the girl's being bullied."

"Are you accusing one of my students of harassment?" Mr. James's reply was sharp. "Has Ava reported anything? Has the . . . *girl* reported anything?"

"Oh, come off it, Ian." Mum's voice was softer now, like she was trying to reason with him. "Any fool can see what's going on."

"Mrs. Dalley . . ." Mr. James said. From the way his voice wavered, I could tell he had risen to show my mother the door. "This girl is just going to have to learn how to get on. You can't come to this country and expect everybody to bend over backward so you feel comfortable."

The door opened wide. My mother stormed out of the office, walking straight past me. I grabbed my bag and followed her down the stairs.

"Racist prick," my mother said under her breath. We walked across the schoolyard following the line of students heading toward my classroom.

I had never before heard her swear.

———

Mum gently shoved me into the classroom, the curious eyes of the rest of the class fixed on me. Mr. Wilkinson stepped out into the cloakroom to speak with her, closing the door behind him. I walked to my desk and busied myself putting away my pencil case and homework book, ignoring the twenty-three pairs of eyes fixed curiously on my back. After a few minutes the classroom door opened again. Mr. Wilkinson gestured for me and Shu Yi to join the two of them in the cloakroom.

"Ava, your mother says Shu Yi has been having some trouble adjusting at school."

I stared at the rows of red schoolbags, all hanging on their hooks. The black kookaburras embroidered on each front pocket glared at me, the school motto trumpeting from each of their beaks: PLAY THE GAME.

"Ava?" Mum sounded agitated now.

Shu Yi was looking at the ground. Her head was bowed so low that I could see the tuft at the back of her head where Glenn had cut a chunk of her hair during art class the previous week.

"Ava," said Mr. Wilkinson gently, "I know you can be relied on to help Shu Yi to feel comfortable at her new school."

Shu Yi raised her eyes from the ground, fixed them hopefully on me.

———

I hurried out of class at lunchtime, not even bothering to get my lunchbox from my backpack. I could feel Shu Yi following me all the way from the grade-three seats up past the staff room. She walked several meters behind, keeping close to the brick wall as if it would somehow camouflage her movements. Glancing in the glass door of the library I saw her behind me, stooping to place her red lunchbox on the library steps before quietly following me in.

As I made my way to Fairy-tale Corner, all I could think about was that round red lunchbox out there on the library steps. I could taste vomit in my mouth. Shu Yi probably knew nothing of bulls and flags, or the breadcrumb trails Hansel and Gretel left when they were led into the dark forest—she probably thought leaving food outside was good etiquette.

A shadow fell across where Snugglepot and Cuddlepie were sitting on the eucalyptus log on page four of the book that was balanced in my lap. Shu Yi was standing in front of my bean bag. Her slim shadow moved, and cast the Banksia Men into darkness. I clenched my hands around the open cover of the book, willing the girl to walk away.

The library door opened. Footsteps clattered onto the foyer linoleum, then padded onto the reading area carpet. I knew without looking up what kind of company we had.

"Please, I sit here with you today." Usually when Shu Yi spoke she scrabbled for words, eyes rolling inward as if searching the far reaches of her mind for a translation. This request came stilted but sure. As if she'd been practicing that morning before her bathroom mirror as she brushed the rice porridge from between her slightly crooked teeth.

Shu Yi glanced behind her as Melinda and her mates semi-circled around us, turned back to me pleadingly. I slammed the book shut and whispered—the loud, hissing kind of whisper you really want everyone in the room to hear—"Fuck off, you filthy Chink."

Melinda laughed, repeating my comment to the tittering group of kids.

Shu Yi's eyes locked with mine. A thin trickle traveled out from the bottom of her uniform and down the inside of her legs, soaking slowly into her frilly white socks.

Railton Road

HIS FIRST night at the rebel squat, Solomon dreamed he was ancient Africa, stretched out wide and deep center-globe, cradling a people. On his lower left shoulder in southern Togo, their mahogany faces caked with thick white clay paint, the Anlo Ewe people stamped thanks to the sky god Mawu-Lisa. The blood of young goats was a warm iron-filled offering, sinking into the sandy earth of the villages spread across his muscular chest.

Solomon dreamed he was Africa, and the Songhay people were conjuring spirit Hauka which danced light-footed across the black-earth ridges of his startled nipple, trapped inside the bucking bodies of taken tribespeople. Village messengers, *djembes* slung across their backs, gently drummed their cryings up and down his rib cage, rocking him back to sleep. Solomon dreamed he was ancient Africa, and his history had no beginning. He dreamed he was forever, remembering more than centuries.

The rebel hub at 121 Railton Road, Brixton, was inhabited by fiery like-minded black youths from all over England. The occupants of Railton Road were bell-jeaned, dome-Afroed, Doc Martened and muscle-teed: as bad and black as they could possibly muster themselves to be, with yearning amber eyes filled with each other and runaway tongues tripping with talk of equality.

Railton Road was a hive of activity. The squat's many bedrooms were wall to wall with mattresses and tatty multi-colored blankets. The shop in the property's lower half was busy twenty-four seven with placard-making tables and the day-and-night thunder and thud of an aging printing press. The cauldron-like pot in the informal cooking pit of the small garden was always brimming. So much so that almost a hundred random brown folk with little aspiration toward black empowerment regularly dropped by the place as if it were a soup kitchen, trading an hour's work manning the printing press or distributing pamphlets for shelter on a bitter night or a steaming hot-pot meal.

In response to ongoing police harassment and eviction attempts, the hand-painted sign permanently tacked to the front of the property read: *Legal warning: this property has been occupied by squatters. we intend to stay here. if you try to evict us, we will prosecute. you must deal with us through the courts.* Time and again the Railton Road Panthers were arrested for squatting on the property, but despite double deadbolts, police barricading, and barred windows, they inevitably scaled, fought, or burrowed their way back in on release.

"This is *my* property. And the law says I have to waste my valuable time attending court to get these hooligans evicted. It's bloody outrageous!" the landlord seethed into the BBC camera as he forced his shoulder hard against the front door, to no avail.

An upstairs window was wedged open noisily. A slim young black woman shimmied her legs over the sill and dangled them down toward the road, frowning at the noise. "Away from the front door, mister, you're breaking the law," she yelled down at the landlord. "We're trying to *learn* some shit in here."

The property owner stared up at her, then bent down suddenly, removed his shoe, and hurled it up at the window. The shoe's trajectory peaked two meters short of the woman. It hurtled back down to fall at the man's feet.

"Hey now, we're right peaceful in 'ere. Why you gotta be so violent, Babylon?" The woman flicked up her middle finger in disgust.

A police car pulled up outside the property, and the cameraman about-faced to film its arrival. From the still-open window, a black canvas sandshoe came rocketing in the direction of the landlord. Missing its mark, the sneaker startled the cameraman backward.

"Away from the window, Liv," Solomon cautioned from inside the makeshift classroom. His chalk-dusted hand was poised above the enormous black-painted wall he used as a board for his Black History classes. Struggling to maintain his frown, the young man turned his face back to his writing. It was difficult not to laugh at Liv's antics as she balanced pre-

cariously on the windowsill, preparing to make a missile of her
second shoe.

The fire of the Railton Road rebel women was legendary.
Along with their flares and clingy velour long-sleeved tees,
they wore handmade African jewelry of exaggerated propor-
tions: wooden carved giraffe earrings as large as the ear itself,
and elaborately beaded necklaces long enough to hang to the
navel even when wrapped around the neck several times. You
didn't want to catch yourself messing with these sisters, Solomon knew from experience.

She was beautiful, though, this Olivia, with that cheeky
sass and no-nonsense glare—those round, full cheeks and
treacle-colored skin. Her left eye was glazed light blue, had
been blinded in a scuffle with the cops at the national gathering six months ago in Birmingham. But even after that, Olivia
was still breathtaking. Breathtaking and, Solomon was sure,
starting to come round to him.

Solomon finished scrawling the chapter number of the
sermon, threw the chalk down on the ground and turned back
to face the fourteen or so students who were dotted around the
shag-carpeted room in various positions: on tatty cushions,
sunk into wilted bean bags, resting their backs against the
walls. He wiped his hands on his thighs then paused to look
down at the thin layer of chalk dust finger-painted onto his
black cords. His Doc Martens, threaded with the standard-
issue yellow-flecked laces, were badly scuffed.

Solomon suddenly looked up. "Genesis nine, twenty to
twenty-seven," he announced, his eyes stilled with the gravity
of his task.

The rebel students clapped in anticipation. This definitely wouldn't be another church sermon of the kind they'd been avoiding from their grandparents and various community do-gooders all school break.

"In Genesis nine, twenty to twenty-seven," Solomon continued in the booming oratory of a Baptist preacher, "Noah tilted his face toward the east from where he stood on the fertile African soil of the border between Libya and Algeria."

The classroom hushed. Angry voices wafted up from the street below, buzzing mosquito-like through the quiet.

"From where he stood on the border between Libya and Algeria, Noah's gaze swept across to Afghanistan: over the dry Egyptian desert, through the raging rivers of Jordan, and out through Iran."

"Hallelujah, that *ain't* no Bible story," an approving voice came from the back of the classroom.

"Dis man im prophet, praise de *Lawd*!" a young cedar-skinned Bajan girl with short spiky dreads chuckled behind her hands.

The rest of the class shushed them to silence.

Aware now that he had their full attention, Solomon threw everything he had into establishing the opening tableau. He bent forward as if leaning on a walking stick with one hand, mimed stroking a long beard with the other. "Noah's gaze swept across to Afghanistan: over Egypt, through the rivers of Jordan, and out through Iran. His dusty white robes curtained down from his prophetic hand, as he turned and put the voodoo hex on his son Ham, through his grandson Canaan." Solomon paused and looked slowly up at the class from his hunched-over position. "What did Noah say to his son?"

The young Bajan woman stared at him, eyes wide. "Canaan's curse," she whispered quietly from behind her hand.

"You, girl." Solomon pointed at her with a sudden start that caused half the room to jump. "Repeat. Louder!" he barked.

" 'Let your bloodline be cursed with servitude, for you betrayed me, son.' " She recalled the sermon by rote, in the singsong recitation of a girl who'd been churchgoing since early childhood but never had the inclination to roll the words around in all her consciousness.

"Let your bloodline be cursed with slavery . . ." Solomon straightened his back and paced up and down the worn tan carpet, weaving in and out of the seated students. "These are the words the antiabolitionists, the slave traders, the missionaries hung the annihilation of the African continent on."

Solomon's sermon was electric, and the students were enthralled, but Solomon was running on autopilot. More important things were clouding his mind than the Genesis lecture and all the raucous goings-on outside. The Railton Road Panthers were expecting an important visitor from their brothers down at the Black House on Holloway Road. Solomon was waiting for De Frankie, or whatever the shapeshifter chose to call himself today. Solomon had been running the Black History classes at the Railton Road squat for almost twenty months now, a position he'd snagged as a result of his modern history degree, and which guaranteed him floor space to sleep on and scratch meals but was otherwise unpaid. Talk had it De Frankie was on his way to sound Solomon out for the position of Minister for Culture for the rising London Panthers.

De Frankie came from the Old World—Port of Spain, Trinidad. The man had done time, lots of it. That much Solomon knew. Drugs, racketeering, attempted murder, rape: talk varied as to exactly what he'd been in the lockup for but seldom as to whether the charges were bona fide. A recent issue of the States brothers' *Black Panther* newspaper at the Railton Road library showed De Frankie bumping fists with Malcolm outside a barbershop in Harlem. Malcolm fucking X. Their own Black British version of the paper, *Freedom Now*, sold on street corners from Brixton to Walthamstow, had recently documented the man's supporters. The list filled a quarter-page column. Lennon and Yoko were on it—*Lennon and Yoko, for crying out loud!* Thousands of pounds, they'd donated.

Solomon delivered his closing rhetoric then quickly dismissed the class. Roll on, De Frankie. This man would bring the revolution, Solomon was sure of it. He could hear the fiery thing approaching: the sound of a million kettledrums; of quiet rolls of thunder; of tough, dark hands beating down against hard pigskin leather. Africa was stirring. In Jamaica, in Barbados, in Trinidad. In Haiti, Guyana, Rhodesia. In Brazil, Botswana, Antigua. In Kenya, Rwanda, Ethiopia, Africa was slowly rising.

The fear and wariness Solomon and his contemporaries had encountered upon their birth into the New World was in many ways predictable. Over time, though, it had suckled on itself, mutating into a bloodthirstiness that enraged Solomon. His uncle Markie, his father's elder brother, had been buried back in Jamaica, but had fought and died under the Union Jack. Solomon's own parents, pity their blind trust, had been persuaded to migrate by immigration barkers planted on the islands by the very country that now refused to acknowledge the white hate that stalked black children on its streets.

Solomon knew the whole country could feel the Black discontent lurking beneath the surface, readying itself to launch at them. All over England, whites were gathering themselves against it. He'd even noticed a change in the growing-up National Fronters: the way they drew themselves upright now when they passed by him on the street, in a step of entitlement, once-scrawny plucked-chicken bodies filled out into broad shoulders and lean hard muscle. It was as if, over time, the Front had nourished a part of the misfits previously starved of the nutrients they required to thrive.

The Fronters would come for them sooner or later. Solomon and the other rebels could feel it. They were sick with the hopelessness of it all: the sit-ins, the placards, the letter writing. They were tired of the Special Patrol pat-downs and Met curb-cruising. And it seemed to Solomon that the world was with them, the brown world at least, rallying for their dues, fighting for freedom. Across the ocean, Malcolm had been taken. King too. And still the anger kept rolling—gathering and collecting until it seemed so large and universal that all of them felt electric with it.

———

De Frankie thoughtfully stroked his thick beard. There was a wildness in his eyes that told Solomon he was dangerous.

Not that kind of big-lipped, coal-faced dangerous the London newspapers implied when they spoke of "racial unrest" in the north, but a yellow-flecked iris insanity that said he was well prepared to kill, and maybe even already had. Solomon had expected anger, hate for sure, but not this kind of chilling skittishness. He'd been in De Frankie's company for close to two hours and still felt on guard. They sat over their fourth whisky on ice at the kitchen table on the second floor of the Railton Road headquarters.

"So. Three years at the Tech. In modern history. White history. Man like you, well schooled in Babylon's lies. And you want a brother to trust the culture of the movement to you?"

"You gotta know what they believe in before you can dismantle it," Solomon replied carefully, lips slurping round an ice cube. His head was swimming. *Stop drinking. The man wants you off balance.*

De Frankie refilled Solomon's glass, carefully placed the bottle back down on the worn wooden table. Nerves getting the better of him, Solomon reached out and raised the full glass halfway to his lips. De Frankie quickly leaned forward and caught his elbow. Whisky slopped over the side of Solomon's glass and onto his wrist. De Frankie's fingernails dug into Solomon's skin as he stared him in the face.

"What is it *you* believe in, Solomon?"

Solomon breathed in sharply.

"Tell me what this doesn't." De Frankie let go of Solomon's arm and tapped the three-page manifesto Solomon had been asked to write in preparation for the meeting.

"What that doesn't tell you, you don't need to know." Solomon spoke firmly.

De Frankie looked irritated. "I heard you got children."

Goddamn. Motherfuck that. Solomon set his glass down on the table. He'd been sure that any disagreement between them would be around religion. Most of the brothers were into all the Muslim shit; he quietly went along with it as much as he had to, but anybody with half a mind could see he was a skeptic. There was no lack of loyalty in that, as far as Solomon was concerned. It was just that he didn't need some religion to back his claim to what was rightfully for his people. But the *babies.* Fuck.

"Haven't got no children." He knew that shit would bubble to the surface sooner or later. He'd never heard from either of those white girls since his mother had kicked him out of the house on Curtis Field Road. He'd just figured they'd had themselves taken care of or each given their baby to some bleeding-heart bourgeois black couple. What kind of simple-minded white English girl wanted to keep a little brown baby and end up all alone and talked about till kingdom come?

"Some sweet little white girl that's got a baby lookin' jus like your ugly mug says you're a dadda." De Frankie looked at Solomon knowingly.

Solomon had read all about the man's views on the matter, heard him on the radio talking about betrayal and lynching black girls who take up with white fellows, making mockeries of black men. Solomon couldn't understand it, really. One glance at the man and you could tell there was ivory close to the bloodline.

"I tasted that candy once. The milk-bottle kind. It's poisonous. Rots you." De Frankie frowned at Solomon.

Liv entered the room then, nodded at them, shuffled around in a kitchen drawer for barbecue tongs.

"Nobody told you to knock around here, sister? We're talking, innit!" De Frankie boomed, relishing the young woman's startled expression. His eyes were fixed on the underwear outline showing through the seat of Liv's camel-colored flares as she retreated from the room.

De Frankie sucked on his teeth, grinned at Solomon. "Now that's the kind of health farm I'd like to visit. Real wholesome. That warm little cornmeal bowl would fix me up good, don't I know it. Amen!"

Under the table, Solomon clenched his fists.

———

Following De Frankie to Railton Road came the new Panthers crew—a thug-squad assortment of ex-cons disillusioned with the academic leanings of the movement. Their step was heavy, with the can't-lose confidence of having already sacrificed everything for that growing, pulsating black anger. Their eyes glowed like hot coals. They were armed with practical skills that Railton Road badly needed: they were butchers, blacksmiths, mechanics, and builders. The new rebels called for a body count, and it seemed evident to Solomon that the war had finally arrived.

Outside Holloway Road tube station, coat collar up against the cold, Solomon leaned against a brick wall, blew on the fingertips poking out through the ends of his woolen gloves.

He could just make out De Frankie's head leaning out from behind the wooden palings of the terrace on the corner of Holloway and Francis. De Frankie's navy beanie was pulled tightly over his bushy Afro. He was barely visible to Solomon in the evening fog.

The man at the booth selling sweets and newspapers outside the station peered at Solomon anxiously, then squinted through the darkness in the direction Solomon kept glancing. He looked back at Solomon again, checked his watch. Only a slow trickle of factory workers and laborers were exiting the station entrance now. The newsstand man hurriedly stacked the last few dozen copies of the *Evening News*, piled up the boxes of gum and chocolate bars, cased up the cigarettes and locked his booth. With the small duffel bag containing the day's takings clutched to his chest, he headed quickly down Holloway, away from where Solomon was lurking.

Solomon smiled to himself as the shopkeeper peered back over his shoulder. *Fool white man.* Turning and straining through the darkness Solomon could see another brother standing just inside the station entrance, the elbow of his puffy black windbreaker just visible. The brother suddenly stepped out into full view, touched his right forefinger to his right temple, and stepped out of sight again. *We're on.* The hairs on the back of Solomon's neck were standing on end, prickling with anticipation.

The roar of the train faded into the distance, and the woman appeared right on cue, shuffling tiredly through the station entrance with her matted winter coat pulled tight around her light blue factory uniform. She was preoccupied with searching for something in her large bag. Solomon had time to look her over properly, and as he did so he felt a sourness rise in his throat. She wasn't what he'd expected. De Frankie said she'd been tracked. For months, half a year even, the Panthers had been following her. But she didn't look to be a kept woman, wasn't chubby and well creamed like he'd somehow expected her to be. Her hair was unstraightened in a natural Afro standing three centimeters high. Everything about her was Black London. She wore flesh-colored stockings that sagged around her ankles. Even the way she walked was familiar—head down, but striding urgently, with purpose. She reminded Solomon of his mother, and for a moment he hesitated. But farther down the road De Frankie was watching, waiting on him to prove himself. The young woman looked toward Solomon, nodded good evening and eased past on those been-standing-most-of-the-day-on-some-factory-line-without-a-meal-break legs.

Solomon paused. He thought of those two girls, of those slim-hipped, silky-haired English girls whose bodies he'd known like he shouldn't have. The girls he'd met at the polytechnic. They'd eyed him in the quadrangle, across the lecture theater, in the cafeteria line, glided friendly up to him all eagerness and curiosity. Solomon had given them what they wanted, exactly how they wanted it. One of them had pushed him inside a specimen freezer in the science lab, pulled him down on top of her like she expected, *wanted* savagery, like she got off on the taboo of him. And when he'd gone at her, pressing down on her body long and tight like drying cement, she'd clutched him to her, pulled him in toward her. She'd thrown her hands back behind the splayed auburn hair that was flared around her face like fire and she'd smiled, daring him to pin them down. And when he had, she'd smiled at him. *Smiled.*

The other girl had offered him a lift home in the car her father had bought her, the leather seats cold under his furious hands as she batted those long brown eyelashes at him. They'd parked behind the Tech. He'd gone at her gentle, not like the other one, but it soon became clear it was all an experiment. *Egyptian eyes*, she'd called them, *Medusan hair*. Until Solomon had felt dissected, scalpel-carved on the ethnographer's table and no more than the sum of his African-originated parts. He had been a foreign country she was apprehensive about visiting but itching to explore. He'd felt her filing the fuck away to reminisce about when times were dull, postcard snippets of the exotic.

And now this sister, this young, beautiful sister, was going home to it—home to some rich white man with a taste for brown sugar. Word was she was going to marry the guy. And he, as De Frankie told it at least, was from some wealthy lot up north. She certainly wasn't dripping in jewels, so maybe they had disinherited the spoiled little rich boy for crossing the race line. In Solomon's book that was worse: that hungry white man, prepared to give up all that wealth and privilege just for a little brown piece of a sister. Of course no brother would stand a chance against that kind of sacrifice. De Frankie was right. She deserved what was coming to her. She made Solomon sick. Solomon quickly stepped up behind the young woman, quietly tailing her as she strode along the footpath. Her house keys were now dangling from her right hand.

De Frankie's shadow was suddenly visible on the pavement in front of them. Solomon took his cue and addressed her from behind. "Miss, scuse me, miss?"

The woman turned around to face Solomon, a quizzical look on her face. De Frankie leaped up behind her, putting his arm round her neck in a chokehold.

"Get off mi. What ye playin' at?" The woman was a fighter, elbowing back at all six-and-a-half feet, fifteen stone of the man.

"Keep still." De Frankie's voice was calm. Solomon stood there, four feet from the scuffle, marveling at the man's composure as his grip tightened around the woman's throat. The woman stared up at Solomon, eyes bulging with fear. Realizing he would be of no assistance, her body wilted and she started sobbing.

"Where your handsome white prince now?" De Frankie sneered at the girl. "Here, let me give you somethin' to help him out." He smirked at Solomon as he bent her down toward the ground, picked up the heavy chains with one hand, flicked the iron collar open and snapped it shut around her neck.

"Patrol. The Special Patrol!" Solomon grabbed De Frankie by the elbow as the lights of a car cruised slowly down the road.

De Frankie backed quickly down Francis Lane into the alleyway behind. The white heels of his sneakers flashed in and out of the darkness as he ran.

Solomon stepped back onto Francis Lane, staring at the sister. She was on her knees now, clutching at the thick, flat metal ring around her neck, tears streaming down her face.

She was gasping for breath, despite the metal collar hanging wide enough for easy breathing. The two-meter link-chain attached to the slave pacifier was heavy. De Frankie had made Solomon try the thing on. He knew that for the sister to walk without the neck plate digging into her neck, she'd have to lift the chain and carry it three blocks to the filthy harem flat she shared with that cracker boyfriend of hers.

The patrol car was getting closer, slowing as it neared them. Any minute now the lights would be on her, and Solomon knew if they saw her they'd catch him too. There wasn't time to run. Solomon stooped down, gathered up the chain, grabbed the woman by the waist and pulled her into the dark alley. The police car drew level with them, slowed. It sat for a moment with its engine humming. A pale face peered out through the passenger-side window. Shrinking back into the shadows, Solomon could feel the woman's hot breath against his palm as he clamped it tightly over her mouth. Finally, the vehicle moved on down the road.

Solomon released the woman and sighed with relief, collapsing against the concrete wall behind him. The woman was crumpled in a heap on the ground. She lifted the chain with her fingers, moaning quietly.

"Why ye gatta do dis?" she sobbed at him. "Dat udda man insane. Mi know im an dem rebel bin watchin' mi. Followin' mi aroun. Is it nat enough we haffi give up everytin an everyone? Ye gatta teyk it off. Please. Teyk de chain off!"

Solomon straightened up and looked at the girl, begging up at him. He hated her. And anyway, he couldn't take it off. Bala, the Railton Road blacksmith, had crafted the slave collars in the firing pit down the far end of the squat yard and they were impossible to open without the key. He hated the girl even more because he wanted to have the key. She would have to walk home like that, back to *him*, through the backstreets, holding that chain. It would have to be cut off her, probably at a hospital. Solomon imagined her sitting in a crowded waiting room full of crackers, the chain gathered up in her lap. He imagined the doctors laughing at her, maybe making her wait longer just for the spectacle of it all. Solomon hated her, and he hated himself. He wanted that key in his pocket. De Frankie was right about him. Much as the thirst kept rising in him, it lulled and peaked, dipped and climbed. And when Solomon's commitment wavered, Babylon came a-calling.

Solomon turned away from the woman and walked slowly down Francis Lane.

Gaps in the Hickory

FOR SILVANO

ELLA LAUGHED when Delores said this, rolled them big brown eyes-a hers. "Ain't nobody roun here gon mess with me, Delores. They knows I can take care-a myself. An sides that, they knows they come anywhere near me, my mama gon hunt them down an break every bone in they sorry body. Sides that too, they all seen me hangin' roun with y'all an know I got a white lady lookin' out for me now."

Delores warn Ella last time that if she snuck in at night again she was gon confiscate her key, lock her out so she like everybody else an need an invitation to come in an visit. In truth, Delores got no heart at all to do that, an that sweet chile know it damn well. Ella share a bed with one-a her li'l sisters: a nervous thing that wet the sheets jus bout every second night. When her sister get to wettin', Ella creep out the cold an

109

stink-a their bed an sneak cross the hall to Delores. Set herself up on the mattress that's stashed under Delores's bed an stay the night.

Delores turn to the window, her long silver-gray hair fallin' from her face. Lef the curtain open last night she did. The sun's shinin' yellow on her cheek, so hot it feel like she jus opened the oven an ducked her head in to check on one-a her butter cakes. The crooked gum side her window is standin' steady, only the slightest rustle-a leaves every now an then. The large red an yellow carnival flags strung up from the telephone pole out her window, they hangin' limp, like they used-a be livin' but now they dead.

Delores sigh, put a wrinkled hand up into the shaft-a light streamin' in the window. She been tryin' to forget bout Izzy these last months—that she gone from this world an ain't never comin' back. She been tryin' to keep busy not thinkin' bout her friend, but now the summer Still done turn up. It's Izzy's Still, really—the dead quiet center-a summer. Izzy the one start callin' it that, way back when they knew each other in Mississippi. Delores can't get her ole buddy out her mind this mornin'. It's like the ole woman's soul is risin' itself up through the drought cracks in the dirt, walkin' toward her from out there over the state line where she done been buried.

Delores rub at her eyes, stretch out. Need a new mattress, she does. She so tall her feet been near hangin' off the end-a this one for years, an besides that she keep wakin' with pain shootin' down her back. She done looked at the shops last week. How these things become so damn expensive? How a simple bed gon break the bank like that? Delores stand up, straighten her long legs an step clear over Ella an her mattress. Chile don't stir none, so she close the bedroom door hind her, walk cross the hall to the bathroom, lif up her baby-blue nightgown, ease down her knickers an lower herself onto the toilet. She stare down at her white thighs, sighin'.

Delores make a mental list as she weein', tally up all the things she gotta do today: for her own self, an for organizin' the carnival. Damn. She done tole Ella they gon have a Beauty Day together. She cut for time, but Ella been so lookin' forward to it. First things first, though—her smalls gotta be washed. All the machines in the laundry room broken, so she been cartin' her bigger clothes to the Laundromat, but not her underwear. She look down at her knickers. They hot pink with purple lace roun the bottom.

"Too saucy for an ole woman like you," Ella said when she saw them hangin' up dryin' on her balcony last month. Delores don't pay her no mind. She several years past sixty now, an done with worryin' bout people talkin'. She gon damn well wear whatever she want. Them saucy knickers restin' on the bathroom floor now, roun her ankles, half coverin' them normous feet-a hers. Why she gotta be born with such hoofs, Delores always be wonderin'. Can't never find women's shoes to fit the things. She mostly end up buyin' from the men's section, replacin' the borin' brown laces with pink ribbon.

Delores kick her knickers off, reach down to pick them up, scrunch them in a ball an toss them cross the bathroom into the pink plastic laundry basket.

———

Jeanie carry the cane clothes basket into the kids' room, rest it on top Lucy's bed. Few thin, sweat-soaked strands-a hair fall loose from her ponytail. Jeanie take a sharp breath in, blow the blond threads outta her eyes. The room's hot, unbearably stiflin'. The summer Still's here in Mississippi meanin' business, so ain't no open window gon offer no respite. Some-a the brightly colored squares on the crocheted blanket spread cross Lucy's toddler bed, they startin' to unravel. Multicolored loops-a loose wool ring the larger holes. 'S the way Lucy digs at Izzy's blanket when she fallin' asleep: sticks them li'l fingers through the gaps in the thick, woven wool an clutches the thing to her as she driftin' off. Always with that bastard right thumb jammed deep in her mouth. Damn thumb suckin's bucked out the chile's front teeth. Real looker their Lucy woulda been. Now she's gettin' to appear rabbitlike. Jeanie touch the blanket, sigh. She never been one for mendin'. Praise the Lord it's summer, cause come winter she gon have to find a way roun to fixin' it, now her mama-in-law, Izzy, passed on. So many things been broken an not made good again since Izzy not roun no more to fix 'em.

Jeanie tip the washin' basket on its side. Small jumble-a clean kids' clothes fall out on the bed. She separate her son's clothes from her daughter's: warm rainbow-a reds, pinks, yellows, an purples on the one side, khaki, denim, blue on the other. Jeanie sigh to herself. Lord know what she gon do bout that boy-a theirs.

She pick up one-a Carter's T-shirts, fole it in half vertically. She fole both sleeves back together, bring the bottom hem up level with the neckline, place the folded shirt on the bed, start again. Cotton in the next shirt's worn tissue-thin. Nother spin cycle in their ole top loader it'll mose likely rip through. 'S what they find at the thrift store these days for wearin'. Been like that a long time, since Jackson los his job. Near four years go now.

She start on the shorts, foldin' 'em vertically, stackin' the clothes in two small piles. These days Jeanie drive halfway cross the county, searchin' out the smaller charity shops where she ain't gon bump into folk they know, folk who gon tell Jackson where she been shoppin'. Ain't no shame in bein' poor, far as Jeanie's concern, though sometimes there's misery in it. Shame oughta be on 'em people who talk. All-a 'em know the welfare don't go far. Half the households in Newmarket los an income when the meat plant close down, not jus hers. Still, her Jackson has his pride—his damn southern pride—an she guess she gotta least leave him have that.

Once, years back, Jeanie made the mistake of lettin' Jackson know they been thrift store shoppin'. Carter proudly show his daddy the new picture books she made sure to get him after the teacher said he gettin' behind on his readin'. She been in such a hurry to get dinner on the table she forget to take the damn store tags off 'em.

"Now you listen here," Jackson hissed at her, after Carter an the baby was tucked up in bed. "I mighta been outta work five months, but that don't mean my children gotta be playin' with some nigger's leftovers."

Jeanie'd wanted to ask him what made him think any black their end-a Mississippi was so much better off than them white folk was. Stead she nodded, promised to buy from the Walmart next time.

Openin' Carter's side-a the wardrobe, Jeanie lower the small stack-a folded T-shirts into the second-to-top drawer, open the third drawer an stuff in the two pair-a shorts. She move back to the bed an start sortin' socks—stuffin' one inside the other till they all paired off. How Jackson spect her to feed four people an clothe 'em new with nothin' at all comin' in she ain't never gon know. She ain't one can work miracles. Still, what her Jackson don't wanna know, she jus gon try her damnedest to make sure he don't catch wind of.

Kids' bedroom's a peculiar shape. Front wall juts out slanted-like so the window overlook the front door an porch. 'S as if the bedroom's tryin-a scape from the rest-a the house. From where she standin', Jeanie can see all the way down the long dusty drive. Out on the front lawn Lucy's swirlin' roun in a circle, tangled hair flyin' out behind her, wigglin' her shoulders in some kinda showgirl shimmy. Window's closed, but Jeanie can see Lucy's li'l mouth openin' wide in song. Jeanie's husband's sittin' on the porch bench, can-a beer perched nex to him, readyin' those damn torch sticks-a his to go ridin'. Carter's on the porch steps, back turned to his sister's dancin' ways, talkin' to his daddy.

Jeanie gather up the pile-a pink an white socks, pause a moment as she stare out the window at her son. Carter's doin' that thing with his nails again. Lord have mercy. Boy's clenchin' his fist over an over as he look at his daddy, makin' red half-moon welts in his palm with his fingernails. Ever since his gram Izzy passed on, her Carter's been fadin'. Hurtin'. Carter's skinny white legs swimmin' in his cutoff army pants, makin' him look smaller than his nearly ten years. Kid's skin an bone. Jeanie ain't seen him eat a full meal in months. Without Izzy roun, she ain't quite sure how to handle the kid, even though he hers. Can't figure him for tryin'. Come from nowhere, their Carter had. Least nowhere they ever be willin' to discuss.

Out the window, Jackson's chattin' to Carter, pointin' to the pile-a sticks at his feet as he barkin' at the boy. Carter's turnin' away from his daddy, lookin' down at his own feet.

———

Delores stop inspectin' her long, tapered toes an get to finishin' her business. She flush the toilet, move over to the sink an wash her hands, lean in an stare at her face real close in the mirror. She gettin ole. No matter how much mail-order miracle cream she use on 'em, these wrinkles not gon let up. No how, no way.

"Y'all starin' in the mirror again miring yourself, Delores?" Ella push into the bathroom, sit down on the can, the plaits in her hair all stuck out an crooked from lyin' on one side while she slept.

"What I tell you bout sneakin' in here at night?" Delores ask, turnin' to face the chile.

"Well, what the Lord teach your damn self in the Bible bout pride a sin?" Ella answer back, pullin' on the toilet roll. "An here you be, preenin' in the lookin' glass anyways."

That chile don't watch her mouth, it gon bring her all kinds-a trouble. Delores shoot her a look like death warmed up, but Ella jus stare back at her with one eyebrow raised up.

Delores leave the room while Ella's on the toilet. They all friends in this buildin', an Delores lived here twenty years now, ever since she leave Newmarket, but you never can be too sure who gon accuse you-a what where there's a li'l pickney concerned. Whenever Izzy came to visit, she warn Delores bout gettin' too close to the girl. Only thing much they ever argued bout. Surprisin', given the years an history an heartache hung between 'em.

"Y'all need to make peace with your son so's you can get to see them beautiful grandpickney-a your own an stop takin' in strays from next door," Izzy'd scold her. "He's a grown man now, an it's gotta be time he saw the truth. Could be it change things between you."

"Y'all call my Ella a stray one more time I'm gon throw you off that balcony to meet your maker right here in the middle-a Orleans," Delores seethe.

Was all well an good for Izzy to say. She had her grandpickney livin' right there under her own goddamn roof out in Sippi. Weren't no way Delores baby would get to talkin' to her again. Specially not enough to let her see them kids-a his.

When the toilet flush an the tap start runnin', Delores open the bathroom door again. She make her way over to the mirror cabinet while Ella dryin' her hands.

"Y'all wanna try one-a my face masks this time, Ella?" She slide the bathroom mirror cross, pull a glass jar-a green goop from the shelf, unscrew the top an dig in a finger.

"Can't be bothered. Too hot." Ella screw up her nose.

Delores get to smearin' the gunk over her face, smoothin' it roun with two fingers. Waitin' for the thing to harden she notice Ella starin' at her in the mirror, lookin' at her mighty serious, like she wanna say somethin' but can't muster it to come.

Carter's daddy's starin' over at him like he wanna say somethin' but can't get it spit out.

"You gon have a stab at this, son?"

"Nah. Can't be bothered. Too hot." Carter's relieved that's all his daddy asked.

He watch him draw back his spit, hock it hard. The saliva hurl through the air an arc right off the side-a the porch like a spat cherry pip.

"No sign-a brawn in you, kid. No fight at all, an you damn near ten." Carter's daddy shake his head. "Place like this, you better toughen up real quick. You been mopin' roun ever since Granma Izzy die. Was already on the cards, Cart. Woman were half shriveled an ready to go anyways. Buck up bout it, eh?"

Ain't no buckin' up gon cover up how much Carter miss his gram. She with the angels now, his mama say. Knowin' Gram an her contrariness, Carter ain't so sure bout that prediction. Sides, maybe she even like to be down where the heat is, given how she went an all.

Cold got Gram Izzy. Least that's how Carter's mama say it, whenever anyone ask. 'S odd to think bout it now, with this summer air so thick with bein' heated it feel like you're walkin' through water. *Cold got her.* Like she was hunted down. Like the cold was some kind-a assassin creepin' icy an cruel through gaps in the elm an hickory, dodgin' through the sweet gum trunks till it hit the Mississippi Delta. Carter magine the killer cold burstin' clear of the forest, headed fast for their cabin as it snag on the thistles, leapin' eager over the knee-high grass fields an skimmin' bove the oil-slicked tar an boggy dirt roads. He magines the cold spinnin' toward them, like the stones he an his ma used-a race over the river come summer. They ain't gone stone skippin' since way back fore Carter's daddy lose his job. Back when there was less baked beans, an everythin' was better.

Gram was sittin' in the rocker in her room when the cold creep up. Slept there mose nights cause she grown not to like lyin' flat. Her old bones didn't like it, she said. Cold must've unlatched the window somehow, snuck up on tippy toes an strangled her real quiet. Gone near as soon as she close her eyes, the men who came to get her body say. They knew cause it was hard to straighten her onto the stretcher. They lay her on her side, body still curled in sittin' shape like a question mark, pale skin already tinged gray.

His mama order him out the room, but Carter'd watched from the hallway, green eyes wide. Not scared, mind you. Jus interested. She wasn't super ole, Gram Izzy, but well over sixty, with her heart tired out, an all ready to meet her maker. Carter an his gram had talked bout it. She been well ready, even if he hadn't quite been.

Carter's daddy'd watched him, watchin' them carry out his gram's body, had sipped on his morning beer as he slapped Carter on the back. "That's it, son, no tears, y'all toughen up," he grunt, then turn an slowly follow Gram's body out to the van.

Carter let it all out then, soon as his daddy's back was turned, tears streamin' down his face. He banged his forehead gainst the hallway wall again an again, till his ma came an put her arms roun him, tight, like she hadn't done since he was real li'l. Without his gram, Carter'll die. He know that, sure as he now breathe.

Carter's daddy shake his head as he stretch out a piece-a cloth, cut away at the edge of it with the thick black-handled scissors till a long, four-inch-wide strip falls away.

"One day you gon have to learn how to do this, son. One day real soon, so y'all can come ridin' with me." His right foot's knockin' gainst the pile-a tree branches. The sticks shift 'mong themselves like they livin' things.

Ridin'. Carter hate it how his daddy an Nate call it that. Like it's back in the good old days an they screamin' through the forests on horses, white hoods lit up gainst the black night. When he was five, Carter thought his daddy had a horse somewhere, for *ridin'.* Thought the animal mus be tethered on a neighborin' property. Didn't think it was fair that his daddy always rode at night, while he was in bed. He went along one day, hidden in the back-a the truck with the canvas cover over him, bump along terrified till the car reach the end-a the road an veer into the forest. They went hurtlin' through the darkness, screech to a stop.

Carter can't remember it so clear now, but his daddy's friend Nate was there, an lotsa other men from roun town. They was all dressed in ridin' gear like his daddy's—red or white hoods, matchin' capes. They held long sticks: tree branches with burnin' ends. He seen his daddy wrap them same branches with rags that very mornin'. The men was singin' songs an spittin' an sayin' *nigger* a lot. *Nigger that. Nigger this. Fucken niggers.* Flags with stars on them was strung up from the trees. The men touched their burnin' torches to a tree, crowdin' roun it. Then Carter realized it wasn't a tree, it was a giant cross. The cross lit up like hellfire an Carter scream an scream. His daddy foun him, dragged him out the back-a the truck an drove him home, silent nex to him in the front seat. His worried-sick mama got a yellin-at when they got there, like it was all her fault. Then his daddy drive right back out into the velvet black.

Carter recognize the material his daddy's cuttin' now. White flannelette, pink stars, blue clouds. His sister Lucy's old nightgown. His daddy hold the strip-a material tight, pick up a long stick, wind the length-a material tight roun one end an he tie it in a knot. Fear snakin' slowly down Carter's spine. It jus don't seem right that his daddy's gon take that li'l sliver-a sleepwear ridin' with him—that he gon dirty up those dainty stars an clouds that used-a wrap cozy roun li'l sleepin' Lucy. Carter like that nightgown. Real pretty it was, with a tiny heart-shaped pocket on the front made-a light blue lace. He reach down, scratch a squito way from his ankle. When he look roun, his ma's standin' at the bedroom window, starin' at him strange, like she got to doin' lately. Carter watch her a moment.

"Nearly there, son. Gonna be a good night for it."

His daddy's not really talkin' to him. Carter been sittin' out here for well near an hour, keepin' his daddy company while he's sat up on that bench, preparin'. Whole time the conversation been lopsided.

Carter look down at his hand. Small cluster-a red crescent shapes are pressed into his palm. Lucy's singin', down there on the lawn. She's singin' an twirlin' in her dress, singin' that princess song, the one Gram Izzy taught 'em. Carter can croon the words by heart. He wanna twirl with her, to dance with the burnt grass crunchin' under the soft bottoms-a his feet, swingin' his hips an curtsyin'. Carter close his fist again, dig his fingernails in hard as he can, wincin'.

Feel like his daddy's takin' near forever to up an go ridin'. He been preparin' things since early this mornin'. Carter, squintin' at him from his bedroom window, was peerin' through the dawn light, past the double row-a Mickey Dee Superman figurines on his windowsill. His daddy lope the perimeter of their ole wood an wire fence, barley sack in hand, bendin' every now an then to pick up branches. His daddy's six-foot-an-some self set gainst the flat fields'd looked giant-like: eerie an wrong.

Carter stare at his daddy's hands as he double knot the material roun the stick an tuck in the ends, tuggin' at the length-a cotton to make sure it ain't gon come off easy. His daddy's a big man; lean an large like Carter's heard tell his grandaddy was. Carter ain't never seen his grandaddy, though he heard plenty bout him from Gram. Nother woman lured his gramps away when Carter's daddy was small, an he ain't never been heard-a since. Lef that lanky largeness hind him, though, bloodlined in Carter's daddy's genes an on its way to passin' right on down to him. Got large, strong fingers, his daddy has. Long enough, Carter reckons, to wrap themselves roun a grown man's throat an touch tips on either side.

Carter's daddy look down at the rest-a the butchered night-gown, pick it up from the porch, tear it quickly in half. The sudden rip of it make Carter squirm, like when his teacher run her fingers down the chalkboard. The sharp sound done startle Lucy from her song.

———

Delores quickly rip the small waxin' strip from between her eyebrows. "Auugh!" The sudden movement make Ella near jump out her skin.

"Shit, Delores!" Ella say, from where she sittin' on the edge-a the bathtub, supervisin' Delores's beauty regimen.

"You watch your language, sweet chile." Delores secure the pink leopard-print scarf holdin' back her long shimmery mass-a silver hair, pull at the knot to be sure it ain't gon come tumblin' down. She stretch back her long neck, press nother sticky wax strip to her chin, smooth it down over her wrinkled weather-worn skin. She lif the end-a the wax paper with her right thumb an forefinger, brace herself, pull away real quick.

"Eeeeeeee!" Don't matter how many time she do this, she always end up squealin' like a li'l schoolgirl. Almost seventy she be now, an lately that damn hair been springin' up more stubborn, in the mose darn inconvenient of places.

"Now Delores, if y'all don't stop screechin' like that, the whole-a New Orleans—hell, the whole-a Louisiana—gon be up here in the flats askin' what in the hell is goin' on an who it was done got murdered."

"Sorry, darlin'." Delores turn to face the girl. "Them nasty hairs bout gone now?"

Ella spect Delores's chin, peerin' through the stickiness left hind by the waxin' strip. "I think so. Y'all gotta wash that goop off so's I can check properly, though." The girl absentmindedly twirl one-a her black plaits. Few strands-a Afro-curl spring free from one-a the thick red elastic bands her nappy hair's been stretched into.

Delores run a face washer under the hot water, wipe at the stickiness on her chin. "That hair-a yours is tryin' to break free again, Ella," she laugh. "It's Beauty Day today. Remember? Why don't y'all let me tease it right on up into that beautiful big Afro crown-a yours?"

Ella stick out her bottom lip, cross her arms over her chest. "My mama said y'all even try to come near my hair again, she gon jus bout slit your throat, Delores."

Delores laugh, a deep rumble that echo roun the tiled white-a the bathroom. That damn chile six goin' on seventy. "Well, if your mama say she gon kill me, then I damn near believe that lady will."

Ella's mama's a force to be reckoned with, an ain't no way Delores inten to commence that kinda reckonin'. Keep them five children-a hers on the straight an narrow like you wouldn't believe, an all on her own to boot. Ella, she the only renegade in the whole bunch-a them: cheeky an stubborn, with a confidence Delores like to bottle if she could. Delores got two li'l grandpickney-a her own that she ain't never lay eyes on, but damn, she love Ella like she hers.

Make an unlikely pair, the two-a them—Ella small for her age, still buried in puppy fat, with smooth skin the color-a coconut husk; Delores, tall, slim, an pale as light, even under this summer scorch. Graceful as Ella clumsy. Least that's what folk tell Delores—that she graceful—an it sure what she like to believe. Taken her a long time to complish that grace, so why in hell shouldn't she have some pride in it?

Make Delores smile when they nex to each other, her an this chile, for no reason at all than the unlikeliness of it. Sight to be seen, the two-a them, down the market an roun bout the backstreets-a New Orleans, Ella haulin' the shoppin' basket, helpin' push the laundry, eatin' from the doughnut cart down Waters Boulevard.

"Your friend ain't come down from Sippi to visit in a while." Ella ease herself off the edge-a the bathtub an down into the empty bath.

Delores can't bring herself to say out loud that Izzy's passed on, let alone break it to Ella. Once a month, Izzy used-a drive her way cross the state line an into Orleans an the three-a them would cook an eat up a storm. Izzy'd bring Delores all the news, talk bout what was goin' on out there in Newmarket, give the lowdown on all the small-town craziness that son-a hers insist on raisin' his poor babies on up in.

Delores been thinkin' bout them children lately, Carter an Lucy. Izzy always swore she was gon get them out that place fore she went, sell up an move her grandpickney all down here. Aches Delores's heart to think bout Izzy's Carter. Soun to Delores like the kid might be headed straight for trouble. Spittin' image of his gram, the boy was, judgin' from Izzy's photographs. Cept for the sheer lank of him. Delores know how it feel not to be able to stop that kinda growin'. She pull the wet flannel way from her chin, straighten her tall self up from in front-a the bathroom mirror.

"Ella. I been havin' trouble tellin' you somethin'." The

words feel hard an sharp in Delores's mouth. "Izzy pass away last winter. Five months or so now." She sit on the edge-a the bath, stare down at the girl.

Ella's lyin' flat gainst the cracked yellowin' porcelain, lay out like she in a coffin, restin' her back gainst the cool. Bath's gotta be the mose comfortable place in the house, what with the Still havin' crept its way here cross the delta last night. New Orleans trap this kinda heat: it collect on the concrete an brick, sink into the tar an breed more of its own. Ain't no way to scape this kinda hot—they jus gotta wait for the breeze to break it some way.

"Oh Delores, I know she gone, I done figure that out months ago." Ella pull herself up to sittin', put a hand on Delores's leg. "How you doin' bout it?"

Delores sigh, reach down to touch Ella on the head. Can't put nothin' past this chile. "I'm doin' okay, Ella. I'm doin' okay."

Sides Ella, Izzy's one-a the only people come in or out Delores's place on a regular basis. Delores ain't ever tell Ella how her an Izzy got to knowin' each other. The last time they together, though, after Izzy leave, Ella say, "Delores, when Izzy's here, y'all act different. Like me with my own kin. Like love an hate all a-rolled-up into the same hug."

"Get to be like that, when you know a person down to they bones," Delores'd said.

Izzy talk bout her grandboy Carter a lot, bout them queer ways he had that Delores couldn't find her way to thinkin' was so strange at all. They talk too much, in front-a Ella, forget that she an her big ears was roun sometimes. Izzy'd talk bout

Carter's daddy, Jackson. How even though he her own son, she scared right down to her bones bout what the man gon do when he find out bout his kid.

"I'm glad you doin' okay bout Izzy, Delores," Ella say. "Cause I been wonderin' when we gon get to goin' out to see Izzy's Carter. You know she want us to check on him. Seem to me now's good a time as any."

———

Seem to Jeanie now's good a time as any to get to doin' somethin' bout the Carter situation. Somethin' go wrong out here with him, she ain't never gon forgive herself, an that boy might not forgive her either. Jeanie pick up the empty washin' basket, rest it on her hip for a moment, look out the window again. The wiry gray tufts at the back-a her hubby's cropped hair seem to be growin' faster than the rest. Jackson's head disappear from sight for a moment as he bend to pick up nother torch stick.

'S gettin kinda creepy, this whole Klan business. That half-wit Nate got Jackson into it after the plant shut down. Tole him it was the blacks why he couldn't get no other job. Said the blacks was used-a livin' on near nothin', livin' in their own filth. That they was ready an waitin' to undercut any bona fide American who wanted to work for a decent pay envelope.

But that was three years ago now, an Jackson's still not lettin' up with it. 'S pig shit, though, what them Klansmen sayin'. Jus the way life is in Newmarket, Mississippi: god-awful hard no matter what color you made in the womb. Roun here you lucky enough to find yourself a job, Lord knows you better damn well hang on to it for dear life. Only way you find nother's if somebody up an leave town or die, an even then you better get to the boss real quick with some kinda bribe to be first in line.

Jeanie ain't worried bout Nate an his lot botherin' the blacks roun here, though. Ain't none-a them gon get strung from a tree or burned alive like they used to. Nate an his li'l Klan all bull an no bravado. Mose they gon do is light an angry fire in the woods an yell roun it with their ugly selves. 'S her Carter Jeanie's worried bout, his daddy findin' out bout him.

Puttin' the basket down again, Jeanie turn back to the kids' wardrobe. She open Carter's side again, thrust a hand into the underwear drawer, scrabble roun, prayin' she ain't gon find anythin' out the ordinary this time. She curse when her fingers hit smooth plastic. She pull up her hand, stare at the necklace. 'S one-a Lucy's: small orange hearts strung tight along the thin black elastic. Jeanie's belly bout tips upside with fear. She look up, out the bedroom window. Carter's standin' up on the porch, starin' in at her with empty eyes.

Jeanie push the washin' basket aside, sit down on Lucy's bed, close her eyes a moment. She ain't sure who or what she believe in no more but she ask the Lord, if he do exist an he up there listenin', to help her out with this one. She lie back on the bed, the springs creakin', her legs hangin' off the end. She examine the cracks in the ceilin'.

Carter's gram Izzy knew she were on her way out this world. 'S why she come to Jeanie bout Carter. If Izzy'd stayed roun till the boy was ole enough to get outta here, ole enough to run from Newmarket, maybe even Mississippi, to run like

Lot an never look back, then Jeanie mighta never been landed with this problem. She mighta never hadda choose.

Jeanie turns her head to stare over at Carter's side-a the room. Izzy's woolen blanket's coarse gainst her cheek, a kaleidoscope-a color framing her vision. Carter's plastic Superman figurines, they tacked to the windowsill with gum. His dog-eared comic books, they stacked on the wooden side table nex to his bed. Jeanie miss Izzy like the Mississippi Still miss the fall breeze. Didn't come from strong family herself, an Jackson's mama always treat her like her own. Course, people roun here talked bout what happened with Jackson's daddy runnin' off, but Jeanie never pay it no mind.

Jeanie jam her fingers through a hole in the blanket, push her thumb into her mouth, suck at it like Lucy do. The day Izzy came to her bout Carter, Jeanie was home early—let go from the cleanin' job she used-a do afternoons, cause the office she was cleanin' done go bust. Izzy limp into the kitchen, that bad hip-a hers playin' up, tell Jeanie to follow her. Her mama-in-law'd slowly opened the door to her own bedroom a crack, an there was Carter. His school clothes was lyin' in a pile on the floor—musta took 'em off real quick, cause the sweatpants still had the rounds-a his legs shaped into 'em.

Carter was dressed up in a lacy white blouse an pearls, balanced on a pair-a his gram's old dress heels. His bangs were brushed down over his eyes an his lipstick was put on better than Jeanie could do—blotted even, it looked like. That angel-voiced gal Carrie was croonin' a country tune on Gram's old radio as the boy sashayed an strutted. Carter'd moved like a real lady. Dainty, as if he weren't really a boy chile at all. They closed the door quiet, crept back to the kitchen. Jeanie'd sat down in a kitchen chair, closed her eyes an swore like buggery. Made sense to her then. Made god-awful sense.

Jeanie take the thumb out her mouth, lets go the piece-a blanket, ease herself up.

"Jeanie," Izzy say quietly, "he been like that forever. Y'all known it since Lucy was born, jus never wanted to see. I love my Jackson, an Lord knows y'all mus love my Jackson. But our Carter's a good li'l kid, a real sweet kid. An one-a these days, Lord help that honey chile, our Jackson is gon find out bout him." She press a piece-a paper into Jeanie's hand. Jackson's daddy's address—Carter's grandaddy—in New Orleans. Jeanie surprise Izzy even know where her ex-husband was. Far as she knew, Jackson an Izzy ain't heard-a the man since he run off decades back. Jeanie hid the paper way, under the mattress in her an Jackson's room, case one day it would prove useful.

Jeanie look over at the empty washin' basket. There's a story she heard a ways back, when she was a chile in church. Bout a li'l baby boy call Moses. What she remember, some harm was comin' to the boy sure, so his mama, she put him in a cane basket, tuck him in real tight. An that mama, in the Bible, she float that baby right on down the river, away from the strife that was headin' to him, even though it broke her heart.

————

Delores shuffle to the kitchen, fill the kettle with water, set it on the stove an turn on the gas beneath it. She thinkin' bout the Still—bout the way it creep up on Newmarket an lay on top the land like some kinda smotherin' blanket. Way the air is eerie an it seem like every wounded ghost who ever set foot in the place be roamin' invisible roun the forests.

It broke Delores's heart to leave Mississippi, get way from the strife that was surely headin' to her. Broke her heart, though she love New Orleans, Louisiana, like a second chile: jus as fierce, but without the terror an apprehension. 'S always the firstborn you remember: the trouble they gave you in the dark-a night, how you worried so very much bout gettin' it right.

Was Izzy who persuade her to leave in the end, even though Delores been so deceitful bout things in the firs place. Was Izzy tole her no one out there was gon 'cept ways they thought was so strange. That she better run herself right outta town fore somebody found out bout her. If they did, Izzy said, Delores wouldn't end up nowhere but stuck beneath that small town forever, in a seven-foot wooden box. So Delores hightail it outta there, an lef Izzy to deal with the mess.

Delores set out a large cocoa mug for Ella, a dainty rose-rimmed teacup for herself. Izzy gave her the teacups an saucers. Say she foun them real cheap in a thrift store downstate. They was part of a set that came with too many saucers an cups, so Izzy brought some up to her. The cup's a delicate thing, hand-painted roses roun the outside an inside rim. Izzy laugh when she tell Delores bout bringin' the dinner set home—how Jackson'd stormed out, sayin' he weren't gon eat off some used-already plates some nigger mighta spit on. Delores didn't find that so funny at all, even back then. Thought sooner or later some doubts oughta raise themselves in Izzy's mind bout the capabilities-a that son-a hers. An sure enough, eventually they did.

Cross the table Ella's slurpin' at her cocoa, so loud an deliberate Delores gotta stop herself from scoldin'. She look down instead, at the inside rim-a her teacup. She put it gently down on the saucer, trail her fingertips over the rose pattern. She still can't stop thinkin' bout the way she turn Izzy's life upside down. Bout how Izzy never falter from bein' there for her anyways. Bout that family-a hers, still out there in Newmarket. Bout that dear li'l Carter.

Delores got tears streamin' down her face. She get up real quick, fore Ella can see how upset she is an start worryin' her bout the cause of it. The chile don't notice none; she drain the cocoa from her cup an start jumpin' up an down.

"It's Beauty Day, Delores. C'mon, when we gon get the nail varnishes out?"

———

Lucy's jumpin' up an down now, one hand holdin' the pale blue headband onto her head. "Why Daddy cuttin' up my clothes?" she ask.

Carter been tryin' not to look his sister's way, forcin' himself not to watch, but now he turns. Smiles. He like the way the dress fits, fallin' down from the spaghetti straps, tight till jus below chest level, then cascadin' loosely to the knee. He dig his fingers into his palm again, can feel his fingernails this time, cuttin' through the skin. Gram Izzy bought the dress for Lucy last summer. Carter remembers it comin' home with his gram after one-a her visits to her ole school friend in New Orleans. Two sizes too big for Lucy it was, an elastic enough to fit a body much bigger. Gram'd winked at him as she hung it in the wardrobe.

"They old clothes I'm cuttin' up, Lucy love, don't you fret." Carter's daddy's tone change when he speak to Lucy. Carter never hear him speak so softly, so gently, any other time. Never even to his ma.

His daddy tie a length-a twine tight roun the material on the end of a torch stick, pick up the pile-a rag-wadded branches an walk over to the truck. He dump the torches on top the pile already in the truck bed, look at his watch. He turn to face Carter an Lucy, hitch his too-baggy blue jeans up at the waist. "It's almost eleven. Y'all done have a snack yet?"

They shake they heads.

"Jeanie!" their daddy yell toward the house. "These kids hungry, y'all get 'em somethin' to eat, you hear?"

When his daddy drive away, the heavy wheels-a the truck fling the dry dirt every which way, till all Carter an Lucy can see is a small storm-a beige dirt, movin' slowly away through the endless Still. Carter's stomach turn over as he an Lucy move into the house, her skip-stumblin' up the front stairs, him a half step behind her, marvelin' at the way the ruffled red-pink hem-a her dress bounce an sway.

Carter love Lucy. Way she moves in that easy way li'l girls do. Part from anythin' else, Lucy'd made him *know* what was wrong bout him. He can still remember the way he felt so swallowed up in with the other boys when he first started at school—way their snotty noses an clumsy, loud ways made him black inside; the sweaty, sour smell-a the boys' washroom that still make his tummy turn itself inside out.

Then his ma's belly got big, an tiny li'l Lucy came home from the hospital with her. An with Lucy came the *things*: the hair clips an the tiny pink bears, the dolls an those sweet-smellin' flower-shaped baby soaps. When folk came to visit, they brought pink cardigans with ribbons on them, lace-ringed baby bonnets. They was things Carter's ma, lovely as she is in her jeans an T-shirts an woolen jumpers, never had roun the house before. Outta nowhere, Lucy'd come, an she had made Carter *know*, made everythin' okay.

Even back then, his daddy'd been bothered by it all. His mama'd thought there weren't nothin' odd bout it, jus he was a mite curious. "Leave him alone, Jackson, he jus a tiny boy. He don't know them things ain't s'posed to be for him," she'd kept sayin'.

But Carter weren't a boy, he knew it right back then; way that word felt like a shotgun, aimed dead center-a his head. *Boy.* Like a cocked barrel. Like some kinda threat.

Carter's learned to secret things away, find quiet corners where he can play with his sister's toys, learned to wear hats to hide his hair growin' jus that half inch longer. He push bracelets high up his arms an hide 'em neath the baggy sleeves of sweaters. Once he even pinch a jar-a sparkly purple nail varnish from the drugstore, tuck it into his sock when his ma was busy with Lucy. He paint his littlest toenail under the covers that night, keep it hidden neath his sock for a week, then scratch off the glittery varnish the night fore gym class.

Delores take the lid off the blue bucket, tip the small glass jars-a nail varnish out onto the couch. They clink gainst each other as they tumble: reds, yellows, greens, purples. Some-a the jars unopened, plastic still ringin' the lids, waitin' for they Beauty Day debut. Ten years she been workin' on this collection. Long as she got the dollars in her pocket she buy up a new shade every time she stumble on one. Got glitter polish, glow in the dark, even press-on silver stars she bought five years ago on vacation in Las Vegas. Her collection prove handy for the performers, come carnival time.

"Perfect day for it." She turn to Ella. "Heat like this, our varnish gon dry in no time at all."

Ella don't answer. She miles way. All the excitement done disappear an she look like she sulkin' or somethin': her bottom lip pokin' out so far it's damn near draggin' on the polished wood floor. "Delores," she say, "I just still can't believe you not gon go check on Izzy's boy. After how long you known each other? An you damn know that boy got no one out there that understand him."

"Chile, I don't wanna hear nother word of it. There jus some things y'all li'l ones can't understand. You gotta take my word for it." Delores don't often hold things back from Ella. Fact, she can't remember the last time she properly did, but the goddamn chile won't let up. "Y'all gon choose a color, or what?"

"Bet Carter'd love our Beauty Days an all."

"Ella! Quiet yourself!" Delores ain't mean to raise her voice. Sounded so much harsher than she intend.

"Y'all cryin', Delores?" Ella's lookin' at her now, starin' real close, worried.

"I'm sorry, Ella. I think maybe we should go on an cancel our Beauty Day today. I got a lotta sewin' to do for the carnival an I ain't gon be able to pay my rent less I got the costume work all done." Delores get up from the couch so the chile can't see her face but Ella follow her, cranin' her neck to see if she really upset, touchin' her arm.

Been years since her days in Newmarket came to Delores like this, so clear an unforgivin'. She can smell the dry rot-a the wooden house, hear the sassafras out front rustlin'. Can taste Izzy's pie—the one she always got to makin' for her an Jackson from the mulberry tree cross the way. Back fore Delores properly existed. Back when Delores were still Denver, an Denver were still Izzy's husband.

Denver an Izzy been married nine years an already had Jackson by the time Izzy found out bout Delores. Delores can't even remember Denver clear now. Not how it felt to be him. Not every day carryin' that brawn, or that clumsiness—not the men's jeans an bulky shirts, the furry all-over hair. In Delores's memory, Denver jus facts, jus details. Not a man an a body that actually used-a be her.

Denver work in senior operations at the meat plant. Denver came home six nights a week stinkin-a flesh an bone an blood. Denver love his wife, an adore his son. Denver were a good, hard-workin' southern man. But Denver been so miserable inside that if he didn't become Delores some way permanent, not jus the nights he stole Izzy's fake pearls an drove to edge-a-town bars, he was surely gon die. Make Delores ill to think bout it, so she don't much let herself now days. Denver ain't her no more. He jus the man her best friend Izzy married then split from. He jus somebody she used-a know, long time ago. The real her was born when she came to Orleans. Real her is Delores.

"Don't cry." Ella's hands are huggin' roun her waist. The li'l girl's starin' up at her, holdin' tight. "I jus can't get to un-derstandin' why you not gon go get your grandbaby," she say, shakin' her plaits furious. "Specially when y'all gotta know what it be like out there."

"What you talkin' bout, Ella?" Delores ask sharply. She take a hanky from inside her sleeve, wipe at her eyes. Must be she hearin' things, she so upset.

"Delores," Ella say, that cheeky dimple-a hers dippin' in an out her chubby cheek, "I know you all woman these days. But truly, ain't no real-life born-in-a-lady's-body woman got feet an hands that damn big." Ella's smilin' now, gigglin' up at her.

"Your mama know?" Delores sniffle.

"Everybody in this part-a New Orleans know you wasn't born in a Delores body. Don't nobody care roun here. You Delores now, an Delores the only way we knows you."

Delores tuck her hanky back up her sleeve, look down at Ella. Small as she is, that chile sure talk some sense. "You hun-gry? What y'all want for lunch?"

"Tin spaghetti," Ella grin back, "if y'all got some."

———

Jeanie open the pantry, stare at the small stash-a tin food, pick out a can-a spaghetti. She pull the ring top, peel back the metal lid, tip the contents into a bowl, press a few buttons on the microwave. She jus don't understand what turn her husband to this ridin' business. Her an Jackson been together since high school. Used-a be he were a reasonable man. Then the grime an the ghosts an the gloom of Mississippi, they got inside-a him. Long years, these last few been with him.

She open the fridge door, unwrap two slices-a cheese, fetch a loaf from the bread box an pop a couple pieces into the toaster.

"Getti, getti, yum yum! Spaghetti for my tum tum!" Lucy bang her fork on her white plastic high chair tray.

"Settle down, Lucy."

Carter's sittin' at the table opposite Lucy, in front-a his empty plate. Jeanie pop the toast up, put a slice on each plate, spoon the spaghetti on top, place a slice-a cheese over the hot pasta.

"You all right, Cart?"

Carter look down at his plate. Jeanie swallow hard, reach out to the windowsill bove the sink, pull a cigarette out the packet. Izzy's voice, it ringin' an ringin' in her ears. *One-a these days, Lord help that honey chile, our Jackson is gon find out bout him.* Jackson ain't never hurt a soul, far as Jeanie know. Never raise a hand to her in all the years they been together. But even his mama, who know him like the back-a her hand, say he weren't gon handle this. Somethin' in him now. Somethin' wrongful.

Jeanie flick the cigarette lighter on, watch the flame for a second. Take her three goes to light up, her hands shakin' so damn much. Cigarette burn down fast, glowin' red end eatin' away the white paper of it. She got no words to explain it all to Carter. Jeanie ain't no good at this kinda stuff, an don't understand it much herself. Kid's gotta know she loves him, though, don't he?

Jeanie toss the cigarette butt into the sink, reach fast for nother, hand still tremblin'. Carter's watchin' her again from the corner-a his eye, like he know somethin's comin'.

Carter wipe the sweat off his brow with the blue-an-white-striped dish towel that's sittin' on the edge-a the kitchen table, look up from the gooey mess on his plate an over at his ma. She standin' by the kitchen sink, cigarette in hand, thin shoulders bony neath her light green T-shirt sleeves. Hind her, the kitchen window look out onto the half mile-a brown grass that separates their property from their nearest neighbors'. From the shoulders up, set gainst the windowscape like that, Carter's ma blends with the scenery. Like she risin' sorrowful from the middle-a the Still.

A thin gray cloud-a cigarette smoke hover in front-a her face, decidin' which direction to take. Ain't no breeze, even though the large window's been slid wide open. The smoke slowly dissolves, his ma's features grow clear again.

"Eat it, Carter. Ain't nothin' else."

Carter ain't hungry. He lif his glass, take a long drink-a the cool water, shift in his seat, unstick his sweaty legs from the vinyl seat covers, wincin' as his sof thigh skin peel free. Carter never eat much in the Still. The Still: name's stuck now. Was Carter's gram who started callin' it that, this eerie forty-eight hours or so in the middle-a summer when all the delta hold steady. These strange few days every year when the ragin' river seem so paralyze with heat that the currents dull to a whisper, when even the sassafras out front-a the house quits movin': every branch holdin' straight an sniper-silent.

———

Ella's slurpin' up her lunch like she ain't eaten in weeks. She peel the tin lid herself, say she don't even need no plate or to have the pasta warmed up.

"Things all right over there at your mama's?" Delores ask. "Y'all got enough to eat?"

Ella stop shovelin' the food in an look over at her. "We got plenty, thank you," she damn near snarl. "Y'all don't have to worry bout callin' the welfare or nothin'."

"Ella," Delores say firmly, "y'all know that ain't why I'm askin'."

Kid put her face right back in the can, use her finger to wipe the sides clean. Ella don't never ask for no food. One thing she always polite bout. Delores remind herself she gotta get more vigilant bout offerin' it up.

Ella jus bout finished her meal when they hear the knock.

"That be one-a yours callin' for you, Ella," Delores warn. "You wanna take some more-a them cans over to your mama's? Don't know why I got so many-a them anyways. Take them all with you, chile. Must be I pick 'em up by accident, 'cause I damn hate the way that tin spaghetti get squashed 'tween my teeth." Delores lyin' like the FBI, an they both know it. Times, they still hard, an couple less cans in the cupboard mean a couple less meals for Delores.

Ella's makin' sure not to look in Delores's face as she puttin' the tins in a paper bag. The knockin' start up at the door again. Noise make 'em both turn they head to stare.

"One-a my own ain't gon be knockin' like that," Ella say. "Not less somebody drop dead or somethin'." She put the bag down on the table, rush cross the kitchen, through the small living room an over to the balcony doors. She step outside onto the balcony, hang her nosy head down over the edge. "Mail truck's parked jus down a way, Delores. Think it might be the mailman!"

Delores shuffle over to the balcony, peer down at the street, curious. Soon as she step out the glass door, the sun burn up on her like fire. The washin' lines strung from the balconies opposite, they still filled with clothes, 'cause ain't nobody on her street braved the Still to take them in. Seem like the city be all heat an angles: doors an balconies an windows an pavements, with jus a smatterin-a trees an people sandwiched in between.

"Well I never. I wonder what he got for me that ain't gon fit through the slot. Ain't no mailman ever come up here personal before." Delores don't wanna open the door. Anythin' can't be written in a letter, well, that jus gotta be bad news, ain't it? She don't know nobody much from back in Newmarket no more, an nobody she know in the city gon waste money on postage when they all can jus pick up the phone or drop on by.

Less it's bout Carter. Delores's stomach knot up. She double over, reach out her hand so she don't topple off the balcony. What her Jackson done? What that gettin-evil son-a hers gone an done to that precious li'l born-into-the-wrong-body boy?

Delores lef Newmarket when Jackson was roun Carter's age. Hardest thing she ever did, but her an Izzy both decide it was for the best. Boy was too young to understand it all. Delores had run from that backward place, from the whole-a Mississippi. Izzy say the boy ask for his daddy every day for near a year. Broke Izzy's heart to tell Jackson his daddy run off for nother woman, but in a way that was God's own truth.

Jackson come to visit Delores once. Delores never tole Izzy, an it weighin' heavy on her mind now she gone. Jackson visit bout four years back. Musta been soon after the meat plant close down, fore he move the family into Izzy's place. Could be he want Denver's help to try an keep the house or somethin'. To cover the mortgage. Come right up to the door, Jackson had, ridiculous early in the morning, like he'd hadda knock fore he chickened out or thought better of it. Delores open the door, still in her nightgown. Her son glare at her, annoyed.

"I'm lookin' for Denver Macleod," he say.

Sound of Delores's old name, shape of it in the mouth-a the man she raise but now don't know, sight-a her li'l boy's face stretched cross the bones of a grown-up man, made Delores panic, bile risin' in her throat. "Denver ain't roun no more," she choke.

"You his woman then?" Jackson spit, mistakin' her horror for guilt, or somethin' near it.

"Hello, Jackson," Delores say, almose without thinkin'.

He look confuse a moment. Off-balance. Then he look in her face, real close, an back away. His grown man's mouth done open wide in shock.

Then on, all Delores hear from Izzy bout Jackson was things to worry for. That Klan nonsense, the way he start has-slin' that poor li'l boy. Jackson clearly ain't tell Izzy he come to find his father, an Delores saw no point in tellin' her either. Better the boy stayed thinkin' his mama didn't know none-a what her ex-husband run off an become. Better he still had one parent he thought he could trust.

"You gon get this door, or what?" Ella yellin' at her now, from back inside the partment.

Delores hear the chain unbolt, look over to see the girl turnin' the door handle.

"Delores, y'all got some registered mail you gotta sign for!"

Delores straighten up, move slowly off the balcony.

———

Carter run a finger roun the edge-a the chipped porcelain plate, tracin' the pink rose pattern. Gram Izzy pick the plates up at the thrift store. Had an argument with his daddy bout them all eatin' off-a them. Carter musta been bout seven at the time. Was back when Lucy was jus a crawlin' baby, jus after they moved in with Gram. He help Gram scrub the plates clean in the kitchen sink with steel wool an washin' liquid.

"Where you get them plates from?" his daddy ask at dinnertime, as he spoon some bean stew onto his plate an break off a piece-a Gram's cornbread.

"Bought 'em today," Gram Izzy answer, ladlin' some stew onto Carter's plate. "Real cheap too, down the thrift store, good as new."

His daddy's face freeze. He spit out the mouthful-a stew-soaked cornbread. "You tellin' me you gon have us eat off-a some plates which been on someone else's table, which some filthy nigger family mighta licked clean?"

"Oh, for cryin' out loud, Jackson," his gram laugh, "y'all

gotta quit this crazy Klan business. You done got near some black folk's spit in your time, even if you tryin' your damnedest to forget it. You remember that cute li'l Taneesha with the pigtails, way back in the third grade?"

Carter never seen his daddy so angry. He didn't say anythin', but his face jus close up with hate. He lef the house an didn't come back till the mornin'. Only reason his daddy didn't usually argue with his gram Izzy, an the only reason he didn't throw her out the house mose likely, was 'cause she own it herself.

————

Jeanie inhale again, hold the smoke in. Carter's sittin' starin' down at his plate with a strange smile on his face. She not game to ask the kid what he's thinkin' on that finally cracked that dismal face-a his.

Lucy's thrustin' her fingers into her lunch, laughin' at the squidgy feel of it. Jeanie exhale the smoke, frown at her. Lucy quickly take her sticky hand back off-a the plate; she wipe it cross the high chair tray leavin' hind greasy orange lines of sauce, pick up her spoon.

Jeanie don't know how she gon cope out here without her boy. Beggars belief how she never saw this comin'. Course, there was li'l things shoulda warned her. Big things, now she think bout them.

————

The mailman look Delores up an down, sweat beadin' on his brown temples as he hand her over the yellow envelope, pass her the clipboard to sign. "That your little girl then?" he sniff, flickin' a thumb at Ella.

"Manner-a speakin'." Delores hand him back the clipboard.

The man linger for a moment, like he gon say somethin' else.

"You got a problem with that, nigger?" Ella glare up at him with one hand on her hip.

"Sweet holy Jesus, you a rude li'l chile sometimes," Delores say. "You watch your lips an pologize to the man right this instant! Else I'm gon drag you cross the hall by your ear an tell your mama to give you a wuppin'. An you damn well know she do it."

"Sorry." Ella hang her head to the floor.

"Sorry what?" Delores prompt.

"Sorry for bein' rude, mister."

Mailman shake his confuse head all the way back down the hall.

"What is it, Delores? What he bring us? What we got?"

Delores's hand shakin' roun the envelope. She lock an bolt the door, carry it to the kitchen, get a butter knife out the top drawer. Ella's hoppin' from one foot to the other like she so excited she gon wee in her pants.

Delores ease the papers out the envelope, get to readin', don't stop till she turn every last page.

"What's goin' on, Delores? What it say?"

Delores put the letter down, move to the sink, rinse out the chipped rose teacup an refill it with water. Get to gulpin'.

"Shit, Ella. Sorry bout the swearin'. Shit. It's from a lawyer down in Sippi. Seem Izzy done lef me her house."

Even as she say it, Delores know she can't go back. Not to Newmarket. Not ever. When Delores leave, she walk out in not a thing but the clothes she borrow from Izzy. She leave Denver behind, leave his home, leave his family, leave the body he was born into an everythin' he acquire since in life. Delores don't have no claim to none-a that now, not what woulda belonged to Denver. Izzy surely had to've known she wouldn't be the least li'l bit interested.

"Y'all gon move back down there then, Delores?" Ella soun real worried.

"No. I don't know why she—" An then it hit her. Carter's out there, in that house with his father, with her Jackson. Carter, who's gettin' older now. Carter, who maybe can't keep locked up inside himself much longer. Izzy say they strugglin', Jackson an that wife-a his, doin' it real tough. Could be Izzy jus pass Delores a way to save her grandboy. Could be Izzy right now is reachin' out from past her grave to help the boy.

Delores pick up Izzy's cup, fill it again, drink from it till it drained. Could be Izzy know only one way for Delores to get to savin' that li'l boy. One way to be sure she got a hold over Jackson.

———

Each rosebud on Carter's plate shaded with least four different tones-a red, from the blood-color petal tips to the tomato base. The plate remind Carter so much-a the airs an graces Gram Izzy always pretendin' she had, when all the county know she born an raised in the delta an hadn't lef to go nowhere an get them fancy manners in the first place.

Carter's gram never did have many friends in Newmarket. Somethin' to do with Carter's grandaddy, an the lady he done lef Gram for when Carter's daddy was a boy. Carter know nothin' bout his grandaddy or that lady friend-a his, 'cept that his own daddy hate the man real fierce for what he did, hate him certain as the Devil hate good.

Carter lean over the plate. The roses, they swimmin' now, blurrin' into each other. He breathe in, breathe out, clench his fist under the table, press gainst the welts he done already dig into his palm. Smell-a the tinned food make him wanna throw up. The toast underneath the tinned spaghetti already sogged through, an slowly saggin' outward, swellin' with red-orange sauce. The slice-a cheese his ma place on top the spaghetti done melted then cooled, coatin' the squidgy pasta like shiny yellow plastic. Carter dig at the meal with his fork.

"That or plain toast, kid." His ma take nother long suck-a her cigarette.

Carter hate it when she call him that. *Kid*. Like he some chile she's never met, some boy she jus found wanderin' the supermarket or somethin'. Like he don't have a name, an like she never chose it for him herself. *Kid*. Carter hate that even more than when his daddy call him *son*. He put the fork down.

Cross the table, Lucy spoonin' tin spaghetti an cheese into her mouth hit-an-miss. The plastic tray-a her high chair all smattered with spaghetti worms. She smile over at Carter, sauce drippin' down her chin. "It's yummy getti, Carty." She grin.

Carter smile back at her as she scratch at her wild mass-a curly blond hair, spoon still in hand, spreadin' sauce cross her bangs. The high chair's done got small for her now. Her chubby three-year-old legs, they hangin' down past the footrest.

"Cryin' out loud, Lucy!" His ma stub out her smoke in the sink, rush over to his sister with a wet cloth.

While she occupied, Carter quickly pick up his plate from the table, move toward the kitchen door, scrape his lunch into the garbage.

"Starve if you like, Cart. Keep throwin' way your food like this you be skin an skeleton fore you hit eleven." His ma's leanin' over, wipin' the food from Lucy's hair.

Carter lay his plate in the sink, run his fingers through his bangs a few times to make sure it sit properly to the side. He been wearin' a baseball cap over it when his daddy's home, so he don't take the clippers to it. Carter want the bangs long. Long enough to flick from his eyes when he get to dancin' hind the thick trunks-a the sweet gums up back-a the yard.

"When's Daddy comin' back?" he ask.

His ma's rinsin' out the cloth in the sink. "Fuck, Carty!" She turn to face him. She know what he's gon do—know the reason he askin' bout his daddy. Her bottom lip shakin'.

Carter love his ma. Love her so much his heart hurts.

He walk out the kitchen, down the corridor, into his an Lucy's room. He slide open Lucy's side-a the wardrobe. Lookin' up at the hangin' rows-a pink skirts, down at the flowery sandals, make him feel like everythin's gon be okay. Lucy's side-a the wardrobe even smell different. Like flowers an sunshine, like that kiddie perfume his ma done bought her last Christmas that Lucy don't know yet s'posed be sprayed on real sparin'.

Carter move to shut the bedroom door. His ma might

come on in, or Lucy might get to bangin' on it, but this time he don't care. Let his daddy come home. Let all-a them see. He pull the navy-blue T-shirt off-a his head, rummage through his sister's drawer till he find the red T-shirt. 'S a size five—too big for Lucy now, but it fit him real snug, jus the way he like it. Tiny roun sequins sewn on the front in the shape of a heart. When Carter wriggle into the top, his whole body get to singin'. He stand up straight, look in the mirror. His mind unfog itself. He stop there a moment, jus breathin'. He only gon wear the thing a minute. Jus a few seconds, then he gon put his other clothes back on.

———

Delores an Ella stare at the papers sittin' in the middle-a the kitchen table, like even touchin' them gon set somethin' other-worldly into a spin.

"Well," Ella's impatience break through Delores's thoughts, "what we gon do?"

Delores wipe her forehead with the hanky from up her sleeve. Blink her eyes a couple times. She feel Izzy there at the table with them, feel Izzy in the room. Izzy's soul done leap through the gaps in the elm an the hickory. It must-a dodge its way through the sweet gum trunks till it hit the wide-open delta. Izzy's spirit done rise up from the soil-a Mississippi an burst clear-a the forest. It done fled on the freeway an floated into Louisiana. Izzy's soul has arrived right here, at Delores's table in New Orleans, sure as her own eyes are green.

———

Jeanie open the door quiet. Carter's standin' in front-a the mirrored doors-a the wardrobe, wearin' one-a Lucy's shirts. Thing's clingin' to him, sparkly an tight, close as a second skin. Carter standin' there with his eyes closed, breathin'.

Lucy's clamberin' roun Jeanie's legs, duckin' an weavin' in an out. "Look at Cart, Ma," she say. "Ain't he look beautiful?"

Carter open his eyes an stare back at his ma. She got a hand on his sister's head to steady her from duckin' in an outta her legs. His ma's lookin' at him like her heart done jus now broke into a thousand pieces.

"Y'all get outside, Carter," she say. "Put your other T-shirt back on. We all gon go for a drive."

———

Carter hole Lucy's hand as his ma back the car out the garage. The li'l Corolla's ole, coated in summer dust. Ain't been on the road for several months. Fact, Carter can't remember the last time they was in it, wonders how the thing even got any fuel in the tank.

Lucy squeezin' at Carter's hand, clutchin' it tighter an tighter like she scared to the bone, even though she don't know what she frightened bout. Carter squeeze at her hand, bend down an give her a cuddle. Strangely enough, he don't feel worry no more. Fear done fly from his body like dandelion wisp—float away curious into the Still. Whatever happen, Carter know he ready for it.

The streets-a Newmarket fall way side the back window-a the car: burnt fields, rottin' fences, dense brown forest an fallin-down houses givin' way to freeway—to whizzin' cars an hot tar windin' far as the eye can see. Carter's window's woun down. The breeze from the car's movement is breakin' through the Still air. Hotness is rushin' at Carter's face, pushin' up his nostrils, down his throat.

On the seat beside Carter, Lucy's playin' with her dolly. She brushin' its long blond hair with a tiny green plastic comb. His ma's been quiet for nearly the whole hour they been on the road, hands clutchin' the steerin' wheel, eyes dead ahead. Carter stare at his sister's Barbie—the painted-on eyelashes, the long slim legs, the pink sparkly princess outfit she wearin'. His ma glance at him in the rearview, lookin' at him lookin' at the doll, but she still don't raise a word.

Must be nearly three hours gone when Carter open his eyes. Afternoon's near darkened to night an the car's stopped in a place Carter ain't never seen before. Tall buildings risin' all roun them, lookin' like lotsa houses all joined up together. Hardly green to be seen, only a couple-a tall trees that look like they tryin' to reach up from the city shadows an find a way back to they forest. In the front seat, his ma's got Lucy on her lap. They playin' some kinda game with the Barbie doll, real quiet, like they been tryin' not to wake him.

"Where we at?" Panic hittin' Carter now, whackin' him dead in the gut like a swung baseball bat.

His ma turn in her seat. Her face, it gone all red an puffy like she long been cryin'. "Carter," she say, "we in New Orleans. Things real hard in Newmarket. Y'all know they are. An we strugglin'. We really strugglin out there. I brought you here so's you could stay awhile with your grandaddy. Before she pass on, your gram say you should come on over here—that I should bring y'all here, if things don't get no easier. Luce, she too li'l. She gotta stay with us—with me an your daddy."

His ma's lookin' back at him the same time as lookin' straight through him. She gon leave him here. With some ole man she don't even know, who abandon his own family. She's dumpin' him on some stranger, some not-so-nice body who ran off an lef his gram on her own for all-a them years. Mus be she can't stand him. Mus be he makes his own ma sick.

She's handin' him a piece-a paper now. He look down an read it. *Denver Macleod*, it say, with an address he guess is somewhere in the buildin' they parked in front of. 'S his gram Izzy's writin' on the paper. Messy blue pen. Fact makes Carter feel better someway.

"Damn, I'm gon miss you, Carter. Give li'l Luce a kiss darlin', will you? We gon come back an visit real soon. We gon stay out here in the car an wait to make sure you get in safe."

Carter don't know what to do. He clutch the piece-a paper tight, open the door, step out the car.

———

Delores hidin' herself hind the heavy living room curtain as she stare down into the street. The dirt-streaked engine-rumblin' car that done pull up thirty minutes back look like the same one Jackson was drivin' that time he come to see her. Ever since she notice the vehicle, Delores been watchin' close to see who it is gon come out. There some movement in the front seat, but sides that, she ain't seen a thing. But now the back door done open. A li'l boy chile climbin' out, lookin' up at her buildin'. Delores draw a sharp breath in, call Ella over from the kitchen.

"What in the hell you been leanin' out that window starin' at, Delores?" Ella ask. "Not bein' rude, but the neighbors gon get to talkin'. Look from here like you maybe gettin' to be some kinda peepin' Tonya."

"Quiet, Ella. I want you to lean outta the balcony door an see who you think that is gotta be standin' on the front path. An mind you don't get seen, pretty thing."

Ella screw up her nose, hang her head out the balcony door. All a sudden the girl start screamin', wavin', hoppin' on the spot, leanin' forward an hangin' her body over the balcony. "Izzy's Carter!" she squeal. "Izzy's Carter! I reckonize him any-where from them photos she used-a bring. Must be his mama drive him down here, 'cause I can see her an that li'l sister in the car too. Carter! Carter! We up here! We up here!"

Delores put a hand on Ella's shoulder, pull her back into the living room. "Quiet, chile. You gon scare him away! That pickney don't know us from Adam." But even as Delores say it, she know it ain't true. Minute that chile an her lay eyes on each other, they gon know they kin. It's gon feel like they finally home.

Carter's lookin' up toward them now, cranin' his neck to see where the shoutin' come from. Delores move back to the table, like she on automatic pilot. She take up the letters from the lawyer, suck in a deep breath an get to unboltin' the part-ment front door.

Big Islan

NATHANIAL ROBINSON lean out ovah de water, shake im head an look-look down pas im grubby dungarees an im heavy leather work boot, an inte de water below. Im a large man, Nathanial, big-big bone like im bloodline done come right down frum Goliath in de Bible or sometin'. Large, an iv ye nyah know how gentle de man is at heart, den maybe im even seem a likkle ominous, standin' on de pier like dis, wid im black shadow castin' down ovah de light blue-a de bay water below.

Kingston Port nyah changed. It same-same as it always is in de easy afternoon affer im knock off down de docks. Same-same as it always is every weekday afternoon wen de young man stan on de edge ov dis beloved islan country-a his, look-lookin out te sea.

Same blue 'pon green 'pon navy 'pon khaki water. Same flat-flat horizon line dat seem like it stretchin' way-way beyon wat im eye can si, runnin' an runnin' forever an a day. Same familiar husky whisper-a de sea breeze, dancin' an teasin' aroun dem broad black shoulder dat hidden beneat im torn work shirt an im baggy overall. Same-same Kingston.

Small air bubble travelin' slowly up out de water, as dem fast-tail fishie flit jus below de surface. Wen Nathanial a-sigh-sigh an squint-peer past de ships, it de same seaweed shadow patterned out in de gettin-deep reaches. Same yellow affernoon glintin' off de ripples. An dat same crazy-fresh islan air, so clear, despite de many cargo ship bout de place dis evenin', dat every breath feel like it flowin' down-down te de very bottom ov im lung an a-comin up new an reborn.

Same everytin but yet, somehow, it nyah de same anymore at all. It big-big change. Since *J fe Jamaica*, everytin aroun Nathanial seem like it nyah quite de same. Since *J fe Jamaica*, de ocean bin callin', nyah calmin', de young man. Sun seem shifted somehow. Im used-a feel it blarin' warm on im back in de hot season, coverin' im gentle like an ole chilehood blanket, an makin' im feel safe an protected. Now, more often dan nat, im fine de sun in im eye, an imself squintin' away de sheer annoyance ov it. Evah since Nathanial learn *J fe Jamaica* de fishie dem seem a likkle less translucent, tiny schools-a dem dizzy-swimmin' in circles, an nyah wid de same purpose anymore. Evah since *J*, dem fancy cargo ship bin *passin' tru* Kingston, nyah *comin' to* or *leavin' frum* it. Evah since *J fe Jamaica*, much as im continue te tell imself nuttin' change, Nathanial carry nyah small amount-a unease deep deep down in im own self skin.

"One lettah per week," im wife, Clarise, had insisted.

Was twelve mont back. De woman was standin' at de kitchen counter preparin' dem Sunday meal.

"We startin wid *A fe ackee*," she seh, her fingers removin' de blushin'-crimson flower frum outside-a de ackee, snappin' off de cedar-black seed at de end-a de cream-color fruit.

Im wife, she had im trace dat firs lettah. Hundred damn time, in de lounge room while she cookin' up de food. Nathanial large frame was crouch down on de floor, hunch aroun de glass coffee table Clarise parents bought dem fe dem weddin' present nat three year before.

A is fe ackee.

Im clumsy fingah clutch tight an awkward roun de gray lead. De likkle lettah *a* was a roun circle wid a stick attach on de right-hand side. De big lettah *A*, de *capital one*, she call it, was pointy at de top, like it some kinda arrow. An Lawd, im sure wan stab de woman wid it dat evenin', she frustrate im so.

A is fe acrimonious.

Is ironic dat dem start it all wid *ackee*. Nathanial nyah even like de way Clarise cook up de fruit. She leave it so long in de pan it go all bitter an mushy. Serve it wid saltfish dat nyah bin soak ovahnight. Fish so damn salty dat im haffi drink a gallon-a water te get de ting down pas im throat. Leave a fuzzy film a-sittin' on im tongue.

A is fe acrid.

"Let's teyk our time wid dis alphabet, Nathanial," Clarise insist. "Ye haffi learn each lettah properly, an start like ye mean te finish. Like ye gwan get so keen at readin' ye gwan eventually be able pick up any classic in de city library, an nat bat an eyelid bout de level ov difficulty."

But it nat Nathanial idea in de first place. It Clarise dat obsess wid educatin' im. Obsess wid de more money she seh it gwan bring. De big home. Sometime Nathanial look at im wife, an im nyah recognize de likkle pigtail girl dat used-a sit beside im in de Baptist school near twenty year ago now. Way back fore im fadda die an im haffi go inte de fields te help wid puttin' de food on de family table.

Dem reconneck wen im come back home one year. Only in de meantime, Clarise use dem intervenin' year te grow spectacular. Wen im return, Clarise more stunnin' dan evah im seen a woman. Nex ting Nathanial know, im puttin' ring 'pon de woman fingah an she sayin' she wan move te de city, she wan get out dis small likkle country nat-even-can-call-it-a-town soon as is possible.

Affer *A is fe ackee*, dem had gone te de supermarket. Clarise'd made im point out de *A*s on all de packages. Nathanial had oblige, sidle up te de brightly colored packets, quickly flick im fingah at de lettah so de udda shoppers nyah catch on wat im doin. Him gat it mostly correct, but wrong some-a de time. Pointed te *M*, an *N*, even a *Y* wen im start gettin' embarrass an tired. Clarise was enjoyin' herself. Was dere in de puddin—in de loud way she speak, makin' sure everybody in de whole aisle listenin' in.

"Dat fantastic, Nathanial! Nex week we gwan get started on *B*. An by half-year's mark, we gwan have de whole alphabet down. Si. It nyah so difficult affer all, dis readin'." Each word-a praise like an open-palm slap on de back ov Nathanial head. Disguised rebuke. Only time since dem marry dat evah im feel like raisin' im voice or im hand te de woman. Still, im guess she owed no small amount-a smugness where im readin', or lack dereof, concern. Most likely im wife still smartin' cause im conceal im readin' problem till dem already wed. It was sneaky, true, but Lawd, im damn payin' im dues now. Amount-a damn trouble it cause im since, im gatta be nearly done wid im penance, sure as im standin' yere.

In any case, it nat only imself dat was cookin' up de porkies fore dem wed. Clarise, she swore im was de firs an only. But a few mont after de weddin' im cousin foun out frum a friend dat de girl bin roun de track several time before. Nathanial too much a gentleman te raise it now an embarrass de woman. But sometime she push im so-so close te clumsy spillin' dem beans all ovah de place. It nyah matter much te Nathanial who Clarise bin wid before, but im grown tired ov de woman's growin' righteousness. Act like she de only one never can do nuttin' wrong.

Nathanial pat down im Afro an close im eye, im workfilthy hand clutchin' de railin' ov de wooden pier. Wen im get home, Clarise gwan get on at im bout dem dirty hand. She like dem sof an clean: uncalloused. Like de men who work behind de counter in Jamaica Bank down de main street, Nathanial imagine. She wan dem hands, like im nyah seen a day ov honest work in im whole life. Nathanial fingahs, dem line wid toil. De grime ov de ports sink inte de tiny likkle skin-ridges ov im palm an fingahtip, pattern dem black wid grease an dirt. Clarise buy scrubbin' brush an special soap. Send im out de house wearin' heavy work glove one day. De udda men down de dock, dem had laugh demself te tears.

Nathanial raise up im face te de warm, gentle wind. De breeze curl up an whisper roun im ear, like a chilehood sweetheart. Lawd, ain't no smell at all like de salt, blowin' off-a dis clear, clear sea.

It almos a year now since Clarise teach im *J fe Jamaica.* Nathanial im has move far an fas beyon de lettahs, an on te de soun ov de words an de sentences.

Laughter an *faster.*

Dark an *heart.*

Water an *daughter.*

Love an *grub.*

So many-many opportunity fe error. So many place te stumble an fall.

On de day he learn *J fe Jamaica,* affer im practice makin' de curve half-smile ov de lettah cross a page ov line paper, Clarise teyk de small globe down frum de bookshelf in dem tiny lounge room, point out de small cluster-a West Indian islan, ask Nathanial te look fe de *J.* Nathanial, im shock inte silence, starin' at de small speck hoverin' halfway down de world. Tiny-tiny it was. Im had te squint te si it proper. Clarise stood ovah de top ov im, one hand on a hip, watchin' right in close te de man's face, makin' sure im understood.

"Dis a small, small islan we livin' on, mi husban," she say, an she leave im dere, sittin' on de saggin' lounge wid de whole world a-tremblin' in im hand, starin' at de likkle *J fe Jamaica.*

Nathanial's already done wid unloadin' down de dockyard fe de week. It Friday so, as im always do, im rewardin' im weary-tired bone wid an easy stroll aroun de port. Monday te Friday de hustle an bustle ov de place meyk it feel like it de center ov de world. Down de export yard, crates unpack an pack, ships move in an out. It Nathanial an im coworkers' job te smooth ovah de process—meyk it run like de inside ov a clock, windin' an turnin' easy. Dem load up de banana boats wid wooden crate, imaginin' de still-green fruit slow-ripenin' te yellow on de journey, reachin' de London market jus in time fe sweetest-ripe.

B is fe banana.

L is fe London.

V is fe voyage.

S is fe safe harbor.

Crates ov coconut an tin ackee an sugar cane all load up on top one unudda, like dis islan produce feedin' half de hungry world.

Clarise bin naggin' Nathanial te get a new job. Im bin wid de Port Authority ovah three year now an no sign ov promotion. Im nyah know why de woman relish rubbin' it in—she know damn well why im overlooked all de time. Im workin' on it every moment im get but it nyah easy, grown-up man like imself learnin' te read well enough fe secure promotion.

E is fe effort.

A is fe audacity.

I is fe impossible.

In any case, dis harbor home te Nathanial now. Im nyah care dat it a tiny-small speck in de middle ov de world. Im cyant tink ov nowhere bettah im like. Im seh dis te Clarise yesterday, wen she start on at im again.

"Mi nat gwan resign, Clarise. Mi love workin' de port. It de center ov everytin comin' an gwan te dis islan. Feel like mi know de workins ov de world wen mi at de port. Ye know, like mi own self is part ov de globality ov it all."

"*Globality* nyah even a word, ye great fool," Clarise huff. "Jamaica a small-tiny islan, like dem always seh it is, an iv we stuck yere long enough, den small is de only ting our likkle minds evah gwan be."

Nathanial grit im teeth now, tinkin bout it. Im taken te ignorin' de woman wen she get in dat way—shuttin' off im ear an lettin' im mind wander te udda ting. Soon as im put de ring 'pon dat eager slim fingah-a hers, Clarise busy herself up wid nag, nag, naggin'.

But right now, on dis yere sunny Friday affernoon, de workin-week rush is slowly dyin' down, an even de thought ov Clarise all up in im face bout travelin' away frum dis place an climbin' up in de world ain't near enough te dampen Nathanial spirit.

Most-a de big boat already pull out fe dem journey, but a big ship still hoverin'. It de largest Nathanial seen in some time now. Great hulk ov a ting, wid swirlin' letterin' on de side all black an fancy. Nathanial stare up at de hulkin' sea vessel.

"*W . . . i . . . n . . .*" Squintin' inte de sun, im try te soun out de lettahs de way Clarise bin teachin' im. "*Windr . . . Windrush Three.*" Nathanial shake im head dismal.

W is fe Windrush.

De name tell im all im need te know. De ship boun fe Inglan, no less. Nathanial bet im fellow citizen gwan scramble te get in line fe boardin' an set sail te where dem true-believe dem streets jus a-pave up wid gold.

E is fe Inglan.

O is fe opportunity.

Wen im look up Inglan on de globe, im surprise at how

teeny it is. Likkle place like dat rapin' an pillagin' de whole rest-a de world. It a madness unheard ov.

Nathanial young wife would have de two-a dem board big boat like dis, if evah de woman could be so persuasive. Night an day she carryin' on bout how dem gettin' on now in age, thirty only a few short year away. Clarise seh before de two-a dem settle inte children dat she wan go on adventure, chasin' bettah dream.

"Huh. De woman crazy. Bettah dreams!" De foamy wave cap rise up gainst de pier, sprayin' onte Nathanial shoes. Im wife talkin' like dat Kennedy on de wireless, whose government jus teyk office in America, cross de sea. Already, Kennedy an co have announce dem intent on sendin' men te walk up on de moon.

"Pfffft. Madness. De *moon*." Nathanial step back frum de spray, shield im eyes wid im hand, an stare nasty back up at de *Windrush III*, suckin' furious on im teeth. Im older brother depart six year ago, on de firs ship dat came te teyk Nathanial young countrymen away.

F is fe foolishness.

Dem-a call dat boat de *Windrush* too, de firs an original one. Used-a be banana boat, Nathanial hear tell. Still travel de same journey. Only now it exportin' de people. It nyah matter, de cargo's still a-gobble up abroad by foreigner—still peel back te flesh on arrival an swallow whole. Nevah te be seen again.

Im brother Curtis was all dress up in im Sunday finery, standin' anxious-happy an full up-a dizzy hope, on dis very same pier fe im Inglan journey.

B is fe bon voyage.

P is fe possibility.

D is fe dreams.

"Lawdy Lawd . . . seem like it so-so long ago now im gone." Nathanial heavy sigh, jus tinkin ov de years dat gone by. Im move away frum de ship an stare out again inte de open sea. "It jus invitin' hardship an trouble te go always a-seekin-seekin."

C is fe courage an carriage an change.

S is fe steadfast an stubborn an staid.

Out on de ocean, aquamarine meet cobalt, cobalt greet turquoise, an turquoise got itself all busy-up hailin' good afternoon te de jadest ov greens. Some part de harbor so clear-clear green-blue dat it seem im could jus reach out in front im face an touch de sandy sea bottom. Light ray ripplin' off true-gentle wave, like de ocean itself is carryin' de sunshine inte Kingston Beach.

"Oh, dis *islan*," Nathanial Robinson whisper softly te imself. "Any red-blooded man on God's own eart gwan get excited bout de view stretch out before mi." Im nyah crazy fe wantin' te stay on de islan. Fe refusin' te budge imself, wen almos every udda young man im know wid de means fe doin' so desertin' de place sly-sly an quick like a fox de firs time opportunity come a-brazen knockin'.

"Cha! Searchin' fe bettah ting. May de Lawd shine down im mercy on de whole sorry lotta dem stuck in cold grimy Inglan!" Nathanial sigh, turn on im heel, saunter off down de boardwalk a-headin' fe de Friday chicken an yam im know Clarise sure te be cookin' up. De woman always burn de chicken black, cause she ovah-marinate de ting an den cook de pieces ov de bird too close te de grillin' plate. Used-a bother

Nathanial, but strangely nough im slowly growin' inte eatin' it like dat.

"No way, no how Nathanial Robinson leavin' dis islan," de young man reassure imself. Im walk down de pier, cross de beach an onte de esplanade. De newspaper vendor give a nod-nod as im pass. Vera, de woman dat sell saltfish by de roadside, raise her hand up in polite salute. De road workers rollin' out de bumps in de tar, dem smile an stop workin' long nough te give a likkle wave cross de way. Nowhere, no how, Nathanial evah gwan leave Kingston, dust-tiny speck on de atlas or no. Nathanial already learn imself *H*, an dat lettah, wid dem two poles dat join up in de middle wid a likkle scaffoldin', it always gwan stand fe *home*.

———

Nathanial sit at de small wooden kitchen table polishin' off de last ov im butter yam. Out de kitchen doorway an in de lounge, im can si Clarise, sittin' foldin' clean clothes inte basket. She a-singin-singin as she smooth an turn de shirt, smooth an turn it ovah again. She singin-singin as she tuck de pairs-a socks inte each udda so dem gwan be easy te find in de drawer ov a mornin'.

"Oh Lawd, wat a nite nat a bite . . . oooooh Laaawd . . ."

Off-key strain ov de market song drift inte de kitchen an beat Nathanial bout de head.

"Carry mi ackee go a Linstead market . . ."

Nathanial cringe as Clarise again fall outta tune. It im own damn silly fault she singin' so. In dem early courtin' days, im used-a tell de woman dat voice she had was big sexy-beautiful.

Meyk de girl smile an swoon wen im say it, so im younger self keep it up. An now she wife te Nathanial, he cyant very well double back an say she soun like a donkey brayin' an im was jus wicked-lyin' all along.

C is fe comeuppance.

K is fe karma.

J is fe just deserts.

Clarise fole de clean clothes inte de laundry basket, one eye on de newspaper dat perch on her lap. Seem she big distracted.

"Ye swoonin' at dat Harry Belafonte in de *Jamaica Gleaner* again?" Nathanial call tru de kitchen doorway, a-teasin'.

"It nyah Belafonte mi swoonin' at," come de big cheeky reply. "Matter ov fact, if ye haffi know, it de whole West Indies cricket team. An mi nat de only one goin' all weak at de knee, tank ye very much, Mister Robinson. So don't ye start comin' across all smug an smart wid mi."

"Lawd, dis woman mi got miself! She nyah know de meanin' ov loyalty!" Nathanial call back, chucklin' big-loud as im remove imself frum de table an drop de crockery an de cutlery inte de sink. Movin' inte de small lounge room, im a-plonk imself down in de armchair. De corroded springs, dem almost give out underneat im botty.

"Ye want te practice readin'?" Clarise pass im de paper, stand, pick up de full washin' basket.

Nathanial stop Clarise readin' de newspaper out loud some week ago now. Im couldn't bear de news dem was reportin': all dem fool politician squabblin' bout independence. Wat on dis fine eart is left te argue bout wen it come te independence frum de British im never gwan figure out. All-a dem years since slavery, an still wen de master say jump, de islan jus gather roun debatin' how high dem gwan lif dem feet.

On de front-a de paper, de West Indies cricket team dem ridin' up back a lorry truck, wavin' dem cricket bat aroun fe de camera. Cheesy-big smile runnin' cross dem face. Along de street, people cheerin' wild-wild. In de nex photograph, a group ov young white women starin' on at de team frum behin de security rope. Dem pretty girl mout so wide open Nathanial tink im can si dem tonsil vibratin'. One-a de girl reachin' out te touch Wesley Hall sleeve, lookin' like she gwan faint. De cricketer pay de girl no mind, wide smile cuttin' in half dat big-handsome face ov his.

"Wait a likkle minute," Nathanial call te Clarise, gesturin' te de collage ov photographs. "Tell mi, wat dis? Wat on eart goin' on?" De *Gleaner* most time gat one photo on de front, but yere Nathanial lookin' at photo after photo, all-a de damn smilin' smug cricket team. "Cricket takin' up alla de front page. Wat goin' on?" Nathanial lif de newspaper close up te im eye. Look like de printin' press done struggle wid de photo display. De ink all bled out inte gray, smudgin' in de page margin.

"It de cricketers," Clarise reply. "Seem dem gettin' a likkle famous ovah dere."

"Fool woman. Course it de cricketers. Mi can si dat wid mi own eye," Nathanial snap. De woman well aware im still have trouble makin' out all de words, but dat nyah mean im sof in de head. "Where dem playin' at, Clarise? Dat wat mi askin'." Nathanial bang impatient on de front page-a de paper wid im outstretch index fingah.

"Owstrayleah."

"Where?" Nathanial search im wife face. "Where on eart is dat?"

"Bottom ov de world, dem say. British rule, apparently. Big, big islan. Dem seh de whole Caribbean can fit inside one tiny likkle piece ov de country. Islan so big it also a continent." Clarise walk ovah te de bookshelf, reach up an get de globe frum de top shelf, spin de ting aroun an hand it te Nathanial. Her fingah restin' on a big mass ov land down de bottom. Nathanial cyant believe de size-a de place. Country bigger dan *J is fe Jamaica* an *E is fe Inglan* all roll up together.

"A," im seh te Clarise, "is nat gwan be jus fe ackee anymore," an im bury im head in de paper as Clarise wander off wid de clothin' basket, shakin' her head.

"Oww . . . Owstrayleah," im repeat slowly.

A is fe Owstrayleah.

Nathanial crouch back down te study de newspaper. Long beach is stretch out behind de cricket team, waves breakin' gainst de juttin' rocks, like dem could easy-easy swallow up de roof ov de two-story buildin' Nathanial now sittin' in. It nyah look like de same sea dat Nathanial pass every day. Look rough, an wild, an capable ov anytin. Look excitin', dat sea, an like it a different body ov water altogether. Nathanial survey de faces ov de cricketers. Look like dem in paradise, dem so delirious-happy.

"Wat country dis, dat offah such reception te black West Indian man. Treat us like we kings!" im whisper 'citedly te imself.

In one frame, captain Wesley Hall throwin' im head back, dress all smartly up in im cricket whites an barin' im matchin' ivory teeth. In unudda, Frank Worrell solemnly shakin' hand wid a gray-hair man in fancy suit. Nex shot de whole cricket team lyin' back on towel on de beach, swimsuits so tight aroun dem genital region dat de photograph could belong in a dirty magazine.

Somehow, some way, fe some strong-strong reason, Nathanial feel discontent coursin' an careenin' aroun im veins.

E is fe envy.

Im close im eye fe moment an im tink im can hear dat blue-black thrashin' ocean breakin' gainst de coastline. Im sure im can hear de people ov Owstrayleah cheerin' im on an smilin'. Nathanial peek out frum im fantasy te close-examine de photo once more.

"Well mi nevah. Big islan. Big, big islan."

Few mont ago, wen de South African cricket team tour Inglan, some-a de British, dem protest frum de sideline. Nathanial nyah catch dem grievance in full, but it about dat dreadful partheid business. De protesters dem so angry-loud dem even disturb de broadcast on Clarise wireless. But in dis country, dis Owstrayleah, look like dem happy-friendly an nat givin' an owl-hoot wat color skin ye gat wen ye turn up, like dem gat nat a care in de world bout trivialities like dat.

"Dem bin playin' dere few days now. Whole country done fall in love wid dem. Introduce dem te prime minister an all manner-a important folk. Like dem national hero or sometin." De empty washin' basket a-perch on Clarise hip.

"Dat so?" Nathanial cyant tear im eye frum de newspaper page.

"Dem callin' dis cricket season de Calypso Summer, affer de team. An cause it always summer dere, in dat country."

Clarise a-whistle de Linstead Market tune as she wander back out inte de lounge.

Clarise retire te bed early. Light trickle sofly frum de room. De full, fat moon castin' an eerie brightness ovah Kingston. Nathanial Robinson, who nevah in im life bin all dat keen on de cricket, labor one sentence at a time tru de sport section ov de paper.

————

De Saturday mornin' sun shine hot tru de bedroom window an onte Nathanial face. Smell-a oat porridge an cinnamon drift in frum de kitchen. Empty space in de bed nex te de man, where Clarise already gat up. Nathanial adjust im sleep shorts, roll ovah, sit up, swing im legs ovah side-a de bed.

De *Gleaner*'s fole up careful on de table nex te Nathanial side-a de bed. De still-smilin' faces ov de cricketers follow im as im rise an walk ovah te de window.

Frum up yere, im gat a prime view ov central Kingston. Dat gotta be bout de only advantage ov dis tiny-small city partment im an Clarise have share de past three years. Sunlight pierce tru de dirt-streak window. Nathanial ease de window open, one hand shieldin' im eye. Im gaze ovah de roof ov de town hall, pas Jamaica Bank an down on te de balcony ov de post office buildin'.

Weekend Kingston already alive an fierce-breathin'. Market an shop doors swing to an fro as de city people lazy-bustle about dem business. Motorcars drive erratic aroun de wide street: showin'-off drivers pullin' up sharp te chat outta dem windows wen dem pass familiar face.

It a usual Saturday mornin'. Nuttin' odd or outta place. De city below fidgetin' no more an no less dan usual. But dis mornin', somehow, someway, fe some reason, wen Nathanial Robinson gaze ovah de city im grow te love so-so dear, Kingston feel insignificant small.

R. R is fe restlessness.

The Stilt Fishermen of Kathaluwa

THE OCEAN *hums like a snoring monster, as if at any moment the great olive-green bulk of it could awaken in a thrash of claw and snarl, ready to protect its treasure. Asanka stares out at its rippling scales, tries to ascertain how much time they have before the beast stirs for breakfast.*

In the eerie predawn darkness, all thirty or so of the men seem to be holding their breath. Asanka looks slowly to his left, then to his right. They're standing, the group of them, in a huddle on the deck, thin brown legs poking out of black or blue shorts, narrow shoulders coat-hangered beneath thin cotton T-shirts.

"Do not wear white," the two men had said when they'd gathered the passengers together three days ago for the first leg of the journey, made them search through their travel bags. They've left those bags behind now, in the back of the truck. Asanka wonders what will happen to his things, realizes now how clearly white

would have been seen in the night: beamed across the coastline to government boats, or fishermen desperate or jaded enough to have their eyes fixed on a reward.

Asanka thinks they're somewhere near Galle. Perhaps in some small fishing bay just far enough around the corner from the port to be hidden but not overly suspicious. In a small, still group like this, silent and watchful, backs arrow-straight, their dark shirts casting only the faintest of silhouettes against the charcoal sky, it feels as if they are soldiers on guard. Asanka wonders how many of the other men, all Tamils like him, have been here before, have peered with their makeshift battalions through the dim light, waiting on a town or a city or a people to finally fall asleep— waiting for the blue-black darkness that makes the bloodshed seem less real.

"Bloodshed when night falls is just a bad dream at sunrise," Asanka's commander used to say, inspecting up and down the double-line of soldiers in the morning, slowly pacing the aisle of blood-soaked uniforms.

The two boatmen, whom Asanka's begun referring to in his head as Mustache and Ponytail, start dividing the group. Asanka and the two other boys are ushered quickly over to the front of the boat with the smaller men, bare feet quietly pattering on the slimy wooden deck. The man with the mustache pulls at the door of the fish hold, swings it back on its hinges, nods at them to get inside. The men crowd around, looking down into the small compartment. Asanka doesn't like small spaces, can't stomach close bodies anymore.

The first time he tried to run from the Tigers, Asanka and his little friend Dinesh, they locked both of them in a potato chest.

They made them crouch right next to each other, arms folded across their chests, knees squashed into their chins. Then the Tigers had nailed the lid shut, and the footsteps and laughing voices had slowly moved away. Thinking about it now, Asanka wants to throw up. He can remember the cramping pain, the darkness, the heat, the vibrations of his friend's chest as he heaved air in and out, wheezing and calling for his mother. Asanka knew he hadn't seen her in over a year. After a few hours, Dinesh had peed his pants. It had pooled warm around Asanka's ankles, soaked into his shorts.

One by one the other two boys and the small men hoist themselves into the fish hold, curling into crouched positions next to each other, until only Asanka is left, staring into the square metal cupboard. Mustache looks at Asanka, prods him with the wooden handle of his fish knife. Asanka shakes his head, takes a step away, starts to cry. The tears feel strange welling in his eyes—foreign. They tickle as they run slowly down his cheek. Asanka reaches up and rubs them away, black dirt from his fingers smearing across his face.

The man looks toward the back of the boat, calls sharply to his friend, who is quietly settling the other men cross-legged on the floor of the small cabin. Mustache gestures with his fishing knife. The other man, tall and thin with curly black hair pulled back into a ponytail, makes his way over.

"Get in," Ponytail says.

Asanka avoids looking at them, shakes his head no, closes his eyes, and braces himself for the blow. If they shout at him, they will wake the ocean for sure, wake the snoring beast. Tears are falling, but Asanka doesn't feel fear in the way that he used to.

His stomach doesn't turn itself inside out anymore at the sight of raw flesh, at the naked butchered bodies of nearly still girl-women lying ripped on the roadside. His lost fingers ache, though, when he's afraid, the stumps pulsing like a heartbeat. He rubs at his hand, moves his gaze out to sea. The waves are breaking flat and even. It's as if he could walk off the boat right now, climb across them like giant steps until he reaches the flatness beyond, as if he could just walk across the water and away from Sri Lanka.

Asanka wants to leave, more than anything. His father and mother must have sold almost everything they own to get him here. For a boy traveling alone, the men had asked for double. He could not go back to Dehiwala, not even to see them after so long away. The government soldiers are watching the house, waiting for him. Asanka does not know what he'll tell his father if the men put him off the boat, doesn't know how he will carry the shame. All because of the stupid fish hold.

"Get in!" *Ponytail says, louder now, scanning the beach behind them as he speaks.*

One of the men seated on the cabin floor rises slowly to his feet, ducks out of the doorway. He's a small man, only a palm width taller than Asanka, though he moves like his bones have seen sturdier days.

"Please. Leave him. He's just a boy. I am almost as small as he is." *He hoists himself quickly into the fish hold before Ponytail or Mustache can protest, points to Asanka and gestures toward the group of men sitting on the cabin floor.*

Asanka pads over and lowers himself onto the cold floor, ignoring the annoyed glares of the other men. Ponytail and Mustache move away from the fish hold. They stand in the center of the boat, their heads bowed, talking in whispers. Snatches of the hurried discussion escape from their huddle: "... not good ... leave both of them ..."

There's a break in the argument, a moment of silence. The sea blows through it, cool and salty, smelling of fish guts, damp wood, and seaweed. Asanka runs a finger along the bumps in the deck, imagines the boat post-catch, the entire deck writhing silver and shimmery as a hundred netted herring thrash and wriggle, gasping for air.

Fishing was the first time Asanka ever saw death close up. When he was a very small boy, he used to holiday at his grandparents' place in Gampaha. His poppo would take him night fishing on a secret stretch of the Kelani River. On their first trip ever, when their small haul of fish was upturned onto the deck, five-year-old Asanka had stared with wide eyes as the terrified squirming creatures grew limp with defeat. He'd grimaced as his poppo slid his knife along each of the fish bellies, scraping their red-jelly insides over the side of the boat. Each plop of their guts into the deep blue below had made him feel like vomiting.

Mustache walks over to the open fish hold, scans the group of men for Asanka's rescuer. Holding the sheathed blade of the knife, he swings the long handle at the man's face. Crack. *Asanka's new friend clutches at his forehead. A thin trickle of blood dribbles slowly through his fingers.*

"If the boy is old enough to get on this boat, he is old enough to behave like a man." *Mustache swings the door to the fish hold shut.*

Asanka stares at Mustache's face as he bolts the door. Something in the man's expression, in his bowed shoulders, reminds

Asanka of the way he felt after the potato chest, after his finger was taken, of the way he became when his heart had hardened and he'd finally stopped trying to run.

Ponytail moves toward Asanka and the other men crouched in the cabin. He unfolds a large sheet of dirty canvas, shakes it out, lays it over their heads. "We need to look like just a few fishermen," he says, in a nervous voice that makes Asanka feel anxious as well.

There is a tiny hole in the canvas, right near Asanka's cheek. As they navigate their way out of the bay, he sees three figures outlined against the early-morning gray: thin, deformed giants swaying above the shallows. The boat draws closer, closer still to them. Asanka gasps softly, then immediately covers his mouth with his hand.

Three bare-chested men are sitting perched above the water on long poles, clutching to them lizardlike with one hand. They crouch there, several meters above the water, balanced on thin cross-branches, looking as if they're suspended in midair. They stare into the water, each of them moving around a thin fishing rod with their free hand. The plastic bags tied halfway down their stilts are sagging with the weight of their catch.

In one slow movement they turn to look at the boat, smiling at Asanka right through the hole in the canvas. The fishermen nod their heads, as if to wish safe passage. In the darkness beneath the canvas, Asanka can't tell if any of the other passengers have seen them. Asanka had thought they were extinct, the stilt fishermen of Kathaluwa. He learned about them back at school. There were photographs of them in his geography book, perched atop their fishing stilts, the salt-sprayed sinew of their shiny brown muscles *set against a flat blue backdrop. The stilt fishermen of Kathaluwa. Asanka squeezes his eyes shut. Opens them again. The fishermen have disappeared. The glints and shadows of the ocean must be playing tricks on him.*

———

Loretta wakes with Sam's breath on her cheek. Before she even opens her eyes, the stale smell of last night's Jack Daniel's annoys her. *Client drinks*, he'd finally texted her at a quarter to eight, after she and her mother had been waiting at the restaurant for forty-five minutes. Her mum hadn't said anything, hadn't even moved a muscle in her face. She'd been cautious about criticizing Sam ever since she and Loretta had words about it several months back. She hadn't needed to last night, though—Loretta had instantly felt the anger creeping into her own face, flushing the freckled white of her cheeks as pink as marshmallow.

When Loretta opens her eyes, Sam's face is twenty centimeters from hers, his cheek smushed into the pillow as if his nonna's gripping it between thumb and forefinger, pinching a hello. This close up, Loretta can see the pores on Sam's nose, the sparse line of black hairs joining one eyebrow to the other, the dark dots of morning stubble peppering his square jaw. His crow's-feet are deepening. Sam's looking even better as they push toward their midthirties. Somehow this annoys Loretta rather than pleasing her.

Loretta rolls slowly over to check the time on her alarm clock. Ten past seven. She watches the second hand tick around once, twice, thinks momentarily of switching off the alarm. Saturday morning's the only time Sam ever sleeps in. Fuck him, though. He was so toasted when he arrived home last night that she heard him drop his keys on the doorstep three times before he managed to open the front door. She stares again at the thin black clock hand as it ticks a circle one, two, three more times. *Eeep. Eeep. Eeep. Eeep.* Loretta hates the sound the alarm clock makes. It's like the warning beep of a reversing truck. A threat. *You had better come and face your day.* She buries her head in the pillow and groans softly, pretending to have just woken up. She leaves the beeping just long enough to wake Sam, then stretches out and hits the snooze button.

Sam stirs behind her, lifts himself up on his elbow. "Did you just hit snooze?"

"I've got to get out to the center, and I'm still tired." She giggles guiltily.

"Bullshit." He jabs his finger into her back. "You just want to punish me for getting sloshed last night."

Loretta giggles again, tries to divert the conversation. "Why do they even have snooze buttons? Isn't waking up at a set time the whole point of an alarm clock?"

"I thought we were talking about you being pissed off at me," Sam says, laughing. "And anyway, don't be lazy. *I'm* already up." He spoons his body into Loretta's back. The stiffness beneath his boxer shorts digs conspicuously into her left thigh.

"Very fucking funny." She wriggles out of his grasp.

"Fucking. That sounds more like it." He reaches a hand over her waist, slides it under her polka-dot nightshirt and up the skin of her stomach, trails his fingers up to her breast, circles around her nipple.

Loretta sighs, collapses back into him. They've always been like this, she and Sam. Their bodies just somehow fit together. She's listened to her friends over the years, even the ones happy in their marriages, and knows it's rare, what she and her husband still have. Still, great sex is not enough to hang a lifetime on.

Sam's breath is heavy on her neck. He nudges her legs open. His hand moves from her nipple, down her stomach, down between her legs. God. It's not enough to hang a marriage on. He eases a hand beneath her, lifts her up slightly from the bed. It's 7:17 now, on the alarm clock. Her cheek presses into the pillow. Fuck. Sam groans into her ear. Loretta reaches a hand behind her, pulls him closer in. God. It's not enough. Then there's the thing with her job, the fact that he's stopped talking about children. God. It's not enough to make her happy. Shit. Sam's mouth is opening and closing, right next to her ear. He thrashes and gulps and writhes, like a landed fish.

His body relaxes and he spoons against Loretta's back once more, wraps his hand around her waist. The alarm clock's beeping again. Seven thirty on the dot.

"Come on, it's Saturday morning. Just stay in bed. Give it a miss for one weekend." Sam sits up and grabs Loretta's elbow as she moves to get out of bed, curly red hair wild around her face.

"Viv can't go today. I promised I would."

"Shit. You're really going all the way out there again?" Sam flops back onto the pillow, exasperated.

Loretta turns her back to him, steps out of her nightshirt and into the en suite bathroom. She hates this bathroom—the shiny black surfaces that gather dust overnight, the plain white tiles. Sam had insisted on buying off the plan and, against her better judgement, they'd succumbed to the developer's interior stylist. That's what they call themselves these days, interior stylists. She and Sam had laughed about it for weeks. Buttering their morning sourdough had become *toast styling*. Changing the screen saver for their mobile phones, *phone styling*. They'd found such things amusing, back then.

"Black and white," the stylist had said, "never goes out of fashion. You just dress it up with whatever color you want to suit the season. Yellow cushions and wall art in summer, purple throw rugs and candles in winter."

Loretta had wanted everything neutral, to suit the old brown leather couches and assorted coffee tables they already had, but Sam thought she was crazy, since new furniture was already paid for in the package they'd chosen.

The hot spray of the shower hits Loretta's face. She tilts her head up, letting the water run into her mouth. She'd been undecided, actually, when she first woke up, about going out to Villawood. Then Sam had started with his usual shit.

Loretta misses her old job at the Asylum Seekers Center. Saturday volunteering's been her only chance to reconnect with that work. She reaches for the shampoo. Oxfam coconut, still going from the gift basket the girls gave her on her last day at the center. It was Sam who persuaded her to ditch the job.

"We're not getting any younger," he'd said. "It's not just

the pay. You couldn't work around this job with kids. They're always calling you off-hours. If you find a steady firm somewhere, you could work the new job for a few years, then take maternity leave."

A warm feeling had flooded Loretta's stomach when he said that. She'd seen this house, this soulless, monochrome Escher-print display home, completely worn in—knee-height Vegemite fingerprints smeared on the double doors of the giant chrome fridge, the varnish on the stairway banister worn dull from kids' bottoms sliding down it, the spare room ankle deep in toys, green playdough squished into the carpet. She'd seen their children: a pair of rowdy flame-haired daughters with his olive skin. They were ballsy and loud, with her big heart and Sam's fiery temperament.

Before then, Sam had always closed down the conversation when she mentioned children; killing conversation was a skill he'd excelled in when they first met at law school, and one that's been fine-tuned by eight years of business law at Smith, Thomas & Everington. But it's been seven months now since she left the center, and there has been no more talk about children. Maybe her mother's right: her job had just become an embarrassment to him.

Loretta towels off, wraps the white bath sheet around her hair, tucks the black one around her body, opens the bathroom door. Sam's fallen back asleep, flat on his back, mouth wide open, snoring loudly, arms spreadeagled. Sprawled against the light gray sheets, he reminds Loretta of the giant silver Jesus hanging on the cross above the mantelpiece at his parents' house.

Loretta moves over to the walk-in, steps into her under-wear, picks out blue jeans and a light cotton T-shirt. At the top of her T-shirt drawer is the tiny white baby nightgown Sam's mother gave her on the sly last Easter. Theresa had slid the tissue paper–wrapped parcel over to her with a wink as they sat at the kitchen table salting the eggplant for moussaka.

"I'm not . . . I mean, we're not—" Loretta had flushed beetroot, sat there stammering.

"Pah. The men, they are never ready," Theresa replied as she ground cracked peppercorns with the pestle. "Us women, we just need to give them a little bit of a nudge, yes? Once the baby is growing in your tummy, he will have to be ready."

Loretta had stared at her mother-in-law, mouth open. Was she—Sam's own mother—suggesting she *trick* him into it?

She sits on the edge of the bed, slides on a pair of red san-dals, grabs a handful of bobby pins from her bedside table and tiptoes out of the room.

———

The digital watch the Brotherhood of St Laurence lady left when she visited a few months back is staring down at Asanka. Its bright blue plastic arms are tucked into the springs of the top bunk, ten springs down and eleven across from the headboard. Three down and five across is a rusty, corroded spring. Twenty down and two across is a light green wad of gum. The length of the bunk beds is exactly eight of Asanka's foot lengths, toe to toe, in bare feet. The length of the room is eighteen and a half of these foot lengths. The width is sixteen foot lengths and one thumb tip.

The watch reads 07:44:25. In thirty-five seconds the security seal on the heavy door leading to Asanka's unit will be broken by the beep of an access card. The door will creak, because the top hinge needs oiling. Then, depending on who is rostered for morning checkup, it will either slam loudly or be eased softly shut. One time, Asanka didn't hear the door close. It must have been stuck open, but the room checker hadn't stopped. Asanka had thought of running, of sneaking past the heavy metal door and trying to escape, but he did not know what the Australians would do. The Tigers came back for him after half a day in the potato chest, but these people have locked him up for a year and a half.

Asanka waits. 07:45:00. Beep, creak, pause, slam. *Thunkerr, thunkerr, thunk.* Asanka can tell from the slam and the footsteps that it's the short man with the big belly hanging over his pants. Some of the workers give their names, stop to chat. But not this man. He will move slowly, taking approximately seven and a half shuffle steps between each bedroom door. This man walks unevenly. *Thunkerr, thunkerr, thunk,* as if his toes hit the ground before his heels. Each room will take Big Belly an average of forty-five seconds to check. Asanka starts counting. 07:45:45. *Thunkerr thunk.* Room three: pause, check. 07:46:32. *Thunkerr, thunkerr, thunk.* Room four: pause, check.

Asanka knows every sound in this section of the center. Every creak, footstep, drawer slide, cupboard slam, groan, furniture scrape, and murmur. Every door clang. Every sigh. *Thunkerr, thunk,* pause, check.

"All right, mate, out of bed. C'mon." Big Belly pauses at

the door, then passes on to the next room when he sees Asanka moving under his blankets.

Asanka eases his legs off the sagging bottom bunk. Sits there for a moment. He stares across at the small chest of drawers containing his two changes of clothes. He scratches his head for a few minutes: 07:49:55. Yawns: 07:52:02. Stretches out his legs: 07:52:41. He unthreads the watch from above him, stands up: 07:52:59. He walks slowly across the room: 07:53:25. He stands by the chest of drawers: 07:54:12. Asanka's pajamas are falling apart—threadbare at the seat, two buttons missing—but they are a donation he's grateful to have. The room is quiet. Nobody's been put in to share with him since Chaminda was found dead. They have asked him if he would like to change rooms. As if that would somehow make things better. He opens his drawer: 07:54:28. Gets out his jeans and T-shirt: 07:55:00.

When he stops counting, he will be locked in the chest. They will shove him inside the fish hold. They will shut the lid and leave him there, with the blood and the stink and the smell of fear. Dinesh will be there, next to him, letting go of his bowels and wheezing. Dinesh will be dead, and his face will already be decaying. 07:58:10. Mustache and Ponytail are going to come for him. They will hit him in the face with the handles of their fish knives. They will turn the boat around and throw him to the Tigers.

Asanka puts out a hand, steadies himself. The man who comes to talk to him, the head doctor they sometimes send in, he says it is not real. Nobody is coming to get him. He is safe now. It is all in his head. But, the doctor, he doesn't know.

He does not *know.* They are coming for him. 08:00:00. And anyway, the Immigration want to send him back, back inside the potato chest.

Asanka inches himself sideways, into the gap between the chest of drawers and the wall, stays as still as he can. The footsteps are moving away. The Tigers will never come back for him and Dinesh. They will starve, or suffocate. They will rot. They should never have tried to run away.

Asanka used to stay in the bunk bed all day sometimes, but since Chaminda died they've been made to get up by 07:45:00. Ever since then, Asanka's been counting. Trying to fill the day with things. Filling a day with things has never been more difficult. In Gonagala, just before he got away, he cut up three people in the time he now has to make stretch till breakfast. He cut them up alive, while they were still screaming.

08:06:21. Asanka deserves to die. He should have tried harder to escape. He should have taken Dinesh with him, that final time. Asanka has no idea what became of his friend. Dinesh is crouched next to him now. Dinesh is always crouched next to him. But today, his friend's dead body has no face on it. They should have refused to fight for the Tigers, let the Tigers take all their fingers. One by one. A fist with no fingers cannot fight. 08:06:32. Asanka knows why they are keeping him in here. They have found out that he is a monster. He *is* a monster. Only monsters do such things as he has.

Asanka shifts his body around inside the chest, trying to get the leg cramps to stop. Dinesh won't quit wheezing. Asanka feels like thumping the kid. "Be quiet! I want to hear if there is anyone near."

08:08:02. Asanka edges out from beside the chest of drawers and sidles into the small shower room. He balances the watch on the sink so he can see its face. 08:09:23. He undresses, moves into the tiny shower cubicle, turns on the hot water tap, steps under the cold spray. The water warms, scalds, starts burning his skin. 08:10:52. Blood is washing off him, running down his thin brown body and into the silver drain hole. There is red everywhere. He has not killed anybody today, not killed since he got away from the Liberation Tigers. But there is blood all over this shower cubicle, all over him. Somebody will walk past and see him, catch him standing there naked and see the bloody mess he's made. There are no doors in this place—no doors except the ones to keep people from running away.

The head doctor said there was no blood, that he would never be locked in a chest or a fish hold again. But then the head doctor had walked out of here, left him behind, in the chest. He can hear the footsteps out there sometimes, can hear the head doctor going about his business. Asanka cranes his head, looks up. The rusty nail ends are poking through the splintering wood. If he could just stretch out his hand, he could try to push them out. Somehow.

08:10:52. Asanka grabs the bar of soap, rubs it all over his body. The waxy white soap bar turns pink with blood. He raises the soap to his mouth, bites off a chunk. Starts chewing. The soap burns on the way down. 08:11:24. Asanka's stomach heaves and flinches. He does not want to die. He wants to be washed clean, to be clean inside. Like Chaminda.

Chaminda's body lay on the top bunk for a full day before a cleaner found it and shrieked at Chaminda's stillness, his waxy skin and vomit-soaked shirt. Asanka had discovered his friend earlier in the day, when he'd climbed up to bring him breakfast. He'd gently closed Chaminda's eyes and covered his slim body with the sheet. After everything he'd been through, the man deserved some peace. Asanka had only met Chaminda at the start of their journey to Australia, but in the end they were all each other had: family.

Asanka's been watching the news every evening in Common Room B, at 19:29:58, but Chaminda has never been mentioned. Just the politicians, arguing among themselves about more boats coming in. They've taken measures, though, in here. They installed two extra cameras in the common areas last week, and now they padlock the cupboards with cleaning fluids in them.

Asanka leans over, gags, opens his mouth wide to the bile. He watches the soapy food chunks hit the metal floor of the shower, pool around the plughole. Asanka wants to be clean again.

———

Asanka wakes on the floor of the boat, shivering, soaked in salt water. His right hand is still knotted to the bench with Chaminda's shirt. The ocean's sleeping again, lapping against the side of the boat in even ripples, snoring as if nothing ever happened. The sky is slowly tinging back to blue, thick gray clouds dissolving into nothing. Asanka looks out at the dark green ripples in the distance, squints into the wind for signs of movement. Over near the fish hold, Mustache is talking to a handful of the men. Asanka strains to listen as he works away at the knot.

"Little man, can you swim?" *Chaminda had asked him last night, just before the storm began raging. When Asanka shook his head, Chaminda had taken off his long-sleeved shirt, ripped it into a makeshift rope, and tied Asanka's wrist to the bench.*

Something moves in front of Asanka, blocking out the light. He pulls his arm free. Chaminda's standing over him, holding a fish. The fish is half an arm's length long, translucent silver with strange bluish-gray spots on either side of its spine. Asanka wonders if he's dead, or if Chaminda is. Then he wonders if the fish is a mackerel. It looks like one—the small, pointy fin on the top, the fan-shaped crest at the front. But the spots; Asanka's never seen a mackerel with spots like this before.

Chaminda's holding the fish out to him, gesturing for him to take it. He raises his free hand to his mouth, makes a drinking motion. Asanka stares at the fish. It's been slit open, a horizontal gash cut beneath the gills. Asanka takes the fish, raises it to his mouth, places his lips around the hole and sucks the salty blood in through closed teeth, straining out the stray scales and flesh. Three days ago, the last three drinking containers had cracked— they'd been tossed up in the air and flung down against the metal fish hold as the boat slid off the peak of an enormous wave, had cracked at the base, so they couldn't even collect more.

After Asanka's done, Chaminda takes the fish from him. Asanka watches as he raises it to his lips. Orange pulp drips down Chaminda's bare chest. Without his shirt, the sun will surely burn his friend up. Chaminda's been watching out for Asanka ever since the fish hold. Asanka's not used to that—random acts of kindness. Last night he had tried to smile at his friend, pulled his lips back and bared his teeth and gums. "You don't need to do that," *Chaminda had said.* "Just say thank you." *He had sounded so sad that Asanka regretted even trying.*

Along the edge of the boat bench are thirty-five notches. Ponytail has carved one there every day since they left Sri Lanka, every morning when he wakes up. Now, Asanka notices Ponytail standing alone on the roof of the boat. He is scanning the blue around them, turning and looking, looking and turning. Ponytail is awake, but he has forgotten the notch. Asanka wants to remind him, to climb up and grab his leg, drag him down off the roof and over to the bench, demand that he get out his fish knife.

The sea has been restless at night, foaming and heaving and bubbling up around them. Under cover of darkness, it becomes a thing possessed—hissing as if hungry for them. Asanka's convinced they will never find land. The rest of the world has ceased to exist. It's only them, and the boat, and the flat wide ocean stretching forever. Only them and the terrible secrets churning ten feet below.

Four notches ago they lost a man. He was there the night before, and in the morning there was no sign of him. The oddest thing was, no one had realized anyone was missing until the morning head count. Nobody could remember the man—what his name was, when they had last seen him, what he looked like or was wearing. It was as if he had never existed, only there was definitely one less person.

"He . . . he hasn't done his mark there today." *Asanka points to the bench.*

"No." *Chaminda sits down next to him, the half-deflated fish hanging limp in his hand.*

———

Loretta pushes the button for the garage door and slowly backs the car out. At the top of the driveway she stops, presses the remote again and watches the door slowly roll down. She glances in the rearview mirror at the houses across the road. The street is empty; vehicles locked behind double garage doors, families sleeping behind peach-colored blinds.

The garbage workers are on a wages strike, but all along the street rubbish and recycling containers have been placed hopefully out, spaced at even distances apart on the verge, a kaleidoscope of dark-green and sunflower-yellow lids. Loretta sighs, resumes reversing. In about an hour, she supposes, the whole street will rise from their beds and face their Saturday morning. The kids will get Nutri-Grain in front of Channel Nine cartoons. The parents will stand at the kitchen counter as they spread strawberry jam on their Tip Top toast.

Loretta's still staring at the double-story blond brick in the rearview when the side of the car clips their recycling container. The large dark-green bin teeters and then falls over. The yellow lid flies open and empty Lite White milk cartons, an orange juice bottle, a Carman's muesli box, a stack of newspapers, and a clutter of toilet rolls spill out. Loretta pulls onto the curb, brakes. She looks up and down their street again. The blinds of her and Sam's bedroom haven't moved. All the other houses are still. She pulls back out onto the road, leaving the mess strewn across their front lawn.

Forty-five minutes later, Loretta pulls in near Fairfield Station and checks the clock. Twelve past nine. She opens the car door. "Fuck." She's overshot the parking space by almost a meter. Again. She still drives as if she's steering her old car. Last year, on the evening of her thirty-third birthday, she'd gone out to the parking lot after work, and her Ford was nowhere to be seen. A zippy black Mazda was parked in her spot; Sam was standing next to it, jangling the keys. Loretta had smiled and squealed, responding like she thought any normal person would, but what she'd wanted to say was, "I love that car. Where the fuck have you put it?"

The Falcon's vinyl seats had needed towels draped over them in summer because she could never find covers to fit. The car was too wide for most city parking spots, and a real workout to turn. But it had been hers. She and Billy Leung made out on the backseat during the dry Northmead summer between years eleven and twelve. Billy's Coke-bottle glasses had fogged up with shy anticipation, his thin, sweat-drenched fingers trembling as they climbed their way up inside her cotton shirt. The Falcon had driven Loretta to her first day at university, her father's funeral, her job interview at the center, and her graduation ceremony.

Loretta reverses a little, grabs her bag, steps out, and beeps the door locked. Sam's been telling her not to leave the car around this area, ever since the hood was keyed a few months ago. Loretta doesn't blame them, whoever did it—shiny new car like hers.

The Nelson Street bakery's already filled with people. Loretta squeezes into the crowd, the smell of freshly baked Afghan flatbread stirring a growling in her stomach.

"Hungry, are you?" the man next to her laughs, his wide smile lighting his bronze face. A round, mustard-colored hat is pulled down over his gray curls. He makes space in front of him, gestures for her to jump the queue.

"Nah, nah, I'm fine. Not in a hurry." Loretta wonders how he even heard her tummy rumble above the order taking, paper-bag rustling, and general banter of the bread shop.

"That stomach of yours is going to eat you alive if you don't give it something. Besides, the center is opening pretty soon—if you're on visiting duty."

"Oh. Well, thanks." Loretta moves forward, smiles at him. She has no idea who the man is. A relative of one of her clients, maybe. Or perhaps he works in one of the other local shops. She racks her brain, but still can't place him.

Ten minutes later, Loretta carefully steers into the parking lot, taking furtive bites of the warm, spicy-smelling flatbread from the paper bag on her lap. She pulls up right next to the red-and-white Villawood Immigration Detention Center sign, brakes, turns off the ignition, picks up the flatbread with both hands, and tucks in.

There's a crowd gathered at the other end of the parking lot. Loretta rolls down her window, leans out to see what's happening. Gathered by the wire back fence of the Detention Center is a throng of reporters and camera crews. Loretta watches them elbow each other, jostling like primary-school kids in a cafeteria line. Their voice recorders clink against each other as they fight for audio. Loretta rolls up her window, blocking out the muddle of raised voices. She doesn't want to know. She just doesn't want to know.

Loretta glances at herself in the rearview mirror, wipes the crumbs from around her mouth, tucks back her still-damp hair and pushes an escaping bobby pin back into her curls. She rubs her right forefinger across her teeth a few times, grabs her bag and jacket from the backseat. The day's turning dark, gray clouds slowly rolling in from the north. She hopes it rains, that the heavens open and they're forced to abandon ship with their press conference. Huh. Abandon ship.

Loretta thinks of the overturned recycling container on her and Sam's lawn. When it rains, the toilet rolls, newspapers, and cereal boxes strewn across the grass will sog to gray pulp. They'll look like old vomit on the manicured jade verge. Loretta beeps her car door locked and strides across the parking lot toward administration.

———

09:56:26. Asanka scans the library room shelves. They're mostly lined with magazines about cars or nature, or religious books. His eyes rest on a stack of Kingdom of God leaflets. The Jehovah's Witnesses came here once, during visiting time. Asanka was stuck for things to count, so he'd listened to their whole spiel. Nineteen minutes and thirty-eight seconds exactly. No fractions. On the Kingdom of God leaflet, a smiling brown-skinned girl and a blond-haired boy are holding hands, surrounded by all manner of animals: lions, bears, dogs, ducks; it even looks like there's some kind of long-necked furry camel in there. All of the animals look cuddly and friendly.

Asanka saw a lion once. Two of them, in fact, at Dehiwala Zoo with his father. They were pacing the cage, rage in their eyes. They did not look friendly like this. A rainbow stretches through clear blue sky above the impossible animal scene.

Printed across the rainbow in pink lettering are the words: GOD LOVES ALL LIFE. Blood is slowly soaking through the leaflet. Asanka does not know where it's coming from.

09:57:33. Asanka glances at his wristwatch. He's put it on too tight. The buckle's pinching the skin of his wrist. He folds the leaflet in half vertically, smooths the top corners into triangles, folds those triangles to the center crease. The paper's so wet with red that it's tearing in places.

"Hey, that's supposed to be reading material, not craft material." Big Belly pokes his head in the door as Asanka flies the animal-printed paper airplane across the room. Big Belly does not mention the blood that is dripping onto the gray-blue carpet.

10:00:01. The visiting hour bell. Asanka gets up from his chair, wipes his hands on his jeans, walks out of the library. He can never remember what day it is here. Everything is jumbled and confused. Sometimes Asanka imagines he catches sight of people from home, only to find that the bounce in his brother's walk belongs to a Sudanese man in the Blaxland Unit, the upward crinkle around his mother's eyes to one of the center staff.

Sometimes, when the room checker comes to wake him, and his head is still full of sleep, Asanka is fourteen years old again, awoken by whispering. There is a gun to his father's head.

"Your son must come with us," they say. "He must come with us and fight."

"No," his father says. "He's too young. Come back in another year and I'll send him with you." Everybody in the room—Asanka's mother, himself, the three soldiers—they all know his father is lying through his teeth.

"You are a Tamil," says one of the soldiers. "We Tamils are tired of the government treating us like dogs. No?"

"He is too young."

"And so, we must all make sacrifices. Your family must send somebody with us to fight, and you are too old."

"I'm not too old to fight."

"Who is it going to be? Your wife or your son?" The man with the machete had smiled at Asanka's mother.

"I'll go with them." The voice hadn't sounded like Asanka's.

Tears streamed down his father's face as Asanka put his shoes on.

10:02:03. Asanka walks with his head down, staring at the light blue linoleum. The corridor leading from the library room past the common kitchen area and into the visiting area is eighty-nine footsteps long. Toe to heel. Wearing shoes. There are three long windows set into the wall. Seventy-one, seventy-two, seventy-three. Asanka looks behind him at the neat row of bloody footprints.

Asanka has to stop counting, has to stop seeing the blood, has to start breathing again. Or they will put him in the Blaxland Unit. The Blaxland Unit is only for the men who are very sad, or very monstrous, or very ill in the head. Sometimes, they are all three. Big Belly calls the Blaxland Unit *hell*. "C'mon," he'll say when he comes for Asanka and tells him to bring his things. "Today, you are going to hell."

Chaminda told them. Chaminda told them he's just a boy. But the Immigration, they don't believe. Asanka knows why they're doubtful. He is not a boy. Not after what he's done, what he's seen. But Chaminda said they should only judge him by the time he has been out of the womb; they should only take note of the time he has lived.

Seventy-six, seventy-seven. There are eight fluorescent lights set into the ceiling of the corridor. Asanka wants to scale the wall and crawl onto the ceiling, wants to walk wrong side up and measure the distance between the light fixtures. Toe to toe. With shoes on. He cranes his neck upward. The fishermen of Kathaluwa are crouched on the ceiling, upside down. How they're balanced there, he doesn't think to wonder. Clutching onto their stilts, they hang down so low from the ceiling that their heads almost touch his own. Their fishing rods reach almost down to Asanka's waist. He abandons counting footsteps, and ducks and weaves to avoid them.

———

The waves break against Asanka's back at even intervals, thumping him so hard he loses his breath. The water is cold: blue-lips cold, toe-numbing cold. Chaminda and Ponytail are holding the ends of the rope, leaning down over the side of the boat, peering at him. The center of the rope is looped under Asanka's arms, knotted to him. When his bowels open, his whole body buckles against the pain and he can no longer hold on to the rope with his hands.

There is only one toilet on the boat, and Asanka's stomach has been so bad that he's not been able to move away from it when the other men need to go. Then Ponytail said he should not go in that place anymore, as the rest of them might get sick too.

Asanka's not worried—about the sharks, or the waves, or being sliced up by the underside of the boat. He just drags in the water, being pulled along behind the boat, limp, with his shorts and underwear off, letting the putrid mess float out of his body to the water's surface, watching it drift past him.

Asanka's head lolls back. He opens his mouth.

"*Don't swallow the water!*" *Chaminda yells down at him. But Asanka's been drinking only fish blood for nearly two days. His body wants water. His mouth won't close. He tries, but it won't shut. He gulps in the salty seawater. He swallows and swallows, until he doesn't feel thirsty anymore.*

Loretta signs in at the front desk, pushes through the first security door. She places her handbag on a blue plastic tray and pushes it toward the woman working the scanning machine. The woman scans Loretta's bag through the machine, the blue light of the monitor lighting up her face. She leans in to the screen, motions Loretta through the body scanner and over to the other side of the table. Sighing in frustration, Loretta unzips her handbag and empties the contents into the tray.

"Sorry, miss," says the woman. "There was an incident recently."

Heat rises in Loretta's cheeks. Viv had left a message for Loretta the day the center got the news. Chaminda had been one of Loretta's cases.

"Yeah. I heard about that," she says. "As you can see, I'm a real danger." She gestures to the contents of her bag.

The woman picks through the items with gloved hands: Loretta's purse, a stack of envelopes, her car keys, a notepad and pen, some deodorant, her mobile phone, a few bobby pins, dental floss, some tissues, a packet of sweets, several paper bags full of flatbread.

The fluorescent light above them flickers then glows brighter. The woman puts Loretta's mobile phone and keys inside a Ziploc bag, seals the bag, hands over a clipboard. "You can collect these on your way out. Write your name here."

While Loretta's scrawling down her details, the woman puts aside the packet of Minties, the flatbread, and the aerosol deodorant. "And please leave these here."

"You've gotta be joking. The bread and sweets? What are you worried about—they'll commit suicide by diabetic coma?" Irritated, Loretta picks up the blue tray containing her remaining possessions, tips them back into her handbag.

"Sorry. No liquids or edibles."

———

10:05:21. Asanka pauses at the door to the visiting area, wonders if they'll let him in like this—blood all over him, his T-shirt ripped at the shoulder by the fishermen's hooks. He shuffles into the room, sits down on a plastic chair, watches the door on the other side of the room, scanning the trickle of outside visitors entering. He only knows to look for the hair. She will be able to help him, Chaminda told him so. But Asanka's not even sure that he could ever stay alive outside of here, with all that space. He's grown used to being able to touch the sides of the potato chest, used to being just three rope lengths away from the boat. Asanka doesn't know what's out there, beneath the ocean.

10:11:54. Asanka counts: one, two, three, four, five, six . . . There are thirty-six chairs in the visiting area. All made from orange plastic, even their legs. Metal legs could pierce the chest, if you upturned the chair and jumped from high enough. Outside, through the sliding glass doors, there are five wooden tables, long benches attached to either side. The tables are made of heavy wood: too heavy to lift, too heavy to drag over to the one tree in the visiting area yard. Asanka imagines himself standing on one of the tables, knotting a sheet to the tree, swinging in the wind.

There's one picture in the visiting room, stuck on the noticeboard: an aerial shot of the world. Asanka walks slowly over to it. Some of the visitors are staring at him. Asanka crosses his arms, tries to cover up the stains on his shirt. The blood is there. Everybody is looking.

The picture of the world wasn't here last week. Neither was the lawyer woman. Asanka can make out Indonesia, the Cocos Islands, Sri Lanka, the Indian coast. The tiny distance between Galle and Australia does not seem like thirty-seven notches on a bench.

10:12:37. Asanka traces a finger around the circle of the world. When Asanka was a little boy, his father was a high school art teacher in Dehiwala. His dad had showed him a painting of Atlas, the Greek god who carries the world on his shoulders. "Strength is everything, Asanka," his father had declared. "With enough resolution, the impossible becomes feasible."

Such foolish optimism. The weight of the world is too heavy for even a god to bear. No matter how strong, how resolute, Atlas will eventually be crushed beneath it. His muscles will slowly slacken, spine bending ever lower. His tired eyelids will weigh shut. The globe will tilt, teeter, and slowly roll down his vertebrae.

———

"Pull yourself up! Help us pull you up!" *Chaminda and Pony-tail are gesturing frantically over the side of the boat.*

The monster that is the ocean is pulling at Asanka. It is tugging at his legs, dragging him down: it wants to eat him. Asanka wonders what it might be like, being sucked inside the cavernous belly. Warm, he thinks. Quiet, maybe.

The two men are desperately pulling at the rope. Asanka can't hear them now, over the monster's roar. But he catches the look in Chaminda's eyes and his body suddenly feels electric, come to life. Asanka does not want to die. He kicks and kicks, grabs hold of the rope with both hands, winces as its coarse wetness burns around his waist. The raw skin on his hands stings in the salty spray.

On the way up to the boat, Asanka's body bangs into the hull. He is so numb he only vaguely feels the bruising. When he is high enough, Chaminda and Ponytail grab hold of him. He teeters on the edge of the boat, then thuds onto the deck. The men crowd around him. Asanka is so cold he is burning. Every breath he takes is ice-fire.

"What were you doing?" *Chaminda sounds angry.* "You were supposed to go to the toilet and wash off. Then we pull you back in."

"Sorry." *Asanka genuinely is. Seeing Chaminda angry with*

him makes him short of breath. "I was just—we were talking. I was talking to them."

"To who?" *Chaminda sounds confused.*

"To them." *Asanka points over the side of the boat to where the fishermen are balanced, wet rags tied over their heads to shield them from the hot sun, fishing bags full, ready to dislodge their stilts from where they're wedged into the reef and ferry their catch to shore.* "I was talking to the stilt fishermen."

"Oh." *Chaminda and Ponytail exchange strange glances. Asanka shivers at them, wonders when the two became such close friends.*

"Uhhh . . . what did they say?" *asks Ponytail.*

"That there's a boat coming for us." *He points in the direction the fishermen had shown him.* "And there's land. Over there." *Asanka's legs won't stop cramping. He straightens them, then flexes them at the knee, stretches them out again on the wet, salt-crusted deck.*

Ponytail stares at Asanka for a moment. "He needs water," *he says to Chaminda.* "He needs water. We need to get him fresh water."

Chaminda looks like he's going to cry.

———

"I'll get it stamped and post it on Monday." Loretta picks up an envelope and carefully copies the address from the scrap of paper she's been given.

"You will post it." The man holds her freckled right hand in his tanned ones, smiling into her face, nodding. "You are a good girl."

Girl. Usually she would bristle at that—at the sheer condescension of it—but right now she feels like a small child: helpless, insignificant. Besides, when this man uses that word it doesn't sound patronizing. The man raises her hand to his lips, kisses it quickly, and walks slowly out through the door of the visiting room, calling a casual greeting to someone as he passes them.

Loretta tidies the stack of envelopes on the table, absentmindedly taps her pen a few times, looks around. At the table next to her, two men in smart suits are chatting animatedly with a new arrival. By their name tags and the heavy black books they carry, Loretta guesses the two men are from a religious group of some kind. The misery of this place feeds the nutbags. They flock to the unhappiness, like bowerbirds to blue.

A shadow falls over Loretta's notepad. When she looks up, a young man, seventeen or eighteen maybe, meets her gaze. He's tall, skin and bone, thick, wavy black hair falling into his eyes. Loretta stands to greet him, smiles, but he doesn't reciprocate—just stands there, in the middle of the visiting room, slowly taking her in.

————

10:16:55. Asanka waits until the lawyer lady is seated again. She has red hair, like Chaminda said. Not red like blood, though, orange-red like sunset. Asanka hasn't seen that before. Not in real life and close enough to touch.

In this country, you look at a person and you know them. It is the inside-out way the people of this country wear their soul. In their eyes you can find civilizations of honesty or sweeping fields of lies. It's taken some getting used to but now Asanka likes it—this casual unguardedness that comes from never really knowing fear.

10:17:10. It takes Asanka only a few moments to commit her to memory. The Tigers taught him that—scanning for threats in a single moment. But the Tigers are long gone and he's still doing it now, in here. He will never be rid of whom they have made him. Never. Asanka wants the bar of soap in his mouth again, wants to feel the burn of it traveling down into his stomach.

She looks new, this lawyer lady. She looks new all over, and neat, and clean, and shiny. She looks like her clothes have just come from the shop, as if she has just run a comb through her hair this very minute. Her skin is pale and flecked with light brown freckles. It reminds Asanka of his mother's kukul mas curry, of how the tender chicken looks when the gingery sauce has been slurped off, of soft meat that will fall apart on his tongue.

10:17:51. Asanka wants to reach out and touch her. In this place, something so unbroken does not seem real.

———

Ponytail shakes his head as if he thinks Asanka's crazy, but Chaminda runs a hand over his graying hair and turns to look in the direction Asanka's pointing. He walks toward the cabin, the boat lurching as he goes. Asanka watches after Chaminda as he reaches out to steady himself, trails one hand against the outside wall of the cabin for balance until he reaches the small ladder.

His friend climbs slowly up the rungs, crouches precariously on the roof.

Asanka drags himself shakily up to kneeling position. His stomach has stopped convulsing now. His naked legs ache. The wind is cold around his private parts. They flap in the wind like a flag. One of the other men laughs, gathers Asanka's discarded shorts and underwear from the deck and throws them at him.

———

"Chaminda is dead," the young man says, looking her square in the face, and Loretta realizes who he must be.

"Asanka." The boy she's heard so much about. The boy Chaminda insisted *was* actually a boy. She's heard that story several times before at the center—enough to assume this particular young man might also be spinning Chaminda and Immigration a yarn about his age.

"You need to come through to the bedroom and see Asanka," Chaminda had begged her on one of the last occasions they'd met here.

"Chaminda, I'm really sorry. I can't go into that part of the center. You'll have to get him to come out here." She hadn't taken it any further. Hadn't asked after him.

Asanka's sizing her up, staring unblinkingly, the shiny black of his pupils indistinguishable from his cloudy black irises. "Yes. Chaminda, he told me about you too," the young man says. "The red-haired lawyer who is going to get him free." He glances quickly at his watch then—an ugly, bright blue plastic thing that looks like it might have come from a two-dollar shop. He looks back up at her, then down at the watch again,

as if time's passing too quickly and he's in a hurry to be somewhere.

"Do you want to sit?" Loretta gestures at the chair. It's
right in front of him, but he doesn't seem to see it. He looks
so young. So young. And now Chaminda's not in here with
him. Ever since she heard, Loretta's been trying to push the
whole thing to the back of her mind. The night she came back
from the new job and heard Viv's message on the answering
machine she'd collapsed on the kitchen floor.

Sam had found her there half an hour later. When she told
him why she was so upset, he'd lost it. "Jesus, Lorri! For fuck's
sake, I thought there was something really fucking seriously
wrong. These people, some of them just aren't right in the
head. It's not surprising. But really, it's ridiculous to be blaming yourself."

"I'm . . . not . . . blaming . . . my . . . self." Loretta was sobbing. "I'm just . . . fuck, Sam, I'm upset. Somebody I know . . .
knew . . . liked . . . is dead." It'd felt like ice-cold fingers were
closing around her lungs.

Chaminda's case file had been almost closed the day Loretta
left the center. The departmental recommendation was that he
be placed in the community within the month. Release mem-
oranda had a habit of getting lost on their way down from the
Secretary of Immigration, so Loretta had taped a fluoro-green
reminder note to Viv's computer monitor. She should have
fucking known, though—better than that. It was emergency
after emergency at the center, every working minute. Post-its
got scribbled over, knocked off noticeboards, stuck to soles of
shoes, used as coffee coasters, inadvertently ignored.

"Yes," Asanka says. "I will sit." Sighing, as if under the sheer weight of this decision, he slides into the seat across from her, looks quickly around the room then back at his watch again.

10:19:09. The lawyer woman looked sad when she heard Chaminda's name, the cloud moving across her face like the promise of rain. 10:19:19. She asked him to sit, so he is sitting. But Asanka wants to kneel down. He wants to put his arms around the lawyer lady's waist and lean his head into her shoulder. He wants to feel her feathery hair brushing against his cheek. He wants to cry against her blue-and-white T-shirt. She is comforting to Asanka somehow, like the smell of slow-cooking kiribath.

Chaminda made them both kiribath the night before he died. He'd begged the volunteer worker from the Brotherhood of St Laurence to bring in the coconut milk and rice. The grains had been firm from using the common room microwave. Still, when Asanka sat down to eat it with his friend, rice scalding their eager fingertips, steam swirling round their heads as they bent over the red plastic bowl, it was as if they were digging their way back home.

"How are you?" she asks.

10:20:03. Asanka stares at her thin white fingers. Her eyes are the color of the ocean when it is very, very calm. Her cheeks are coloring now, slowly turning red, like the just-sliced throat of a fish. How is he?

"I'm sorry—"

"Thank you for asking me," he says, looking down at a small wad of blackened chewing gum squashed into the visiting room floor. "I am not good."

———

Asanka's legs are still numb with cold. He sits on the bench and rubs at them. The rest of the men gather at the side of the boat, staring across the ocean. The other boat is not like one Asanka has ever seen. It looks like it's made of metal, a dull-bullet gray. The boat swoops into a sharp point at the front—it is all lines and triangles and scaffolding. The boat steers closer, riding low in the water. It's almost camouflaged, even this close up. The other men laugh, pat each other on the back. Two of them are crying.

"How did he see this boat?" *Mustache says to Ponytail.* "From so far away."

"The stilt fishermen," *Asanka says.* "They showed me."

They both turn to look at him.

"Everybody be reminded," *says Ponytail to the men,* "do not say anything about us. We will make sure your families are notified that you have arrived. Remember: do not say anything about us."

The other boat's moving toward them faster now, as if beneath the surface the ocean's many fingers are hurriedly passing it over to them. Asanka stands, pain shooting down his legs. He moves closer to the huddle of men at the side of the boat. If they had a boat like that other one, they could have come here in just two weeks. They would have had enough water if they had a boat like that. They would not have had to drink dead fish.

The boat pulls up alongside theirs. The two vessels float next to each other for a few minutes. The men on the fishing boat run to the side, pointing and laughing excitedly. Suddenly, Asanka notices weapons trained on them.

"They have guns! They have come with guns!" *There are guns pointing at them. Big machine guns stuck to the roof of the boat. Asanka lets his body fall, hits the deck hard, crouches into a ball. He screams and screams and screams. The men on the other boat are not Sri Lankans. They are not Tamil, and not government soldiers either. They are wearing uniforms. The men on the other boat are soldiers. Asanka has been a soldier, knows what soldiers are capable of. The wail comes from deep down inside his belly, but Asanka doesn't recognize the sound. The sound is not coming from his body, but through it. Something is howling through him, through his mouth.*

Chaminda's kneeling next to him. He pulls Asanka into his lap, holds him to his chest, clutches him so tightly he can barely move. "There are no guns," *Chaminda says.* "There are no guns, little man. They are government people. And the government people in this country are not like they are in our country. They will help us."

"You going to help me get out of here?" The young man shifts in his seat, scanning the room skittishly.

"How old are you, Asanka?" Loretta asks.

"I don't know," he says, glancing up at the bare white ceiling as if expecting to find something there. "When the Tigers took me, I was fourteen. I forget how long it's been since then. There have been no birthdays. On the boat, we were thirty-seven days before they picked us up. I have been put in here for four hundred and twenty-one. I know this. I make marks. I make them inside the top drawer in my room. To count. The department saying they're sending me back to Sri Lanka, but Chaminda said you can get me out of here."

She can't get him out of here. She can't even try. It's not her job anymore. He wouldn't understand, even if she explains it. He's just a kid. He *is* a kid.

"Chaminda said you would help me." He fidgets his legs around under the table, checks his watch again. Then, with a suddenness that startles Loretta, Asanka stretches out both arms before him, splaying his hands across the writing pad in front of her. The thumb and pinky finger of his left hand are missing.

"When the Tigers first made me fight with them, they brought me a girl from one of the villages. They told me I needed to have her, but she was so little and frightened that instead I helped her run from them. That day, the Tigers took my thumb." The young man rubs the thick black stump at the inside edge of his hand. "The other finger they took later, when they caught me trying to run. There was no medicine. I used sewing needle and thread."

Loretta stares down at Asanka's mangled hand, bile rising in her throat.

"They keep coming, the Immigration," he says. "They are asking me the same questions. They don't listen. It is like I have no tongue." His eyes are shadowed with that hopelessness that makes Loretta remember why she had wanted to do this work in the first place.

"Uhh . . . I had a bag of sweets, but they . . . they made me leave them at the door." As soon as she speaks, she feels foolish for even mentioning the treats.

Asanka motions to where her handbag hangs over the back of the plastic chair. Loretta passes it over to him, embarrassed. Inside, there is almost nothing: purse, tissues, bobby pins, dental floss. Asanka rummages around, quickly pockets a few items, pushes the bag back toward her.

"Sorry," she offers again.

There's a commotion at the doorway of the visitors room. A group of six or so men and women, mostly suit-clad, are making their way into the room. They stop a few meters inside the doorway, quietly talking among themselves.

"Why are they here?" Asanka gestures at them, looks at his watch again.

That bloody watch. Chaminda was right, the kid is like a caged animal. Still jiggling his leg, he looks over at the notice-board on the wall. Loretta follows his eyes to the aerial image of the earth. The globe is tilted to show Australia and the whole of the Pacific region. It's been ripped out of a *National Geographic* or something. Loretta swears under her breath, wonders whether a staff member has placed it there as a taunt.

"I'm not sure." She sits for a moment, watching Asanka survey the well-dressed group.

"They're filming again. Outside the yard there. The government people." He says it softly, as if talking to himself. Loretta can feel the heat of his anger from across the table. She reaches up, tucks her hair behind her ears, doesn't know what to say next.

Asanka cocks his head to one side, smiles, stares up at the ceiling. "I have to go now," he says.

Loretta stares after him. He walks in the opposite direction to the new visitors, heads through the doorway leading back into the center. When he reaches the hallway he slows, looks down at his feet, places one directly in front of the other, heel touching toe, as if balancing on a tightrope.

––––––

Asanka turns on the tap, lowers his head, takes a long drink. No matter where he drinks from—bottle, shower, tap, face upturned to the rain in the recreation yard—the water always tastes like fish blood. Like sand and salt.

Asanka searches his jeans pocket and pulls out one of the lawyer's thin black hairpins. He peers closely at it under the fluorescent lights. Two wavy red strands of the lawyer's hair are caught in its crook. With his good hand, Asanka carefully pulls the hairs from the thin piece of metal. He watches, mesmerized, as they float to the floor.

Asanka bends the pin straight. There's a plastic bubble on one end of it, to stop it from hurting her head when she pins her hair back. Asanka drags the rounded end of the hairpin across the brick bathroom wall. He coughs loudly to disguise the sound. He scrapes and scrapes until the round plastic ends have come off, keeps scraping until the metal underneath has been formed into sharp points. Coughs. Holds the hairpin up to the light, jabs the pointy metal ends hard into his finger until he punctures the skin. He can't feel anything. He is already dead. He does not exist anymore. If he slipped quietly into the water in the dead of night, if he disappeared off the boat, then in the morning, people would wonder whether he was ever actually there at all. They would not even remember his name.

Asanka can hear the fishermen swishing with their rods, can hear their stilts shifting against the wind. He looks past the bathroom entrance, scans the bedroom, but he can't see them anywhere.

He searches his pocket for the teeth-cleaning thread. There is a red sticker on the small white plastic packet, showing a white lady's chin. Her mouth is lipstick-red. Her teeth are white and straight, and she is smiling. It does not look like a pretend smile. The smile looks real and happy. Asanka tears off a long section of teeth thread with the metal cutter, winds the middle of it tightly around the center of the bobby pin six or seven times.

The ends of the hairpin are sharp now, but the center of it is still so thick that the flesh on Asanka's bottom lip bulges shiny-tight as he makes the first incision. He pulls the pin all the way through his lip. It leaves a bloody hole, but does not hurt. Not like his fingers did. Asanka moves the hairpin in and out, dabs the blood away with the tissues from the lawyer lady's bag. The tissues are so soft in his fingers. Asanka hasn't felt tissues this soft since he lived in Dehiwala, in his parents' house. Asanka wonders if his father's still alive. He checks for the time. The watch isn't on his wrist. He checks the bathroom sink, but it's not there either. It could be in the hallway. Maybe it fell off while he was talking to her. Could be the fishermen hooked it off his wrist as he passed under them.

Asanka leans forward, blood all over his fingertips, dripping into the sink. He clumsily ties a knot in the thread, drawing the stitches tight, tugging his lips together. Beads of blood gather beneath his bottom lip and above the top one, ringing his mouth in red. He doesn't feel anything. The head doctor was right—the blood isn't there. He is safe. He stops for a moment, admiring the eight perfectly vertical mint-scented stitches. They remind him of his mother, of the embroidery she used to do on the dish towels she made for their kitchen.

Asanka holds a wad of tissue to his mouth, bows his head low as he walks back toward the visitors room. The fishermen are back. They are waiting for him, upside down, on the ceiling. They wave, smile, shake their fish bags at him.

The government people are in the outside visiting area now, by the tables and chairs. Asanka holds the tissue to his mouth, walks quickly past the people gathered in the visiting room, steps through the sliding doors to the outside area. He can't feel the ground beneath his feet. The whole world is quiet, distant. From the other side of the silence Asanka can hear Atlas, gasping for breath.

———

From the deck of the Australians' boat, the fishing boat Asanka came on seems so small. The Australians are climbing over it, roping it behind their boat. The fisher bobs up and down as if trying to escape, as though if it could only break free of them it would be able to find its way back home. It wants to backtrack through the black, uncertain, violent nights, through the impossibly golden sunrises. It wants to bob home unmanned across the flat, to that deserted beach just around the coast from Galle.

The blanket the Australian wrapped around Asanka is scratchy against his raw, wet skin. They are passing out bottles of water, unscrewing the caps. The way they move about from person to person, speaking softly to them, handing out blankets and water, makes Asanka realize they have done this many times before.

"Was there anybody else?" *the tall man in the white uniform says, in a casual drawl Asanka's only heard before through radio or television.*

The passengers from Asanka's boat look over at Mustache and Ponytail, but the two men just look around, as if confused.

"Yes," *Chaminda says, talking around the clear plastic bottle that's wedged between his lips.* "We lost a man. In the night. Several days ago."

The Australian closes his eyes: not for much longer than a blink, but Asanka catches it. "Do you know his name? Who he was?"

Chaminda glances over at Ponytail and Mustache. They stare blankly back at him. "No," *he says.*

The Australian looks around the boat—at Asanka, at Chaminda, at Mustache and Ponytail, at the other men and boys scattered across the deck. He turns on his heel and walks into the large room in the center of the boat, talks quietly to a few of the other Australians. He unclips a small machine from his belt, raises it to his mouth, presses a button and speaks into it. He pauses. Puts it to his ear. Listens. A voice crackles back to him.

Chaminda gets up and follows the man, then waits until he has clipped the transmitter back to his belt. "You are the Australians. We are going to Australia, in Australian water," *Chaminda says. Asanka's surprised at how firmly his gentle friend has pressed the uniformed man.*

The Australian looks at Chaminda, at Asanka, now standing a few meters behind his friend. He takes in a deep breath, turns his eyes away and scans the water. "Yes," he says. "Yes."

The deck is moving beneath Asanka, rippling like the sea. The tall Australian man is a stilt fisherman, crouched two meters above the water. He is staring down at Chaminda, at Asanka, at the whole boatload of them. They are tiny fishes, flitting about his stilts, unaware what crouches above them, and he is quietly suspended, waiting.

———

Loretta sits behind the wheel of her stationary car. Asanka had walked away so strangely, so forlornly. And she'd left him in there. Wasn't even in a position to help anymore. She doesn't know what will become of him if he has to stay there much longer, or even if he's sent back. She should get out of the car, turn back around, talk to the kid some more.

Tears stream down her face as she watches the cameras flashing and microphones jostling at the other end of the parking lot, where the razor-wire fence adjoins the visiting area. The Mazda windows are closed, but she can still get the gist of the press conference spin. Hopelessness burrows into her chest again, its fingernails digging into her lungs, slowly squeezing the air out.

Fuck Sam, fuck having a baby, fuck her new job, and fuck this stupid fucking car. Loretta doesn't even know who her husband is anymore. She's even more uncertain of why she's sitting here, crying about her *husband*, in this of all places.

Loretta takes a deep breath and turns the key in the ignition. As she pulls out of the Villawood parking lot, she glimpses a commotion unfolding in the rearview mirror. Cameramen scramble across the gravel, abandoning the startled speaker. They are shouting, sprinting, pointing at a figure moving slowly and steadily toward the fence, across the asphalt of the visitors yard.

Aviation

MIRABEL PLUMPS up the couch cushions, quickly turns over the one with the tiny stain on it, and adjusts it back into place. She straightens up and runs the cotton lounge curtains through her tired fingertips. Mirabel can recall, so clearly still, measuring the windows. It was almost four years ago now. She can remember Michael and her, in the haberdashery store down near Union Square; Michael's eyes glazing over as her eager hands traveled over ream after ream of potential curtain material. Mike had tried his best to look interested, polite as he always was.

"Michael!"

"Sorry!" He'd jumped, startled. "The material all looks the same to me, Bel."

"No. This one's thicker—look here, feel the two of them."

"Who cares how thick they are?"

"It's for the curtains, Mike! The thickness *matters*!"

Michael's face had flowered into sunshine at her obsessiveness. That crooked smile of his had broken. His sea-green eyes had flashed in that amused way they did. Then there was that grin that warmed everything it touched.

"Nesting! That's what it is," he'd teased, reaching around Mirabel's sides till both his hands reached her stomach, chin resting on her shoulder, blond stubble prickling her cheek. It had been just a small bump, but already holding far more hope than any of the other times. They were past thirteen weeks and Mirabel had felt, with the certainty of stone, that this pregnancy would be the one that finally worked out. The women in her family never had any trouble bearing children. The eldest of five, Mirabel can still remember running her hands over her mom's swollen belly when her youngest siblings were inside—the way her mother's almost-translucent pearl-white skin stretched drum-tight over each fast-growing life.

Mirabel steps away from the curtains now, the memory of her husband aching in the muscles just below her abdomen. Two weeks after she and Michael had bought the curtain material, she'd found herself curled up in their bed, bleeding, her entire body contracting with grief. Memory is everywhere in this house. Trauma. And yet, Mirabel still can't bring herself to sell up and leave. *Michael* is here, even though he's gone. Mirabel can feel his presence. In a strange and slightly eerie way, this will always be his home.

She walks toward the glass coffee table and starts tidying up the small pile of magazines and books spread across it. They haven't given her much notice, Child Protection. An hour ago, the woman—Jillian, her name is—phoned. But Mirabel guesses that's part and parcel of the job—the late notice—and the house is never really that untidy anyway. Not now, with just her and the dog rattling around in it.

Mirabel reaches down and picks a few stray strands of grass up off the cedar-colored rug. She hasn't even time to vacuum. She doesn't suppose it much matters, but she wants to make a good first impression. It feels momentous, this: a child, finally in the house.

She stares out the sliding glass doors of the living room. Big Ted has his eyes closed. His goofy black Labrador-cross chin is resting on his oversized paws as he suns himself on the warm wooden planks of the back patio, tail flicking. Mirabel watches him for a bit. Sometimes the dog still wanders around the house, bumbling in and out of each room like he's looking for someone. It's been three years since Michael died, but Big Ted still remembers. Of course he does. Remembers Michael, playing fetch with him in the park across the road; Michael, with the wind rustling through his sandy-colored hair as dog and man tumble over each other, wrestling.

Mirabel moves slowly into the kitchen; lifts the kettle from the countertop; shuffles slowly to the sink. She lifts the cold water tap. Sunlight from the kitchen window bathes her face. Warm. Certain. It was golden outside like this the afternoon everything changed. *Golden*, on what would become Michael's last breathing day. A brilliant yellow light had bathed the whole of Oakland.

"Shit." Mirabel shakes her head, cussing to herself. She wasn't going to think about this today, but she can't seem to stop her mind wandering there. To *him*. She'd been standing at the kitchen sink. Just like this. *At the kitchen sink*, with her long auburn hair twisted up in a silver butterfly clip. She remembers everything: every minute, inconsequential detail. Several disobedient heat-limp strands of hair had clung to the back of her neck, the wet featherweight of them falling just below her ear. Mirabel sets the full kettle down on the stove; decides against another coffee; walks back into the living room and draws her long legs up underneath her on the couch.

It's almost eleven. They'll soon be here.

Through the half-open window she can smell the potted lavender on the back balcony. Sweet. Impossibly fragrant. It was nearly fall, the day Michael was killed, but it had still smelled like summer—like today. The air was thick with newly cut grass and neighbors barbecuing, and the freshly laid asphalt from two streets down the block. And the lavender. The lavender.

The house had been almost completely packed up in large brown boxes: ready for their move, ready for her to join her husband in New York. Mirabel had marveled at the emptiness of the place. The crisp, clean, soaped-down walls and ample floor space visible with most of their furniture already shipped had suddenly made her fall in love with the house all over again. It had brought back the potential she and Michael had seen when they first moved in: before they realized filling the place up with little ones might not be as easy as they'd planned. Before he took the new job, and before she'd decided to give up her teaching position, move across the country with him, and try the baby thing just one more time.

That day—Michael's last—just as Mirabel had been musing on the emptiness of the place, there'd been that knock at the door. *Rappata, rappata, rappata.* A frantic urgency.

—————

Antonio pulls at his shirt collar; runs his fingers nervously through his dark curls. He double-checks the silver house number bolted to the front door; knocks loudly. It's the third door he's knocked on for little Sunni this morning. Antonio looks briefly up to the white cumulus cloud hovering in the endlessly blue sky. *Please. Let this home be the one.* Antonio's eyes fall on the red and white stripes of the flag rising from a pole attached to the roof; the cluster of white stars staring out of the midnight-blue rectangle.

"Here's your new home for the next while; fingers crossed, little man, eh?" Antonio rests a hand gently on the top of Sunni's baseball cap. There's something uneasy about this place. Antonio's come to be able to read the signs in just two years on the job. Something feels slightly off.

Antonio looks down at the child standing next to him on the doorstep. Sunni's arms are hanging straight and still by his sides, as though he's trying to squeeze himself smaller. The straps of his purple backpack are digging into his chubby shoulders. Sunni looks up, searching Antonio's face. Antonio flashes the kid the most hopeful smile he can. He wants to reach down and give the little man a hug, to say: *It's not you, kid, it's them.* But there are footsteps now, moving toward them from inside the house. Antonio takes a deep breath.

This is the kind of moment he talked about last month,

when his daddy and mama came visiting, when his mama had started on at him about getting a *proper* job. Antonio's parents had climbed the narrow set of stairs to his third-floor apartment, and he'd heard his mama complaining before he'd even opened the door. She'd shaken her head, click-clicked that sharp tongue of hers as she wandered disapprovingly around his two-room home.

"Lord have mercy on my sweet, sweet soul. You a half-black, half–Puerto Rican man, graduated top of your class from UCLA, and this is how you're gonna spend that education? Ayah! Running after those troubled kids and living in the most lowdown place you can find, 'cause you gettin' paid no more than pennies for it?"

Antonio's daddy—six and a half silent feet of brown construction-site muscle—had quietly closed the apartment door and wrapped himself around Antonio's tall, slim frame. Antonio's daddy had shrugged his shoulders and grinned at him softly like: *That mama of yours is gonna calm down eventually. Don't worry, I got you, son.*

Standing on the doorstep next to Sunni, Antonio wishes with all his might for that kind of bear-hug love to open the front door. Antonio reaches down, grabs Sunni's warm, trembling hand. His mama's voice circles around the inside of his skull, the way it always does at pressure-cooker times like these. *Ayah! Antonio! This job of yours! Who can really love a child that's not their own? These children, they are lost already. It is hopeless, Antonio. Hopeless!*

———

Sunni fixes his eyes on the wooden front door, straining to bore holes into it with his eyes. If he were Superman, he'd be able to see who was on the other side already. If he were Superman, his X-ray vision would tell him what he needs to know.

The last two ladies at the last two houses, they both had earrings on. *Fancy* earrings. Gold. In Sunni's experience, tiny, fancy gold earrings on white ladies in big houses is never a comfortable thing. Sunni doesn't know if he can take another hushed doorstep conversation, another turning-away. *Nobody* wants him. Sunni grinds the toe of his running shoe into the paved doorstep. Well, he doesn't want any of *them* either. He wants his maa. Just to go home to his maa. What was she thinking, anyway—not arriving to pick him up after school like that. The police officers who finally came to collect him said his maa was in *custody.* Sunni doesn't know where that is. *Custody. Open the door.* Sunni bites at his bottom lip, stares up at the neat silver house numbers screwed to the front door, his hand growing sweaty in Antonio's. *Please open the door. Open the door and be nice.*

Something happened in the Walmart with his maa before she had to go to that *custody* place. Sunni heard the cops at the police station whispering. His maa had been yelling at people in the store, they said. It was as if the cops had decided he couldn't hear them, even though he was standing right there in the room. Sunni didn't like the way they'd talked about her— clustered around the station's front counter in their black-and-gold uniforms. They'd talked about his maa like she was really crazy. Said she'd been throwing things and yelling about the airplanes. She'd been yelling about terrorism, about America.

Sunni had heard her do that before, when folks stared at them on the street.

"It's not our fault. Stop staring. What the hell are you all looking at? I'm American. We're American. We're not even Muslim. We're Sikh. *Stop staring!*" The veins in her neck would stick out.

This time, the cops said, his maa had smashed things; said really bad words. Sunni tries to imagine his maa doing that: using bad words and smashing things, her long black plait swaying to and fro as she tumbles cans of baked beans and glass bottles of ketchup into the store aisles. The cops said she's done it. *Property damage*, they'd whispered. So it *must* be true. She *must* have.

"Your mom, she's done some bad things. We're going to have to find a place for you to stay for a while. I'll make a few calls. A lovely lady from the department will come down to help you. Do you want a soda or something? Some crackers?" The cop had sounded like he felt sorry for him. Sunni hadn't liked that—had wanted to kick him in the shins and run off. In the end, it hadn't been a lady that came down from the department. It had been Antonio.

"Just like Antonio Banderas, but infinitely more handsome. You can call me Ant if you like, little man," the tall brown man had joked to Sunni, shaking his hand vigorously and pressing a chewy mint into his palm. Sunni had smiled and nodded, even though he didn't know what *infinitely* meant, or who *Antonio Banderas* was.

Mirabel readjusts the silver heart necklace on top of her cotton shirt as she walks slowly down the hallway toward her front door. The hardwood floors beneath her feet have turned to royal-blue carpet. Plane seats are laid out in straight rows on either side of her. Mirabel is walking, slowly, toward the cockpit. She puts a hand on the wall to keep herself steady. The hallway is spinning. She's right inside the nose of the beast now, can see over the pilot's shoulder. There are men yelling things in a language she can't understand. The plane is suspended in time, hovering wasplike. The knocking at the front door sounds far away.

Mirabel is close enough to the first tower of the World Trade Center to see through the glass, across one entire floor. She can see thin, French-manicured secretarial fingers flying across a laptop keyboard; a half-finished cup of black tea; a laser printer spitting out reams and reams of paper. *It's not real. It's not real.* Mirabel gasps for air. A lean, scruffy-haired man is scribbling notes on a whiteboard, his back to her, in one of the glass-walled meeting rooms. He turns midsentence, her Michael, and stares back at her through the tower window, through the plane window, disbelief scribbled across his face.

Mirabel fights against the panic attack—blinks the vision back. Not today. Today is a new chapter. The beginning of something. Through the frosted glass, Mirabel can see a tall silhouette next to a shorter one. Her stomach flips. She knows it's impossible, but she feels like this child will be hers and Michael's, somehow. A child of circumstance. Perhaps even with his same tousled, sandy-colored hair, or eyes the exact same cloudy green as San Francisco Bay.

———

The door swings open.

"Mrs. Mirabel Adams?" Antonio clears his throat, uses the firm, friendly-yet-businesslike tone he's learned to cultivate.

"Yes."

Antonio smiles away his surprise. The young white woman is dressed in cream slacks and a white cotton blouse. Her long hair is twisted back into a loose plait. She blinks her clear, light-gray eyes as if surprised to find anyone on the doorstep. Usually, the emergency caregivers are older: grandmotherly empty-nester types. Mrs. Adams's cheeks are flushed pink, as though she's been running or just come from the shower. Antonio's heart closes a little. If not a carer like his dad, he'd been hoping she'd be someone like his mama: all loud opinion and sharp tongue, but fierce love. *Fierce* love. Antonio can hear his mama's voice in his ear. *Ayah. Antonio! This woman! She is wearing cream-color pants. So neat and proper and impractical for life. This fancy white lady. Tell me, how will she love this messy little fat brown boy? How will she love him? Antonio! Use the brains God gave you, child. Ayah!*

"Hi, I'm Antonio." He stifles his doubt. "We spoke earlier on the phone. And this"—he puts a gentle hand on Sunni's back, nudging him forward—"is Sunni."

The woman looks down suddenly, taking in the top of Sunni's baseball-capped, bowed-down-toward-the-doormat head.

"Oh, yes. Of course. I'm been waiting for you. Hello, *Sunni!* I'm so glad you've arrived."

As the woman ushers them into the impeccably tidy living room, Antonio's eyes discreetly scan the place. *Something's not right.* There are photographs on the wall of her and a man. The husband, maybe. The department file said he passed away a while back. Three or four years, maybe.

"Your husband?" Antonio asks, smiling casually toward the framed vacation snapshots.

"Yes."

She seems rattled, a bit defensive even.

"I suppose I'll get around to taking those down, one of these days. Would you like coffee, or tea?" She gestures for him and Sunni to sit on the long leather couch.

"Thanks, that would be great. Tea, please. Black, one sugar." Antonio's eyes move to the carved wooden cross hanging above the mantelpiece. On the ledge below is a photograph of the husband overlaid on an American flag, with the words *September 11, 2001. Never forgotten. God Bless America.*

Sweet Jesus. The deceased husband. That's how he died. Antonio's eyes widen.

Antonio can feel Sunni's leg trembling against his as the boy moves closer to him on the couch, can hear the kid's shallow breathing right next to his ear. He wonders if Sunni's noticed the memorial plaque as well.

———

Mirabel leaves the Child Protection worker sitting on the couch and moves into the kitchen. She fixes two cups of tea, and an orange juice. He's eight, they said, the boy. He's chubby, but he still looks small for his age. Perhaps it's just that he's leaning up against the tall man like that. Almost as though he's afraid of her. Mirabel hasn't even really looked at his face. She'll go back out there and talk to him properly. She hadn't wanted to be too pushy in those first few minutes, but in the process of trying to give him space, she realizes now that she's kind of ignored him. Mirabel puts the drinks on a wooden serving tray with a plate of Oreos and walks carefully back to the living room. She sets the tray down on the table.

"Sunni." She looks directly at him now. His eyes are still staring at the floor. "I'm so glad to have you here. I have a room all ready for you. We can go and have a look at it now, if you like."

The boy slowly raises his dark-brown eyes to meet hers, and she sees him. The chubby brown arms, furrowed black eyebrows. The oversized cap still pulled down tightly over his ears. And something . . . she can see something—*what is it?*—beneath the cap. Something covering his head. Mirabel tears her eyes away from the kid and looks over at the man from the department.

The man clears his throat and stares steadily back at her. "Sunni, you should probably take off your hat indoors, little man," he says.

The kid's bottom lip is quivering. He raises his hand to the front rim of the faded blue Knicks cap, slowly removes it from his head, and rests it in his lap. His face is cherubic: cheeks rounder than Mirabel's ever seen on a child his age. Wound tightly over his head is a piece of black, stretchy material. The material conceals the boy's hair and twists around at the top to form a kind of covered-up bun.

Mirabel takes a sharp breath in, fear rising in her throat.

––––––––

Sunni stares at the lady. She's not smiling anymore. She's screwing up her face in that way people do. Screwing up her face in that way he thinks might have made his maa go crazy in the Walmart, in that way that made it so that now his maa has to stay in *custody*, and he has to stay *here*. Sunni wrenches his eyes away from the lady and looks down at the tray of Oreos. He reaches a hand out: grabs two, three, four of them. He starts cramming the cookies into his mouth as fast as he can, grinding the crunchy sugar crispness of them down with his teeth.

There's a small crack in the glass coffee table where the plate of cookies is sitting. The crack in the glass makes Sunni think about when all of this started: about when his maa first started to go crazy, when the trouble first came.

They were okay. They were okay, his maa and him. Sunni's *pita* took off when Sunni was very little—before he was one year old, even. Sunni can't remember what his dad even looks like. Whenever he asks, his maa says she's burned all the photos. The kids at temple always teased Sunni; whispered that his *pita* had run off with an American woman; a *white* woman. But Sunni had paid them no mind—he and his maa got by okay.

Old Bill and Susie, who live in the apartment next door to Sunni and his maa, had looked after him when his maa was nursing a night shift. He would play on their living-room floor and sleep in their spare room. Sunni could feel that Bill and Susie loved him, in the sure, quiet way they'd let him become part of their everyday lives. His maa said the old couple had no kids themselves, so no grandkids either; that they were *very lonely*. Sunni hadn't minded hanging out at their place. Old Bill and Susie had looked at him like he was special, like he *belonged* to them. Not like this rich white lady is looking at him now.

But everything changed. Everything changed on that one day when Sunni was about five, when the bad men flew planes into those towers in New York. Sunni's maa had let the TV run all morning, and Sunni saw the baddies crash the planes over and over and over again: watched the buildings smoke and crumble. It was like a video game where you had to swerve the plane away at the last minute, and the kid playing the game got distracted and went to the park to play, but the game kept looping and looping.

That same afternoon, while Sunni was playing cars in his bedroom, there'd been a shattering sound. On the street outside their apartment, a car had quickly screeched away. Sunni had paused for a moment, petrified, then run into the living room to see his mother cleaning up broken window glass and the shards of a stray roof tile that had been hurled into their home.

"They think we're Muslim," his maa had said, wrapping the jagged pieces of glass with newspaper. "It will pass."

Sunni hadn't understood. He hadn't understood, and his maa had been wrong—it hadn't passed at all. Sunni used to climb over from their apartment's balcony to the balcony of

Bill and Susie's place. It was a cheeky thing he did: surprising them with a visit, sneaking in through the sliding balcony door to leave a drawing he'd done of them, or some cookies he and his maa had baked. After the bad men in planes, Bill and Susie had stopped looking after him, stopped looking at him with kindness in their old-person eyes. All of a sudden, they said they were getting too old to help out looking after him anymore. They'd said it through the crack in their door, peering above the silver security chain.

The next week, old Bill and Susie had put plants up against the concrete divide where their balconies joined Sunni's place. Sunni pointed the beautiful pink flowers out to his mother.

"You can't climb over and visit anymore," she'd said, her voice shaking. "They're poisonous flowers. That's oleander."

The look on his maa's face then had been the same terrified look as the one on this lady's face as she crouches by the coffee table, staring at him. Sunni quickly swallows the mouthful of cookie.

———

Antonio watches the lady closely. "Are you all right, Mrs. Adams?"

"Mirabel," she says weakly. "Call me Mirabel . . ."

Her face is drained of color. Antonio bites back his disappointment. *Sunni's watching. For fuck's sake, the kid's right in front of her.* Antonio reaches over and hands Sunni the glass of orange juice, helps the woman up, and escorts her into the kitchen. He pulls out a wooden stool for her, folds up a clean dish towel, and wets it at the sink.

"I'm sorry. I wasn't expecting—" She dabs at her face with the wet cloth. "I probably upset him. He looks scared. I just wasn't expecting . . ."

"He *is* scared, Mrs. Adams." Antonio scratches at the back of his newly razored Afro, looks out the kitchen window at the clumsy black dog chasing its tale in a patch of sunlight. "We have you down for emergency care. For *any* child. Did Jillian at the office not explain?"

"Yes. *Any* child. I did say that. But I never considered . . . Jillian said his name was Sunni."

"It is." Antonio tries his best to sound understanding. "His name is Sundeep—Sunni for short. He's a good kid. He really is. You're lucky. I don't think he'll be any trouble at all. It's *emergency care*, Mrs. Adams. Just for the weekend. Then we'll find somewhere a bit more permanent."

———

What would Michael think? Mirabel takes a deep breath, swallows past the lump that's formed in her throat. "Is he— I mean . . . What . . . ?"

They're standing in the haberdashery store down near Union Square. Michael is reaching around Mirabel's sides, both of his hands on her swelling stomach. His chin is resting on her shoulder, his blond stubble prickling her cheek.

The man from the department is glaring at her, judgment in his eyes. Mirabel can see he's doing his best to be calm, but she can sense the annoyance in his voice.

"His family's Sikh. If that matters to you."

The memory of her husband aches in the muscles just

below her abdomen. *Sikh*. Mirabel doesn't even know what that means. She glances out the window. Big Ted is running around now, chasing his tail, tornado-ing around the back lawn.

Michael, with the wind rustling through his sandy-colored hair as man and dog tumble over each other, wrestling.

It's golden outside. A brilliant yellow light bathes the whole of Oakland. The breeze drifting in through the open windows is all cut grass and neighbors barbecuing, and freshly laid asphalt.

This child. This tubby little brown boy. This knock at the door. *Rappata, rappata, rappata.* A frantic urgency. Mirabel looks back through the kitchen doorway to where the little boy is sitting, shoulders curved over, backpack still on.

"Where will he go?" she asks softly. "If I can't take him?"

The man from Child Protection sighs. "Honestly? I don't know. He's a good kid, Mrs. Adams. He's just a little kid."

Mirabel closes her eyes. Plane seats are laid out in straight rows on either side of her. She is walking, slowly toward the cockpit. She puts a hand on the wall to keep herself steady. The hallway is spinning. She's right inside the nose of the beast now, can see over the pilot's shoulder. There are men yelling things in a language she can't understand. The plane is suspended in time, hovering wasplike. The man from Child Protection is talking, but he sounds very far away.

The Sukiyaki Book Club

AVERY IS hanging upside down on the monkey bars. Her blue-and-white-checked uniform is bunched around her waist. Her black bloomers are tight around her chubby thighs. The elastic waistband digs into her stomach. Every afternoon when she takes the sports undies off after school, they leave a stinging pink ring around her middle that looks as if somebody has tried to saw her in two with a blunt knife.

Avery's told her dad that she needs some more bloomers, but when they went to the shopping center last month and finally found Target, her father froze outside the entrance, peered in at all the families on their Saturday afternoon shopping trips and made a small, strangled sound at the back of his throat.

"Here's thirty dollars, love. I'll sit out here on the bench. You ask one of the ladies to help you out, eh? You're a big girl now. You'll be okay in there by yourself. I'll be right here waiting."

But Avery isn't a big girl. She's only seven. She can tie her own shoelaces, climb to the very top of the acorn tree in her backyard and almost ride her bike without the training wheels, but she is definitely too little to buy sports knickers on her own from a crowded department store.

She had taken the money and scrunched it down into her pocket, walked into the store and hid just around the corner behind a tall stack of electric fans. After several minutes she'd come out again, told her dad they'd run out of sports knickers. He'd forgotten to ask for the money back, so every lunchtime for three weeks she'd bought a doughnut with yellow icing and blue sprinkles from the school cafeteria. Her dad wouldn't have minded even if he knew, so it wasn't *really* stealing.

Avery's head feels heavy and swollen. The sweaty backs of her knees are sore where they're hooked around the shiny yellow rung of the monkey bars. The shredded bark on the floor of the infant school playground is playing tricks on her eyes, forming and re-forming into different shapes: a fire-breathing dragon, a princess in a pointy hat, the rabbit from *Alice in Wonderland*, a garden spade. It's like cloud-watching, only wrong way up. And the bark isn't moving; it's her that's swaying back and forth.

Avery's arms feel loose in their sockets. They pull downward, as if they want to detach at the shoulder and tumble to the ground. There's a spot on her back, right between her shoulder blades, that is itching like buggery. That's what her dad says whenever anything's going on with his body he's not so keen on. *Itches like buggery. Tired as all buggery. Hungry as buggery. Drunk as buggery.* Avery wriggles, trying to shake the itch away. The backs of her knees are really stinging now, burning. Her head feels dizzy. Avery does not know how to get down from the monkey bars. She is stuck as buggery.

———

Down the short corridor from my bedroom the Bananas in Pyjamas are talking to each other with their trademark speech affectation—repeating themselves unnecessarily, slapping each other's names onto the end of every sentence.

"Have you seen my shoes, B1?"

"No. I haven't seen your shoes. Maybe we should look for them together, B2?"

"Great idea. Let's look for my lost shoes together, B1."

"Where do you think we should start looking for your lost shoes, B2?"

It's enough to drive even a toddler crazy, but there's no other sound coming from the tiny lounge room—both kids are miraculously quiet. I move over toward my bed, climb onto the thin patchwork quilt cover, peer out the window and down toward the station. From four stories up, we can see right through to the Melbourne skyline. Every night before bed the kids climb up and search for the tallest lights, the Eureka Tower.

"When we move into the next house," Maryam said last week, "can we take the window with us?" At three years old, she has already known four homes. It is always the same story: landlords refusing to fix hot water heaters, home invasions even pest controllers cannot fix, extortionate rent increases.

Down below, Irving Street is crawling with evening commuters. They chat on mobiles and clutch folded newspapers under their arms as they hurry out the station gates, then dash across the road to Footscray Fruit Market to gather extra grocery items for dinner. I shift to the left a little, peer past the rusty corrugated-iron roof of the Dancing Dog Café.

The queue in front of the Peter's Doughnuts van, just outside the station exit, is about ten people deep. Not bad for piping hot sweets on a ninety-five-degree evening. The old Greek man and his wife will be trying to hurry themselves and failing miserably, but nobody in the queue will bat an eyelid. Rosetta will be wearing the same starched white nurse's uniform she wears every workday, her wiry salt-and-pepper hair pulled tightly back into a netted bun. She will be slowly mixing the batter for the doughnut machine, flicking the switch at various intervals to drop glugs of it into the honey-colored cooking oil. The conveyor belt will be straining, sliding round balls of just-cooked doughnut into the shallow dish filled with fine white sugar.

Her old man will be taking change, mostly coins, with weathered olive hands, asking about jam and sugar, rescuing doughnuts from the conveyor belt before they hit the sugar pile. He will be nodding through the tiny window of the rusty white food van, ramming doughnuts onto the metal jam syringe and growing them plump with bright red strawberry syrup, sliding them into white paper bags.

Bananas in Pyjamas is finishing now. The familiar theme song's blaring from the lounge room. The apartment is so small that even with the television turned down low, the program echoes in every other room. The kids are still eerily quiet. It is entirely possible they've managed to simultaneously dispose of each other.

Across the road from the station entrance, the evening busker is setting up: an elderly Vietnamese man who wears a long khaki jacket and pale denim jeans, no matter the weather. He stands on the footpath, between the Vietnamese bakery and the Ethiopian coffeehouse, next to a wire rack of prepackaged coconut buns. The old man's violin is clutched lovingly beneath his chin. His bow hovers an inch above the strings. He closes his eyes a moment. He bows then retracts into straight-backed poise, as if taking a breath with all his being.

I slide the window open a crack, listen for the mournful wail. The glass is warm beneath my fingertips, still holds the day's heat. The music is different this time—not the usual slow, regal, pentatonic pull, not those several yet somehow cohesive harmonies. I listen, squeeze my eyes shut, search for the tune. It is not a Vietnamese song at all this evening. It is Japanese. "Ue o Muite Arukou": "I Shall Walk Looking Up." A song about sadness lurking in the shadows, sadness lurking behind the stars and moon. A song about ignoring the tears welling in your eyes, raising your head high and walking on.

Markie's prep class performed the song for their school assembly item last year. The teacher taught them to sing it jovially, with an upbeat tempo, swaying with joy. "Sukiyaki," his teacher had called it, the easier name the song was given when it reached Western shores. Even after we did the research on the history of the song and Markie presented it for Tuesday Show and Tell, the

FOREIGN SOIL

teacher still insisted on having the kids smile through it, as if they were singing "Happy Birthday": a song about a man overwhelmed with despair.

———

Avery does not know how to get down from the monkey bars. She is hanging upside down, stuck like buggery. She tries to take her mind off her headache by scanning the empty playground. She draws a treasure map in her head, marking herself as the X, dotting a red line directly to where she hangs so somebody will come out of the school and find her.

On the map she is making in her head, Avery includes the two hopscotch grids that are stencil-painted onto the dark gray asphalt of the infants area, and the white plastic skipping rope with bright yellow handles that hangs from a gum tree near the kindergarten seats. She also adds the five lunchboxes that have been left on the wooden benches, colluding in a brightly colored cluster, as if having a tea party.

Avery concentrates hard, sends the mind map out toward the school office. She wouldn't even mind if it was the principal who came. Ms. Lothian is a tall, unsmiling lady with cold gray eyes who reminds Avery of the nasty headmistress in *Matilda*.

Avery's mum gave her a copy of *Matilda* the afternoon of the accident. The new book had been lying on the backseat when Avery got in the car after school. It was in her hands when they screeched through the roundabout. She had already opened the front cover.

When Avery woke up in the hospital after the crash, the

240

Roald Dahl book was lying on her bedside table. Avery wishes she was Matilda now, and she could close her eyes and use her brainiac magic to whirl the playground bark up into a small mountain underneath her. Then she would gently touch her fingertips to the mountain and ease herself off the bars. She would climb down the bark mountain and go and get a drink from the bubblers. Avery is beginning to feel thirsty. She runs her tongue over her bottom lip. Her right thigh is turning numb.

———————

I shuffle back on the bed a little, away from the window. The stifling evening has started to cool, but there are several rush-hour services to pass by before I can open the apartment up properly. On still nights like these, the wind-rush of passing trains carries all the way up to the bedroom windows. The roaring and heaving puts both kids on edge.

The ABC Kids channel is still blaring from the lounge room, but aside from the mellow version of "On the Night Watch" Jimmy Giggle is crooning with his owl puppet friend, the apartment's oddly quiet: a rare gap in the roaring and shaking, a breath in the growling thunderstorm that is Footscray Station. Crisscrossed steel train lines glint in the early evening light, hum and keen, bracing themselves for another arrival.

Jimmy Giggle is mourning the end of a magical day, welcoming the arrival of the moon in a soothing melody designed to entice sleep.

A high-pressure pop sounds, like a plug being pulled from a full sink: Maryam removing her thumb from her mouth.

She will have hurled aside her filthy crocheted comfort blanket and leaped to her feet.

"*And bright da day to a bwand true way . . .*" She sings along spiritedly in wavering falsetto to the last few lines of the lullaby.

Jimmy Giggle will be freshly dressed for bed in his bright yellow owl pajamas, swaying from side to side with extended jazz fingers, smiling that odd wide grin of his. Maryam's big brown eyes will be following him in adoration.

The rumbling outside grows closer, louder, closer still, until the bedroom floor shakes. The walls vibrate for several seconds. The headlights of the train, already glaring though darkness has not yet fallen, beam orange light into the bedroom: two glowing circles that dance faintly across the wall as the train swerves past. The Watergardens to City rambles away toward South Kensington Station in a rush of white noise, the driver sounding the horn three times as he slides the beast out of Footscray Station.

This place was supposed to be temporary. A month, maybe three, I told the owner when I found the apartment online through Gumtree. Single mother. Two small children. Freelance income. After a month of rejections, I'd had to go off the real estate grid. Again. It's been almost a year now. Long enough to be home. Between the three of us, we can recognize almost every evening train by speed, sound, and character. Each driver has their mark. The captain of the 5:36 Watergardens to City is always flamboyant like this in announcing his departure.

"I hate that driver. Why does he always have to honk like

that?" Markie's standing at the bedroom door, knotted mass of curly black Afro curl haloing his head, one leg of his navy school tracksuit pants hiked up around his knee, the other hanging full length.

"You don't *hate* that driver. You don't even know him. He might annoy you, but that's different from *hate*."

"I hate that driver. And I hate being bored. And bored is what I am right now."

"I thought you were reading your book."

A paperback copy of *Captain Underpants* is hanging from his right hand, his thumb wedged in to keep his place. Markie shrugs. "The *book's* boring me. I want to watch television."

"Isn't the television already on?"

"It's *Giggle and Hoot*," he says pointedly.

"So?"

"I'm too old for *Giggle and Hoot*."

"*Giggle and Hoot* is universal entertainment. Nobody's too old for *Giggle and Hoot*!"

He rolls his eyes, walks into the room, dives onto the bed next to me. "Anyway, you said Jimmy Giggle laughs like he's high as a kite."

"What? I did not. When did I say that?"

"I heard you say it the other day, to Alice's mum. And high as a kite," he looks over at me sternly, "means on *drugs*."

"What do you know about drugs anyway?"

"Nothing. Drugs are bad. Miss Walton said so. I don't want to talk about drugs. I just want to watch television. Can I—"

The 5:41 Werribee to Flinders screams in, drowning the end of Markie's sentence. He has become patient with the punctuation of howling freight trains, inured to the crude and untimely interruptions of the whooshing cross-country V/Line services. When he hears a train approaching he closes his eyes for several seconds to block out the flash. It's become an impulse, really: a body brace, a tic. Markie talks a little too enthusiastically, as if constantly straining above engine noise. In his December school report the teacher recommended a hearing test. There is nothing wrong with his hearing that could not be fixed by a change of address.

Maryam has been having nightmares. At five o'clock every morning, a fire-breathing dragon looks into the window of the small bedroom she shares with her brother. It licks its swollen silver lips and glares at her with glowing yellow eyes. She will not believe it's just a brand-new eight-carriage Metro electric: an early-morning train lurching so far and fast toward our building that flying off the rails and slamming through the café below always seems a distinct possibility.

"I hate these trains. I want to go back to our old place. At least it was quiet there."

———

Avery can't pull herself up. She strains for a few seconds to grab the monkey-bar rung with her fingers, but she can't quite reach it and lets her arms hang helplessly again.

Metal garbage cans are peppered around the playground. There's a can only a few meters from where Avery hangs, just outside the bark-covered play area. A wasp buzzes around the small hole in the lid. From where she's hanging, Avery can smell the half-eaten sandwiches sweating in the summer heat.

The garbage can smells like her fridge at home when her dad hasn't emptied it for a while.

Avery does not want to fall. She saw her dad split his head open once. There was a big crack that sounded like a hard cricket ball being smashed against a wooden bat, then blood so thick and red it didn't look real, matted all through the front of his sandy-colored hair. It was after her mum's funeral and everybody had come to their house to drink lots of wine and eat the delicious soft chicken-and-avocado sandwiches her auntie Tina had made. It was like a party, only everybody was sad. Avery's dad had drunk too much wine and started talking funny. He'd come over and sat next to her on the couch in their lounge room.

"It's just you and me now, kid," he'd said, in a slow voice like he was about to fall asleep. "We'll be okay. We'll be fine. No worries, kid." Then he'd got up from the chair and swayed into the kitchen. As he reached for the fridge handle he'd slipped on the tiles somehow. There's still a dent in the fridge door, where his skull hit.

Avery stares down at the bark. If she falls, she might not crack her head, but she will definitely hurt herself. A tear rolls from the corner of her eye, down her forehead, into her hair.

———

Avery is stuck upside down, and for the life of me I cannot figure out what to do with her next.

There could be a man, standing just outside the wire fence of the schoolyard. Both hands might be wedged deep inside his pockets as he stares at the little girl hanging upside down in the empty playground with her dress bunched around her waist. Perhaps he is not supposed to come within eight hundred meters of a childcare center or a school.

The laptop screen flickers. Threads of static crackle across it. If the computer goes, I'm screwed. The bills have been reshuffled and extended. I click to save, and Microsoft asks me to name the document. I pause. This story is not going to be sent out, in any case. Most likely never even completed. Certainly not published and read. Because Avery is hanging upside down, and it will all end in tragedy. The only way down is for a scared little girl to hurt herself. I do not know how to rescue Avery gently.

Slotted into the emerald-green milk crate that I use for a bedside table are printouts of seven very nice, very separate rejection e-mails. They are from different publishing houses, but could actually have been written by the same person. They are curled into paper scrolls, slotted into the diamond-shaped holes of the crate, like echidna spines, literary armor. *We are enamored of your writing. Your prose is startlingly poetic. We have not seen work like this for quite some time. Please could you send some more of your writing, maybe on a different theme. Or is there anything else you're currently working on?*

Your writing is genuinely astonishing, but I'd like to read something you've written that deals with more everyday themes. Work that has an uplifting quality. Ordinary moments. Think book club material. I'd be happy to have a conversation about this if you're interested. I may be able to point you in the direction of the kind of stories I mean. Unfortunately, we feel Australian readers are just not ready for characters like these.

The title character in "Harlem Jones." What can I say? He's intriguing—so raw. But what if he didn't hurl the Molotov in the closing paragraphs? Imagine if that day of the Tottenham riots was ultimately a wake-up call that got an angry black kid back on the straight and narrow? We would be very interested in working with you to bring some light to this collection with a view to discussing its potential publication. These are very minor edits we are talking about. We hope you would be open to this.

Before the song became "Sukiyaki," it was "Ue o Muite Arukou": "I Shall Walk Looking Up."

I have hung Avery wrong side up, alone and afraid. I was not going to do this again. When I first started writing, hers was going to be a story about love.

"*Mum!*" Markie's standing by my desk now, pulling at my arm.

"Just a second. I just have to save this. Or it might disappear." Poor Avery is already almost invisible.

I ease myself up from the wooden kitchen chair that doubles uncomfortably as my desk chair, step into the narrow hallway and stand at the door of the lounge room. Markie follows me, stops and stares smugly at his sister. Maryam is sitting on her Kmart baby lounge, clutching her blanket, thumb jammed into her mouth. She looks over at us for a second, then back at the television screen.

"We're changing the channel," Markie declares, striding into the lounge room.

Maryam slides her thumb out of her mouth. "But I'm watching *Giggle and Hoot.*"

"Jimmy Giggle," Markie says, "is on drugs."

"Markie!"

Maryam stares at her brother, as if assessing his claim. "I don't care. I like Jimmy Giggle. I'm watching it."

Markie moves over to the coffee table, grabs the remote control.

"If you change the channel, Markie," says Maryam, "I will be *very* angry."

Markie pauses, glances at me. Lately, his sister has been taking the terrible twos to a whole new level: stiffening her body and trembling as if undergoing electric shock therapy, howling with despair at the slightest inconvenience.

"Come and help me make some Milo in the kitchen, Maryam. You can stir the Milo powder in, if you like."

"No."

"I'm changing the channel now," Markie declares again.

"You are *not* changing the channel. Jimmy Giggle is my *friend.*"

———

Avery is crying, upside down on the monkey bars. The other children have all gone back to class. They left her there at the end of recess. But not on purpose. They just forgot. The bell went and they stampeded back into their classrooms. Nobody looked back and saw. One moment Avery was sitting on top of the monkey-bar rung, easing herself slowly upside down for the first time in her life, not sure if the dizziness was from the sudden blood rush to her head or from the sheer triumph of the feat. Next, the bell had rung and all the other children had quickly disappeared. Avery hadn't thought to sing out for help.

She is used to being a little bit ignored. Sometimes at home, her dad doesn't even seem to realize she is there.

"You're the spitting image of yer mum, y'know," Mr. Matthews, who lives next door, said to her a few weeks ago. He whispered it over the fence while she was playing with her grip-ball set in the backyard and he was out watering his precious gardenias. "That's mostly why he can't stand looking at yer. Don't take it to heart, little love."

Avery wishes Mr. Matthews was here now. He might be an old man, but she saw him hack up half a tree for firewood last winter. He raised the heavy axe high above his head, swung it fiercely, like he was Superman or something. Mr. Matthews would be strong enough to get her down.

———

"Right. Nobody is watching television. You kids have had enough for one night. It's time you both had a shower anyway. Off. Now."

"But I don't like showers. I *only* like watching *Giggle and Hoot*."

"Mum said *turn it off*."

"No."

"Maryam! Jimmy's on *drugs*!"

"Oh, for Christ's sake, both of you, will you just quit it for a minute? The television is going off. See? There. *End of.* Markie, of course he's not on drugs, and if you mention drugs one more time I will confiscate your *Captain Underpants* book. Though I hear it's pretty boring anyway, so you clearly won't mind. C'mon. Shower time. Both of you."

The bathroom's small, only a few feet bigger than the actual shower cubicle, with a tiny porcelain sink, small metal towel rail, and a mirrored cabinet mounted on the wall. I shuffle in sideways, turn on the shower's hot water tap, wait till it warms up, turn on the cold.

"First one into the shower gets ice cream when they get out!" There's only four spoonfuls left at the bottom of the blue plastic tub, but it will be enough to share between them if I throw a spoonful of Milo powder on top.

The hallway outside the bathroom is a sudden blur of shirt-sleeves, discarded socks and tangled pant legs. Markie squeezes under my arm, steps into the shower with his Spider-Man underpants and one sock still on.

"Markie!"

"What?"

"You've still got clothes on."

"You didn't say we had to take them off. What flavor ice cream do I get?"

"It's not *fair*. It's not *fair*. Markie's being *bad*. Markie still has got his sock on! And he's *bigger* than me. I don't *like* showers." Maryam has thrown herself down on the gray carpet in the hallway and is flinging her chubby brown arms about and howling.

"Oh, stop it. Just get in the shower. You'll get some ice cream too."

The waterworks cease immediately. She wipes her eyes with the backs of her hands. Her green BONDS tank top is bunched around her middle. She rolls it down over her legs and steps out of it, squeezes into the shower next to her brother, squinting and flinching as the warm spray hits her face. "I don't *like* water in my face."

I hand them both a washcloth, slide the shower door shut, grab my laptop from the desk in my room and settle myself on the hallway floor, back against the wall, computer balanced on my knees.

———

Avery is crying now, properly. Those first few tears have turned into distraught sobs. Avery's little chest heaves. She tries to clamp her knees tighter around the monkey bar to stop herself from falling.

———

For a few minutes, the apartment falls silent again. The children stand under the shower, staring down at their tiny grublike terra-cotta toes, calmed by the streams of warm water running down their backs. Then Markie remembers how much he likes singing in the shower.

"Doo wah, doo wah. Doo wah, doo wah."

"It is remarkable," the junior choir teacher at Footscray City Primary School once cornered me, "how a child of his age knows rhythm."

There is no reason for Markie *not* to breathe notation. He is a child of changes, gaps and relocations, of rumbling and shaking, of constant sound and frequent movement. A child of whistles and boom gates and signals.

Rhythmic splashing echoes through the bathroom door, wet thudding in time to the off-key singing.

"Markie, how many times have I told you, darling? No dancing in the shower. It's dangerous. Especially with your sister in there with you."

"*What . . . melody . . . what . . . music . . . possessing something . . .*" "It Don't Mean a Thing (If It Ain't Got That Swing)." He's crooning Ellington, singing about the soul of the music, the uselessness of a melody without a soul.

The Footscray Primary choir mistress is in love with Duke Ellington. From the back wall of her music room, a caramel-faced portrait leans in, hair gelled back black and shiny from his baby face, pencil-thin mustache hovering above that come-hither grin. The junior choir, Markie included, are happy beneficiaries of her impeccable taste.

Markie's deep in the tune now, drawling the words in true Ellington style, warbling about giving everything he has to the rhythm.

I set the laptop aside, lever myself up on my knees, peer around the door and through the foggy shower screen.

"*Doo wappa wappa, doo wappa, doo doo wap.*" Maryam's joining in now, swaying her hips from side to side, clapping her hands together so the trapped water makes a splat noise.

Markie's tap-dancing in the water now. It's splashing through the small gap beneath the shower door and onto the floor mat. He might slip. His head could go through the shower screen. He might fall on his sister and split her lip. We don't have a bath and the owners won't be in a hurry to fix the shower if it breaks. It took them three months to see to replacing the bolt on the front door.

But they are dancing, the two of them, twisting and swaying their small brown bodies under the shower-rain, faces upturned and singing Duke Ellington, Maryam's voice completely out of tune, joyously off harmony. I raise myself to my feet, stand in the hallway just out of sight, peering in at the two children. They laugh, shake the water from their faces, drum on their tummies, go unashamedly ragtime.

———————

Avery straightens her legs. She can't hold on any longer, feels herself sliding toward the ground, braces herself for the fall. She wonders what it will feel like, the playground bark splintering in her head, her neck jarring on impact. Halfway to the ground her body flips suddenly, bending at the waist. Avery gasps, somersaults, lands somehow, both feet facing forward, arms swung out in front of her like the gymnastic girls she and her mum watched together on telly last year when the Olympics were on. Avery pauses a moment in shock. Laughs out loud, flushed cheeks almost bursting. She did it. She looks around the playground, still astonished, then runs off toward her classroom.

Acknowledgments

Thank you to my family: Claudette, Syreeta, Mike, Braden, Mali, Maya, and Ayana. Thank you to Silvano Giordano, with whom I started this journey twenty-three years ago, rewriting *Playing Beatie Bow* while listening to Prince. Thank you to Jeff Sparrow and David Ryding, who gave me rope even when the waters became rocky and who *believed*, way back before anyone else did. To the fellow students and teaching staff of the Faculty of Creative Writing at the University of Wollongong, in particular Merlinda Bobis, Alan Wearne, Anthony Macris, and John Hawke, for pouring petrol on the flame. To the Law Faculty at the University of Wollongong, for the scholarship that gave me the educational means to financially support my writing until it grew to support itself. Thank you to Alice Pung, Catherine Deveny, Tony Birch, and Randa Abdel-Fattah, for being generous and enthusiastic first readers. Thank you to the Melbourne

ACKNOWLEDGMENTS

Spoken Word community, my chosen artistic kin. To my editors, Robert Watkins and Kate Stevens, and to Anna Hayward, Fiona Hazard, Matt Richell, Justin Ractliffe, Kelly Morton, and the entire Hachette Australia family, for adopting me so wholeheartedly. Thanks also to Clara Finlay and Eloise Oxer, for their respective editing and scribing expertise on *Foreign Soil*, and Allison Colpoys for the breathtaking cover design. Thank you to my agent, Tara Wynne, at Curtis Brown Australia, who held the flashlight and the cutlass but let me lead the way. Thank you to Nicholas Walton-Healey, whose lens truly sees.

Foreign Soil was the winning manuscript of the 2013 Victorian Premier's Literary Award for an Unpublished Manuscript, and I would like to thank the Wheeler Centre and the Victoria State Government for sponsoring and administering the award. This award was instrumental in finding a publisher for this collection. I would particularly like to pay tribute to the 2013 judges, Paddy O'Reilly, Sam Twyford-Moore, and Francesca Rendle-Short who, in selecting *Foreign Soil*, made the bravest and most unexpected of decisions where others may well not have. Several stories in this collection, or previous incarnations of these works, were first published elsewhere: "Shu Yi" appeared in short form in *Peril*. "Harlem Jones" was shortlisted for the 2012 Overland Victoria University Short Story Prize, and was first published in *Overland*. "Hope" was published in extract in *Page Seventeen*, and "Railton Road" first appeared in *Harvest* magazine. *Foreign Soil* is dedicated to Australian fiction writers of color: those who paved the path before me, and those for whom these clumsy feet will hopefully help smooth the way.

About the Author

Maxine Beneba Clarke is a novelist and poet living in Melbourne, Australia. *Foreign Soil*, which was originally published in Australia, won the ABIA for Literary Fiction Book of the Year 2015 and the 2015 Indie Book Award for Debut Fiction. Clarke was also named one of the *Sydney Morning Herald*'s Best Young Novelists for 2015 and was awarded the 2014 Hazel Rowley Literary Fellowship. *Foreign Soil* is her first book. Her memoir, *The Hate Race*, was published in 2016 in Australia.